A Maryland Witch

Catherine Mesick

Copyright © 2019 by Catherine Mesick.
Cover Design by Melody Simmons.

All rights reserved. Published by Scofflaw Publishing.

ISBN: 978-0-9986631-5-9

Witches of Crabtree Bay: Book 1

A Maryland Witch

Catherine Mesick

Chapter One

"Good afternoon, miss. Can you tell me what this symbol is?"

I looked up into a pair of dark eyes. The eyes were matched by equally dark hair, and both hair and eyes belonged to a handsome man—he would have been extremely handsome if not for the look on his face.

He seemed skeptical—and challenging—as if he'd caught me at something.

I looked down at the piece of paper the man had placed on the desk. It showed a symbol drawn in black ink—it looked like an uppercase L intersected by another, upside down uppercase L:

I drew in my breath sharply.

"No," I said. "I have no idea what that is."

The man raised one mocking eyebrow. "Isn't this the library?"

I glanced around me, as if to reassure myself. Between the man's good looks and the shock of seeing the symbol, I was momentarily disoriented. But the study tables were full of our regulars, and our books sat on our slightly dusty shelves in quiet repose like they usually did.

We were indeed in a library.

"Yes, this is the Crabtree Bay Public Library," I said a little unsteadily.

"Oh," the man said. "I thought the library was supposed to be a repository of knowledge. And I thought librarians were supposed to be smart."

"Well, we don't know everything," I said, feeling myself bristle. "And just because you've doodled a mark on a piece of paper doesn't mean I can tell you what it is."

The man persisted. "Aren't you Chloe Bartlett?"

"Yes," I said. Despite the man's sneering tone, hearing him say my name made a little tingle run through me. "Yes, I am."

"And you're still saying you don't know what this is?"

The man tapped on the piece of paper, and I glanced down at it.

"No," I said firmly.

"You're lying," he said.

And he was right—I was. I just couldn't help it. The symbol was secret—and sacred. It wasn't the sort of thing you discussed with strangers, and I hadn't expected to see it. Denying that I knew about it was instinctive—I was just protecting my family.

"Let me explain myself, Miss Bartlett," the man said. He drew himself up to his full height, which was considerable—he wasn't short. "I am Mike Fellowes."

"Who?" I said.

The man looked disappointed. "Mike Fellowes. *Professor* Michael Fellowes of Henrietta College. Surely you're heard of me?"

"You're a professor?" I said, startled. "You don't look much older than I am. And I'm twenty-three. And besides, you're too—"

I stopped myself quickly. I'd been going to say "too handsome," but there was no way I was going to admit to something like that now.

I looked at the man before me, who still seemed to be struggling with the idea that I didn't know who he was.

"Oh, I get it," I said suddenly. "You're a TA, and you're trying to make yourself seem important."

I winced a little on the inside as I said the words—I hadn't meant to sound quite so sharp. But then again, I was still reeling from the sight of the symbol, which he kept waving around.

"A teaching assistant?" Mike said. "Me? I'll have you know that I'm *twenty-seven* years old *and* a full professor."

"Congratulations," I said. I meant that sincerely, but somehow it came out sounding a little sarcastic.

"And do you know what I'm professor of?" Mike said.

"No," I replied. "I thought we'd established that I'd never heard of you."

Mike's mouth hung open.

After a moment, he recovered himself. "I'm the new Professor of English and Folklore Studies. I've published several folklore books— all of which are available at Fogerty's Bookstore downtown."

"Well, they're not available here," I said.

Mike scoffed. "And you would know?"

"Yes, of course," I said. "I know my library. There are no books by a Professor Mike Fellowes in the folklore section. It's Dewey Decimal number three hundred ninety-eight right behind you. Check it out if you don't believe me."

Mike glanced around at the shelves I'd indicated.

As he did so, I noticed that several of our patrons were frowning at the two of us—our discussion had grown a little loud.

Mike turned back to me. "That's not the point."

"What is the point?" I asked. "And please keep your voice down. People are trying to read in here."

"The point is," Mike said, "that you believe you're a witch. Deny that!"

He said the words in a loud, ringing voice and then crossed his arms across his chest.

"Shhh!" Mrs. Ludlow hissed. She was one of our regulars, and she was glaring at the two of us over the top of her glasses.

For my part, I was too stunned to say anything.

Nobody knew I was a witch.

Nobody.

That was a secret we had guarded for three hundred years.

Everyone in the library was looking at us now.

I found that I was having trouble breathing.

Mike went on. "You also have two sisters—Alberta and Rafaela Bartlett. And they're also harboring the delusion that they're witches. Is that not right?"

I looked around at all the eyes that were staring at us.

This isn't happening, I said to myself.

Just then, I caught sight of a swift movement nearby.

I turned and saw a familiar figure rounding the corner of the stacks in the graphic novel section. It was Joe Osgood—tanned and muscular, with long, light brown hair that was streaked with gold. He had a bit of a crush on me, and he was often to be found lingering near the comic books and pretending to read them, while actually peering around the corner to look at me. Most days, Joe's presence was a little irritating, but today it seemed as if it could actually be a good thing.

"You haven't answered any of my questions," Mike said, still speaking loudly. "Do you or don't you believe you're a witch?"

"Dude, back off!" Joe said. Suddenly, he was at the circulation desk, and he was wedging himself in between Mike and the desk.

Mike was blocked from my sight for a moment, and then he took a step back. I could see he was startled.

"Did you just call Chloe a witch?" Joe asked.

Mike folded his arms once again. "Actually, that's what I'm here to ascertain. But so far she hasn't said a word."

His eyes darted to me. "So I'm going to take her silence as confirmation."

Joe blinked at Mike. "Look, I have no idea what you just said. But nobody comes in here and calls Chloe a witch. She's my girl—I mean, she's my friend. She's a girl who's my friend. And nobody can talk about her that way."

"So you're the boyfriend, are you?" Mike smirked. "It figures. You're both good-looking and empty-headed."

4

"Wait," I said, startled once again. "Did you just say I was good-looking?"

Mike threw me a scornful look. "Of course that's what you'd hear. I rest my case."

"What case?" I said.

"Shhh!" Mrs. Ludlow said.

"What I'm trying to demonstrate here is this," Mike said. "You're a bubbleheaded girl who believes she has magic powers, and I'm here to debunk this for the nonsense it is."

"Dude," Joe said, "I still don't know what you're talking about."

Mike stabbed a finger in my direction. "She believes she's a witch. And her sisters believe they're witches, too. It's absurd, and it's got to stop."

Joe's expression grew stormy. "I told you not to call her a witch."

Mike waved the scrap of paper with the symbol in Joe's face. "It's what she calls herself. Just ask her."

I was back to finding it hard to breathe again. Every time I saw that symbol, I felt a fluttering in my stomach.

"You know what?" Joe said. "I'm going to call you Professor Mike."

"That's good," Mike said. "Because that's my name."

"Yeah?" Joe said. "Well, that's what I'm going to call you. Professor Mike, Professor Mike! Hey, everybody, we've got an egghead here. Say hello to Professor Mike!"

"Well, you know what I'm going to call you?" Mike asked.

"What?"

"I'm going to call you ignorant."

Joe's face suddenly went brick red. "What did you call me?"

"Ignorant." Mike repeated the word, but he looked a little nervous.

"Are you calling me stupid?" Joe asked. Somehow his face had gone even redder.

If there was one thing Joe hated, it was being called stupid.

I hurried around the circulation desk and stepped in between the two of them.

"Okay, guys," I said. "Let's simmer down now. Nobody here is ignorant or a witch, and please let's try to remember that we're in a library. No shouting or fighting in here."

Mike ignored me. "Being ignorant doesn't mean you're stupid. It means you lack knowledge. And you know nothing about what's going on here. You haven't seen my research—you are entirely ignorant in this situation."

Joe seemed to swell up. "Did you just call me ignorant again?"

I grabbed Joe by the arm and pulled him back a few steps.

I found myself wishing—not for the first time—that the library had some security. If things got really rowdy in here, there wasn't anybody else to take care of the situation but me. I was working alone today.

"Yes, I did call you ignorant," Mike said. "But you're not alone. Society as a whole is ignorant. This town is ignorant."

I kept hold of Joe and looked over at Mike. "You know, you're really not helping."

"But this town isn't the problem," Mike said, clearly warming to his subject. "There are pockets of ignorance everywhere. Pockets of superstition everywhere. And intend to expose them. I'm going to expose everything. I will reveal all!"

Joe grimaced in disgust. "Dude, I don't think you should be talking about exposing yourself. That's just not right."

"I'm not talking about exposing myself," Mike said. "I'm talking about exposing the ignorance and superstition in this town. When you live in a place where the librarian believes herself to be a witch, you've got a problem."

Despite my best efforts to hold him back, Joe took a threatening step toward Mike. "Where did you hear that anyway?"

"Yes, where did you hear that?" I asked. "And how did you find that symbol?"

Mike smiled smugly. "That's easy enough to answer. I've been receiving emails from a man named Charles Tyndall. He spells out everything about you and your sisters—if you'll forgive the pun. I did a little digging, and it turns out he's right. I found corroboration for all of it—every last detail."

"Charles Tyndall?" I said.

"You've heard of him."

"Yes."

"I'm not surprised," Mike said. "In his emails, Mr. Tyndall did indicate that he was rather a prominent citizen."

"When did you get these emails?" I asked. "Was it a long time ago?"

"No," Mike said. He stopped to consider the question, and for the first time he didn't look angry or smug—he just looked thoughtful. "Well, I suppose it depends on what you mean by a long time. I received the last email about a month ago. I've been researching his claims ever since."

The smug look returned as he continued. "As it so happens, I'm a very quick researcher. I was able to substantiate many of his claims about your family's peculiar superstitions in very little time. I doubt many other scholars could have completed the work as swiftly as I did. I'm both quick and accurate."

"And yet you miss the bigger picture," I murmured.

Mike frowned. "And what does that mean?"

"It means that couldn't have received emails from Charles Tyndall a month ago."

"And why is that?"

I took a deep breath. "Because Charles Tyndall died about ten years ago."

Mike looked at me in surprise. "What?"

"It's easy enough to check," I said quietly. "You won't need any great research skills to find out."

Mike stared at me. "You're saying I received emails from a dead man?"

Joe snickered. "You got punked. The emails are fake. Chloe's no witch and neither are her sisters."

"You're saying the emails aren't real?" Mike said. "You're saying my research was based on a prank?"

"It looks like it," I said.

Mike's face went as red as Joe's had earlier.

"I don't believe it," he said. "And it doesn't matter who sent the emails. Even if it wasn't Charles Tyndall, it was probably from someone who wanted to remain anonymous. And my research is still good—the facts still stand. And I'm going to prove that you and your sisters believe you're witches and that you're at the center of a conspiracy of ignorance to keep this town mired in superstition."

"So," I said. "You're going to prove that my sisters and I think we're witches."

"Yes."

"And then you're going to prove that even though we believe we're witches, it's not actually true."

"Yes."

"In that case, you could save yourself the trouble and just skip to the end. Just tell everyone it's not true. Or better yet, don't bother."

"You're impossible," Mike said. "But I'm going to get to the bottom of this. I'm going to bring your crazy beliefs out into the open."

He stormed out of the library and slammed the front door behind him.

Mrs. Ludlow was still glaring at me over the top of her glasses.

"Shhh!" she hissed.

Chapter Two

Everything Mike had said was true. I was a witch, and so were my sisters.

The town of Crabtree Bay, Maryland, was founded in 1718, and my ancestor, Mary Bartlett, arrived not long after. The town was named Crabtree Bay not because of apples—although crabapples were the only variety that grew here back then—but because one of the early settlers thought he could see a crabtree in the shape of the bay the town nestled against. I couldn't see it myself—but then again, I didn't have an explorer's eye.

There were stories—whispers—about Mary back then. And for better or worse, they were true. Mary was a kindly soul—and a witch—who wanted nothing more than to live her life in peace and use her gifts to help others. So Mary had left her native land and traveled far across the sea to a place where she and her abilities would be entirely unknown.

Of course, Mary's abilities didn't remain unknown for long—she was a skilled healer who could also draw on the power of nature to lend additional restorative aid to her patients. But the weather was good and harvests were good for many years, so the whispers about Mary never grew into angry shouts, and even though people could see that her powers were more than ordinary, they still continued to take their children and themselves to see her whenever anyone was ill.

Mary eventually married and had children, and Mary's talents and abilities were passed down from mother to daughter all the way down to our present generation. And all of the girls were given "Bartlett" as a middle name in honor of Mary. I went by Chloe Bartlett, but my full name was Chloe Anastasia Bartlett Delaney—"Delaney" being my father's name. And my sisters—Alberta Bartlett and Rafaela Bartlett—were actually Alberta Bogdana Bartlett Delaney and Rafaela Serena Bartlett Delaney. It was our way of keeping the Bartlett name alive.

And even though Mary Bartlett had had a relatively easy time with her neighbors back in the eighteenth century, she knew that it might not always be so for her descendants. So she created the symbol Mike had been waving around to protect us. It kept a veil of secrecy over everything we did that was related to our powers. People remembered us, but not our unusual abilities. And the symbol was placed in inconspicuous spots throughout our houses—it was even painted in a tiny corner of our door jambs. I also wore a gold ring that had the symbol engraved on the inside, and Alberta and Rafaela both wore similar pieces of jewelry with the symbol hidden on it—Rafaela had a favorite necklace, and Alberta had a couple of different pieces.

But the power of the symbol depended in part on its secrecy—if it became widely known, the symbol would lose its effectiveness.

As I made my way home after work that day, I couldn't help worrying about this last part. I assumed that waving the symbol in public for a few minutes as Professor Mike had done wouldn't really be that much of a problem—or at least I hoped it wouldn't be.

And then there was his threat to "reveal all."

I didn't know how he intended to do that—but he did seem determined.

He certainly hadn't minded causing a scene in a public library.

I reached home in about ten minutes, and as I parked the car, I heard a little jingle from my phone.

I picked it up—there was a text from Joe.

He was just checking in with me to see how I was.

I didn't really think Joe was my type, but he was a sweet—if occasionally irritating—person, and I had been grateful for his presence today.

I smiled as I texted him back.

Then I walked up to the house. The evening was hot and muggy—and I could feel the humidity as soon as I stepped out of the car.

As I opened the door, my sister's cat, Sibyl, came streaking out of the house and ran down the driveway. She then ran back up and twined around my legs, meowing loudly.

"Who's my crazy kitty?" I said, scratching Sibyl behind the ears. She was an elegant cat with sleek black fur and amber eyes, and she was usually very calm. But lately she'd been rambunctious, running through the house at odd hours and vocalizing loudly.

As if to demonstrate this once again, she gave a loud yowl and then ran off into the house.

My sister's cat was quickly replaced by my sister, Alberta.

"Try this," she said, holding something golden brown and sweet-smelling up by my mouth.

"I haven't even walked into the house yet," I protested. And it was true—I hadn't. My feet had yet to cross the threshold.

"Just try it," Alberta said. "I think I've finally got it right."

When people heard that my eldest sister was named "Alberta," and that she was a tax attorney, they usually pictured someone older and kind of dour. But Alberta was twenty-eight with flame-red hair and green eyes, and she was all fire, which made sense since she drew her abilities from the element of fire. Alberta was definitely the fighter in the family, and she had strong opinions on everything—including baked goods.

I dutifully took the bite she proffered.

It was warm and sweet, and then there was a burst of something deliciously tart.

"Wow," I said. "That's good. What is it?"

"Cherry muffin," Alberta replied.

I made a face. "I don't like cherries."

"I know. I figured if I made one that was good enough that you liked it, that other people would like it, too."

"Well, it was good," I said. "I would definitely eat a whole one, cherries and all."

I paused. "Who are these other people you're going to give the muffins to? And can I come into the house now?"

Alberta waved a hand. "I wasn't thinking of anybody specific—just potential plans for the future. And of course you can come in. In fact, I'm so glad you're here. I wish you'd stop looking for apartments and just live with me forever."

She pulled me into the house and pulled me into a hug.

My sister Rafaela walked over to us then and put her arms around the both of us.

"Oooh, random group hug," she said.

Rafaela was twenty-five, and her hair was straight like Alberta's, but instead of red, it was an unusual shade of brown mixed with gold. Her eyes were blue-green, and they were big and soulful. Rafaela, like our ancestor Mary, derived her powers from the element of water. She, too, was a skilled healer, and she worked as a physician's assistant.

And then there was me. My hair was dark brown and wavy, and my eyes were brown, too. My abilities stemmed from all four elements—earth, fire, air, and water—and I had the ability to make things grow—not just plants, but other things—like ideas. Alberta said my powers were vague and unreliable—the result of drawing on too many elements—but I liked being different. I knew there was a lot I could do—I just had to give my abilities time to grow themselves.

But though we all had different abilities and coloring—the result of having one dark-haired, dark-eyed parent with an olive complexion and one blond-haired, blue-eyed parent with a light complexion—there was a very strong family resemblance. People who met us for the first time knew right away that we were sisters.

The hug went on, and after a moment, I began to wriggle out of it.

"Guys," I said, "I think we're letting out all the air-conditioning."

My sisters stepped back.

"Sorry, Chloe," Rafaela said. "We're just so glad to have you here."

There was a ding from the kitchen.

"My muffins!" Alberta cried.

She ran off, and I finally closed the door behind us.

"So glad," Rafaela murmured. She was still staring at me.

"I've been back for three months," I said. "You should be used to me by now."

Rafaela smiled. "I know. But it's good to have you back all the same. And I don't get to see you as often as Alberta does."

That was true enough—I was staying with Alberta until I found a place of my own, and Rafaela had a house about fifteen minutes away. Rafaela also worked long hours and had an unpredictable schedule, so I didn't see her that often. Luckily, she'd planned to have dinner with the two of us tonight, so I wouldn't have to call an emergency meeting to get us all together.

I'd be able to tell both of them what I needed to tell them right away.

Rafaela was still staring at me, and even though I knew she was just reading my emotions, it was still a little unnerving. Her eyes always seemed to get just a little bigger when she did that.

She frowned. "I sense conflict."

"There was plenty of that this afternoon." I walked over to a sofa and flopped down on it.

Rafaela sat next to me. "That's not quite what I meant. I sense two different groups of emotions—I sense happiness and a lot of worry and fear."

"Happiness?" I said.

Rafaela gave me a coy look. "Someone is feeling happy about a boy."

"Oh that," I said. "It was just a text."

"From?"

"Joe Osgood. It was kind of a tough day at work, and he really helped me out."

"Interesting," Rafaela said. "I thought you always said he wasn't your type."

"He isn't," I replied. "Not really. It's just—he was a really good friend for me today. He defended me when I needed it."

Rafaela frowned again. "Defended you? That must be the worry part I sensed. What was he defending you from?"

"Dinner!" Alberta shouted from the kitchen.

"Come on," I said. "I'll tell both of you together. This concerns you guys, too."

Rafaela gave me a puzzled look, but she followed me into the kitchen.

"Out! Out! Shoo!" Alberta said.

I could see about two dozen muffins cooling on the big counter by the sink, and Alberta herself was fussing over two pots on the stove.

"But you called us for dinner," I said.

I glanced over at the little kitchen table.

It was bare.

"Yes," Alberta said. "We're having dinner in the *dining room*. You two go sit down. I'll bring everything out—I don't need any help."

"What's the occasion?" Rafaela said.

"The occasion is I'm having dinner with my two lovely sisters," Alberta said. "And I don't get to do that nearly as often as I would like. Now shoo!"

Rafaela and I walked into the dining room, and I could see that the table had been set with candles and Alberta's good china. There were even cloth napkins and crystal water goblets next to the plates.

"Wow. Fancy," I said.

"Like I said, it's for my sisters." Alberta's voice floated out of the kitchen. "Have a seat, you two."

There were three places set—one at the head of the table and then one on either side.

Rafaela and I sat down across from each other.

She looked over at me.

"What do you think she's made?" she whispered.

I glanced through the open doorway at Alberta, who was upending something into a bowl.

"I don't know," I whispered back. "All I can smell is the muffins. And I can't quite see what she's doing."

Alberta was a great baker but an indifferent cook, and Rafaela and I exchanged worried glances as Alberta dropped something in the sink and then cried out.

"Need some help?" Rafaela called out.

She, on the other hand, was an excellent cook.

"No," Alberta grumbled. "I've got this. You stay right where you are."

After a moment, Alberta appeared with a big, clear plastic bowl full of salad, which she set on the table along with several bottles of dressing. Then she hurried back into the kitchen and returned with a basket covered with cloth napkins. She pulled back the napkins to reveal golden brown rolls—the aroma was wonderful.

"I baked these yesterday," Alberta said. "I just popped them in the oven to warm them up a bit."

She disappeared into the kitchen again, and Rafaela reached for one and began to butter it.

"At least we know these will be good," she whispered.

Alberta soon returned with a big bowl of fettuccine alfredo, which she also placed on the table. Then she sat down herself.

"Dig in," she said.

I eyed the bowl of fettuccine. The sauce looked delicious and creamy, and it smelled good, too.

But I'd had a few bad experiences with Alberta's sauces.

I selected a roll for myself and then began to scoop out some salad.

"So did you make the alfredo sauce yourself?" I asked.

I tried very hard to sound nonchalant.

Alberta scowled at me. "I know how to boil pasta, Chloe. And I also know how to open a jar of sauce and a bag of premade salad as well as the next person."

"So it's store-bought?" Rafaela asked. She sounded relieved.

"Yes, it's store-bought," Alberta replied. "I'm aware of my reputation as a cook. I went with something safe—no experimenting."

Rafaela and I helped ourselves to the fettuccine then, and we both tried it.

"It's good," I said.

"Yes, it is," Rafaela chimed in.

She sounded surprised, but Alberta seemed mollified.

She served herself, too, and soon we were all eating.

"Chloe had a bad at work," Rafaela said to Alberta. "She said she needs to tell us something."

"Oh no, honey," Alberta said. "Was it Joe? Was he staring at you from behind the comic books again?"

"No, it wasn't Joe," I replied. "He was there—but he wasn't the problem."

"Was it that guy who talks to his invisible friend?" Rafaela asked.

"No, it wasn't him."

I looked at the two of them. Then I took a deep breath.

"Someone revealed our symbol in public today," I said.

Alberta had a forkful of fettuccine halfway to her mouth, and she froze with her mouth open.

Rafaela did the same thing with a water goblet.

Alberta recovered first.

"What?"

"It's true," I said. "This guy—Professor Mike from Henrietta College—was waving a piece of paper around with our symbol on it."

I told them quickly about the whole thing—about how Mike had called me a witch in public and Joe had come to my defense. I told them, too, about how Mike had threatened to reveal all and had claimed to have received his information from Charles Tyndall.

"Charles Tyndall," Rafaela murmured to herself.

"Charles Tyndall is dead," Alberta said bluntly. "It must be a prank."

"That's what I said," I replied. "That's what Joe said, too."

"Then I'm sure we have nothing to worry about," Alberta said. "This will all blow over."

"But the symbol," I said.

"It can handle one public outing," Alberta said.

"What about his threat to reveal all?"

Alberta was dismissive. "What's he going to do? Stand on the corner with a megaphone? If he gets too chatty, I'll have a talk with him. That will stop him quickly."

"Charles Tyndall," Rafaela said again. "You know, people used to say—"

She stopped.

"What's wrong?" I said.

Rafaela's big eyes were full of worry.

She went on slowly. "People used to say he was a member of the Crabtree Coven."

Alberta snorted. "Complete nonsense. The Crabtree Coven died out two hundred years ago."

"What are you saying, Rafaela?" I asked. "Do you think Charles Tyndall really could have sent the emails?"

"No, of course not," she said. "He's certainly deceased. And no amount of magic can bring someone back from the grave. It's just—somehow the mention of his name gives me a funny feeling."

From upstairs, Sibyl gave a very loud yowl.

The yowl was followed by a crash.

"Crazy cat," Alberta said, standing. "I'd better go upstairs and make sure she hasn't broken anything."

After Alberta left, Rafaela sat crumbling a roll onto her plate.

"Charles Tyndall," she said softly.

"What's wrong, Rafaela?" I said. "What are you feeling?"

But no matter how many times I asked her, she wouldn't reply.

Chapter Three

The Crabtree Coven was sort of a myth in the area, and there had actually been one once. Shortly after my ancestor, Mary, had arrived in the town, another witch arrived—a male witch. His name was Ezekiel Rapp, and he had with him two female witches whom he called his "disciples."

They were pretty quiet about their activities and didn't really bother anyone until 1730 when Ezekiel tried to take over the town. The methods he used weren't magical—he actually ran for office. But there were irregularities with the votes—when the votes were counted, there were somehow more ballots cast than there were men in the town— and the most vocal supporters of Ezekiel's opponents either fell ill or suffered disasters on election day. The election was declared invalid, and then votes were recast without Ezekiel's name on the ballot. But nothing was done to the man himself—possibly because of his gender—and accidents continued to befall his business and political rivals. When Ezekiel's grandson tried a similar scheme in 1800 with more violent results, the Crabtree Coven was eventually run out of town and never heard from again—they'd agreed to emigrate west in return for safe passage out of town. There had only ever been three of them at a time, so it was pretty easy for the townsfolk to be sure they were gone.

But the rumors of a coven run by a male witch continued to linger, and children still told scary stories to each other about the witches that lived in the town.

My ancestor, Mary, of course, had never been part of the coven and had disapproved heartily of them—she didn't believe in using her abilities for gain or to harm others. The presence of the coven was another reason Mary had developed the protective symbol—she didn't want anyone to associate us with the coven, which wasn't always very secretive about their practices. We were entirely separate from them, and she didn't ever want anyone to believe that we would help them.

I'd heard the rumors about Charles Tyndall that Rafaela had mentioned when I was a kid, and I'd never put too much stock in them. I knew that my mother would have known if there were other witches in town, and she was quite insistent that there weren't. As I grew older, I came to realize that the rumors might have had a mundane source rather than a magical one—jealousy.

Charles Tyndall was a very wealthy man, and there were whispers that his wealth had come from dark magic and his membership in the Crabtree Coven, which he had supposedly revived. While I couldn't necessarily have said how honest his business practices were—and there grumbles about that, too—I did know for a fact that he hadn't used the dark arts to amass his fortune. Again, my mother would have known, and she wouldn't have stood for that.

Still, I had witnessed children daring each other to go near his old house within the last few months. And even though the house was now occupied by Charles' granddaughter Bradshaw, the rumors persisted. Bradshaw, I knew for a fact, was no witch—though she was a very difficult, challenging person.

What puzzled me was Rafaela's reaction to the whole thing. She knew as well as I did that the Crabtree Coven was long gone and that Charles Tyndall had been an ordinary man—albeit a very rich one.

I would have to see if I could catch Rafaela on the phone or even in person and see if I could get her to talk to me.

Rafaela only went silent when she was really worried.

As I stepped out of the house that morning, carefully trying to extract myself from Sibyl, who was winding around my legs and yowling like crazy, I managed to successfully close the door behind me and then immediately tripped over the newspaper that was lying on the front step.

I picked up the paper, along with the bag I had dropped, and glanced at it.

The Morning Cider was allegedly a daily paper, but it sometimes came out every day and sometimes didn't, depending on what staff was available. Times were tough for newspapers in general—and for local ones in particular—and I felt a little rush of sympathy for our local paper as I looked at the copy in my hand. I went to shove it in my bag, but I stopped. I didn't usually read the local paper, but today I felt like I should at least look through it—I had a strange feeling that it was important for me to take a look today. Maybe I would even start reading it again on a regular basis.

The headline on the front page wasn't too promising, however: *Little Miss Fire Prevention to be Crowned at County Fair.*

And right below it was this story: *Puppy Yoga at Civic Center.*

I leafed through a few pages and was startled to see a familiar face leap out at me from the "Opinion" page.

It was Professor Mike. Even in the black-and-white photo, he was still handsome, and I felt my heart flutter just a little.

I found that really irritating.

And then I saw that his picture was next to a headline that read, *Superstition Alive and Well in Crabtree Bay.* Below his picture was a rendering of our symbol.

I stared at the article in disbelief.

I felt a little bit like I was drowning.

But I made myself read on, and my disbelief turned to horror.

Mike knew all about us—my family and our history. And he spelled it all out. He even knew about the Crabtree Coven—he knew about their history starting with Ezekiel Rapp, he knew about their three symbols, the crow, the pearl, and the eye, and he mentioned that someone posing as Charles Tyndall had been the foundation of all of his research.

I finally did shove the paper into my bag, and I made my way down the driveway to my car. I didn't know if Alberta or Rafaela had seen the article, but somehow I doubted it—I knew they didn't usually read the local paper, either.

I considered texting them, but I thought I should give myself some time to cool down first—outrage and texting probably didn't make a good combination. Of course, outrage and driving probably didn't go together very well, either, so I made myself sit quietly for a few minutes before I started the car.

Once I was driving, however, bits of the article came floating back to me, and I found myself muttering terrible things about Professor Mike under my breath.

Realizing I wasn't in the best frame of mind to be operating a three-thousand-pound vehicle, I drove carefully and made sure to watch for pedestrians.

I was likely to be in a bad mood for the rest of the day—I would have to watch myself.

I reached the residential neighborhood in which the library sat—the trees somehow still green and leafy despite the intense heat of the summer—and I parked along the side of the building. The library didn't have its own parking lot, and street parking near the building was sometimes hard to come by. I usually had the best luck when I worked the morning shift—if I timed it just right, I could find a good spot once the neighborhood residents had left for work in the morning but before our patrons started queuing up outside to get in.

This morning I was in luck, and finding a great spot helped to soothe my bad mood a little.

But as I walked around the front of the building, I could see that someone had spray-painted "WITCH" in big black letters on the bricks next to the door.

I stood by the book drop, just staring.

As I had a couple times in the last few months, I suddenly wished I were back in New York City. I'd moved there right after high school so I could attend college, and in my senior year, I was lucky enough to get an internship with a small academic publisher. They hired me officially as soon as I graduated, and I was well on my way to the kind of career I'd always imagined for myself—I was working on books libraries loved, and I was making enough to maintain a small apartment in New Jersey. But times were tough for publishers, and after a year, I was laid off along with ten other people. I looked for other jobs, but I had no luck and money ran out fast. Then I found myself moving back to Crabtree Bay and getting a job as a library assistant. I loved the job, and most people assumed I was a full-fledged librarian—though I actually lacked the proper degree. I was really happy to be back in my hometown, but at the moment, I thought longingly of New York. In a big city, no one cared if you were a witch. And if you were, you were still hardly the strangest person in town.

There were much stranger people in New York than me.

But in a small town—especially one as gossipy as ours—getting branded as a weirdo was something serious that would last your whole life.

And that didn't even take into account the damage the publicity was doing to our symbol.

Everyone would remember who we were and what we could do.

"Oh, honey," said a voice behind me.

I turned to see a woman with black hair and coffee-colored skin dressed in a chic white dress coming toward me. It was Rita Cavanaugh, the head librarian, and even though she worked in a profession that was inherently a little dusty, she somehow always managed to look crisp and fashionable—as if she'd just stepped off the cover of a magazine.

"Hi, Rita," I said.

She walked up to stand next to me. "I'm so sorry."

I gestured to the graffiti. "I gather you read the paper this morning?"

"I read the papers every morning," Rita said. "All of them—including *The Morning Cider*."

"Then you know," I said.

Rita put an arm around my shoulder. "Don't even think about this. I can't imagine what that man was thinking—and he calls himself a professor. We're all going to stand by you and help you get through this."

She paused. "Would you like to take the day off?"

"No, that's okay," I said.

"Are you sure?" Rita asked. "It's seriously no problem. We've all run this place by ourselves, and if we get super busy, I can call Stu. I'm sure he would be happy to come in and help out."

Stu was the other librarian, and he usually worked part-time, coming in only in the evenings and on weekends.

"No, really," I said. "It's fine. I'd rather be at work and have something to do to keep my mind off it. If I sit at home, I'll just stew over it."

Rita stared at me with sympathy in her large, dark eyes.

"All right," she said. "But if you feel like leaving before your shift is up, just go ahead and go. You don't even have to say anything. Just run right out the front doors if you need to."

I smiled a little. "Thanks."

Rita glanced at the big metal box next to us. "Would you like me to get the book drop?"

"No, that's all right," I said. "I want the day to go as normally as possible. Maybe that will help me to forget."

"All right," Rita said again. She gave my shoulder a squeeze. "I guess we'll see what our patrons are made of today. You let me know if anybody says anything."

"I will," I said.

Rita began to walk toward the library.

"At least it's not the first time we've had graffiti on the library." Her voice floated back to me. "Barry will have to get the pressure washer out again."

She went up the few steps, and after unlocking the front doors, she disappeared inside.

I got out my own keys and opened up the book drop. The box, as usual, was full to the top. We were lucky to have a lot of avid readers in our little town.

I grabbed an armful of books like I usually did, and I turned toward the library—I would come back with a cart for the rest of them.

But as I turned, I saw that someone was standing right behind me.

It was a tall, handsome man with dark hair and dark eyes. I was momentarily stunned by his good looks, and then I realized I was looking at someone familiar.

It was Professor Mike.

"You!" I said.

Rita's motherly warmth and concern had helped to soothe my ire. But now that I was faced with the person who had splashed our symbol and our history all over the place, I could feel the anger returning.

The man standing in front of me was threatening my family's safety.

I didn't actually know any curses—but at the moment I really, really wished I did.

"Yes, it's me," Mike said in an irritatingly smug tone. "I take it you read my op-ed piece?"

I looked at the pleased, self-satisfied expression on his face, and I felt my anger boiling over.

"Yes, I read it," I grated out.

"Well, that's good," Mike said, raising a mocking eyebrow. "After the way you acted yesterday, I wasn't sure you *did* read. You didn't come across as very educated."

I resisted the urge to hurl a book at his head. "Of course I read. I work in a library."

Mike smirked. "For a librarian you don't seem very smart. Neither does your boyfriend."

And you don't seem to have any manners, I thought to myself.

On the drive over, I'd thought of all the things I would say to Mike if I saw him again. But now that he was here—right in front of me—I was so shocked and angered by his attitude that I couldn't throw any of the clever insults that I had thought of at him.

He was so smug—so arrogant—and he was so very wrong.

He clearly couldn't begin to understand what he had done.

"So are you ready to admit that you think you're a witch?" Mike asked.

I looked at him. I didn't know any witchy curses, but I knew a few of the other kind.

"Are you ready to admit that you're a—"

I stopped myself just in time as a woman with a stroller went by.

"Good morning, Mrs. Campbell," I said.

The woman raised a hand in greeting, and her baby grabbed his foot and hauled it toward his mouth.

"No, no, darling," Mrs. Campbell said. "We don't want to do that."

The two of them moved on, and I continued, lowering my voice.

"You have no idea what you've done," I said. "You have no idea how much harm you've caused."

"You're exaggerating," Mike said in that same irritatingly superior tone. "This does no harm at all. In fact—"

His eyes drifted upward and he stopped suddenly.

I followed his gaze.

Mike had finally noticed the graffiti on the library.

"Who did that?" he said.

He looked really startled.

"I have no idea," I said shortly.

Mike looked at me. "Chloe, I—"

"I'm sorry," I said. "I need to get to work."

I turned with my armload of books and marched into the library.

Chapter Four

Luckily, our patrons turned out to be very nice about the entire incident.

Many of them *did* mention it throughout the morning—but they brought it up so that they could express sympathy—and outrage. It turned out that more people than I realized read *The Morning Cider*, and quite a few stopped to tell me that they didn't believe a word of it and that they were sorry my family and I had to go through this. And nearly everyone who came into the library expressed indignation that the building could be defaced in this fashion—though as Rita had pointed out earlier in the morning, that had happened before.

Maybe it had something to do with the word "witch"—it wasn't one of the words vandals typically used—and somehow the word stood out very starkly on the red brick.

Everyone seemed to be relieved once Barry, our maintenance man, had pressure-washed the word off the front of the building.

After a little while, our morning rush slowed down, as it usually did, and the library settled into silence. I was just starting to forget all the troubles of the morning when the front door opened, and a tall, dark figure entered.

For a moment, I thought Professor Mike had returned, but as I looked at the familiar figure, I realized that this tall, dark-haired man was a different problem entirely. It was my ex-boyfriend, Andrew Wyatt.

He did come into the library occasionally—I hoped this time he wouldn't notice that I was at the desk.

But I was to be disappointed. Andrew made a beeline straight for me.

I glanced around. Rita had gone to the office in the back. There was no one to cover for me if I wanted to hide in the back myself.

"Chloe!" Andrew said in his deep, sonorous voice.

I closed my eyes and took a deep breath before I looked up at him—he was always hard to deal with.

Andrew had some superficial resemblance to Professor Mike—they were both tall and dark-haired—but Andrew's eyes were a bright, mesmerizing green, and he had a classically handsome face with a perfect profile. He was well-built—a result of his having spent many summers working for his dad's construction company—and his marvelous physique combined with his good looks served him well in the calling that had eventually found him.

Andrew was an actor—and I had also dated him in high school. But he had broken off our relationship when I had left for college in New York—he'd said he couldn't be with me if I couldn't commit to staying with him in Crabtree Bay. I *had* considered attending nearby Henrietta College—but the pull of the big city had proved too strong. I'd needed to get out and see a little more of the world.

So Andrew had left me, and I'd been heartbroken at the time. But eventually I'd gotten over it, and I'd come to realize that we were better off apart—our personalities didn't really mesh well.

And when I came home for vacation the first few times and saw him again, I began to wonder what I had ever seen in him. Andrew was certainly handsome—but there wasn't a whole lot going on behind that good-looking façade.

Eventually, I forgot about him.

Now that I was back in town, however, I saw him from time to time, and the results were always embarrassing. Andrew didn't seem to understand that it was possible for someone to stop being in love with him. He still saw me as the teenage girl who had pleaded with him to go with her to New York—after all New York had many more opportunities for an actor than Crabtree Bay did. But Andrew had stayed behind and had worked steadily as an actor and model all over Maryland. He saw me as the poor, sad girl who had gone off to the big city and lost out on him. And he saw himself as a big success who had launched himself to dizzying heights.

Andrew did work quite a bit, but I had a feeling that much of his apparent "success" actually had more to do with the money he received from his father than with anything else.

It was well-known in the town that at the age twenty-three, he still received a sizeable allowance.

Andrew trained his striking eyes on me. "Oh, Chloe. You don't have to do this."

I fought the urge to roll my eyes, and I pasted a professional smile on my face.

"I'm sorry, Andrew," I said. "I'm not sure what you're referring to. Is there something I can help you with?"

"This!" he said, slapping a newspaper down on the circulation desk in front of me. "This, Chloe. Why have you done this?"

I glanced down at the paper on the desk. It was a copy of *The Morning Cider*.

"Thanks for bringing that up," I said. "I was just starting to forget about it."

"I get it," Andrew said. His expression had become pitying. "I really do. That's why I'm here to tell you it's okay, and you don't have to do this."

I could sense the patrons growing restless, and I glanced around. Our regulars in the morning were largely a different crowd from our regulars in the evening, so many of the people at the study tables and computers hadn't been present for yesterday's scene with Professor Mike. Mrs. Ludlow, for example, was mercifully absent. But even though these patrons hadn't witnessed yesterday's altercation—and even though many of them felt sorry for me this morning—I didn't want another scene to transpire so soon after the last one. There was a lot of gossip in this town, and if I developed a reputation for having unruly visitors during work hours, complaints would soon start rolling in.

I glanced around again. If I could get to Rita, I could ask her to cover the desk, and I could take the discussion with Andrew outside. But Rita was still in the office, and the phone extension back there wasn't working. Talking on cell phones was strictly forbidden in the library, but I could still send her a text. I was just reaching for my phone when I realized that Rita's was sitting just in front of the computer next to me—she'd left it behind when she'd gone to the back to work.

I sighed and looked back at Andrew.

He was still staring at me with pity in his eyes.

"Andrew," I said in a whisper, "I'm happy to discuss this with you—whatever 'this' is—but we're in a library, so we have to be quiet. Otherwise, we're going to upset everyone."

Andrew looked around at our patrons and blinked. No doubt he'd been aware of them when he'd made his entrance—he had an actor's love of an audience—but he seemed to notice them for the first time as people. I could see two emotions at war very plainly on his face—he wanted to have everyone watch him, but at the same time, he didn't want everyone to watch him if he knew it would make them dislike him.

Andrew took the safer route and lowered his voice.

"Okay, Chloe," he said in a stage whisper. "We'll do it your way."

I sighed again. I supposed that was the best I was going to get from Andrew.

"So," I said. "I assume you're here about the opinion piece in the paper that claims my sisters and I think we're witches."

"Yes," Andrew whispered loudly, drawing the "s" out.

"And why would you think that has anything to do with you?" I asked.

"It's pretty obvious. Women without a relationship to keep themselves stable often call attention to themselves—just like you're doing now. You were hoping to get me to notice you. That's why you put that professor guy up to this."

"Andrew—" I said in frustration. I realized I'd spoken out loud, and I quickly lowered my voice again. "That's ridiculous. I didn't put anyone up to anything. I had no idea the professor was going to do this. If I had, I would have stopped him."

He looked at me sadly. "The article mentions Charles Tyndall—Bradshaw's grandfather. This is all about her and me. You're clearly jealous."

"You're insane," I hissed.

"You did all this to get my attention."

"I did nothing of the kind," I said. "Did you even understand the article? It was about my family—it had nothing to do with you or Bradshaw."

"I just want you to know I understand," Andrew replied. "It's been hard for you to get over me. But it's been years now, and you should let go. I want you to let go."

I sputtered. "You want me to—"

"Yes. The time has come for you to finally let go of your feelings for me. My soul burns bright—brighter than most—and you have to let me be free to shine."

I stared at him, stunned.

"You're insane," I said again.

Andrew gave me a serious look. "Despite everything you've done, despite the way you've obsessed over me the last few years, and despite this newspaper stunt you've pulled to attract my attention, I just want you to know one thing."

He paused. "I forgive you."

"You—forgive me?"

For the second time that day, I had to fight down the urge to hurl a book at someone.

"And Chloe?"

"Yes," I said.

"You have nothing to worry about with me and Bradshaw."

"I'm not worried about you and Bradshaw," I said.

Andrew looked puzzled for a moment—as if he'd actually heard what I'd said for once.

Then he went back to his internal script. "Seriously—you have *nothing* to worry about."

"That's great," I said. "Thanks. I'll keep that in mind."

Andrew glanced around then, as if he hadn't quite worked out how this scene should end.

"Take care of yourself," he said in his hoarse whisper. "Even though we're not together, I still want things to be okay for you. That's because I have a big heart."

I had a retort, but I stifled it—I didn't want to risk dragging this conversation out any further.

"Goodbye," Andrew said. "I hope this time you can accept that it's final."

"I have no trouble accepting that," I said.

He gave me one last sad glance with his piercing green eyes and then left the library.

Through the window in the double doors at the front, I could see the back of his head as he disappeared.

I had never been so happy to see someone leave.

A few moments later, a new face appeared in the window, and one of the double doors swung open. Bradshaw Tyndall, clad in white jean shorts that showed off her long, tanned legs and a tank top that showed off her equally tanned arms, walked into the library. Her long, blond hair was perfectly coiffed despite the heat, and she wore tiny flip-flops that slapped the bottoms of her feet as she walked.

She marched right up to me.

"Was that my boyfriend?" she demanded.

Bradshaw was the same age I was, and she'd gone to school with Andrew and me. She'd had a crush on him all through high school, and after Andrew had broken up with me, and I'd left for college, she'd finally been able to get him to notice her. The two of them had been dating on and off for years ever since then, and according to local gossip, the "off" times were usually caused by Andrew's wandering green eyes. Apparently, he was always chasing after other girls.

"Was that my boyfriend?" Bradshaw said again.

"That was Andrew Wyatt," I said, "if that's what you mean."

"What was he doing here?" she demanded loudly. "Did he come here to see you?"

"Not again," I muttered to myself.

Our patrons were eyeing me with disapproval once again.

"Well?" Bradshaw said.

"Wait right there," I said. "Don't move."

Even though I wasn't supposed to leave the circulation desk unattended, I ran around it and hurried to the back.

I threw open the door to the office.

"Rita," I said breathlessly, "you've got to come watch the front desk for a few minutes."

She looked around, concerned. "What's wrong?" Her face darkened. "Is someone giving you a hard time about the witch thing?"

"No—it's not about the witch stuff," I said. "But that article's causing trouble of a different sort—somehow I'm caught in the middle of a soap opera at the moment."

Rita looked puzzled.

"Bradshaw Tyndall is out there," I said.

Comprehension dawned on her face.

"Oh," she said. She got up quickly.

Bradshaw was known to have a bit of a temper, and she had thrown tantrums in businesses and shops all over town.

Rita and I hurried toward the front where Bradshaw still waited.

"Look—" Bradshaw said as we reached her.

"Oh no you don't," Rita said. "You're taking this tantrum outside."

I continued on to the door.

"Come on," I said. "Outside."

Bradshaw whirled around to face me. "What's going on?"

"We'll talk if you want to," I said. "But we'll do it outside. This is a library—we're not putting on a show."

I went outside, and Bradshaw followed me reluctantly.

As we walked across the lawn to the sidewalk, I noticed that a blue car with a yellow lightning bolt painted on the side was idling nearby, as if the driver was waiting for someone. I thought that was a little strange, but Bradshaw didn't give me any time to think about it.

"So what was Andrew doing here?" she said without preamble. "Did he come here to see you?"

"Yes," I said.

"I knew it." Bradshaw's eyes narrowed. "If you think you can steal my boyfriend—"

"I don't want your boyfriend."

Bradshaw folded her arms. "Then what was he doing here?"

"He wanted to talk about the article in *The Morning Cider*."

"The one about your being a witch?"

I was surprised that Bradshaw had read it. "That's not exactly what it says, but yes. That's the one."

"So what about it?"

"Andrew thought I'd set it up to attract his attention."

Bradshaw's eyes narrowed once again. "Did you?"

"No," I said. "A thousand times no."

Bradshaw thought for a moment. "Why did the article mention my grandfather? What did he ever have to do with you?"

"Nothing," I said.

Bradshaw stared hard at me. "This wasn't some scheme to attract attention?"

"No," I said firmly.

"And you're not after my boyfriend? I know he's sneaking around with somebody."

"No."

Bradshaw continued to stare at me, and after a moment, she seemed to make up her mind.

"All right," she said. "I believe you. But you'd better stay away from him."

"Trust me," I said. "If I see him coming, I will walk the other way."

Bradshaw tossed her head and began to walk away across the grass. She kept going toward the side of the building, where presumably her car was parked.

"And not a single word of apology," I said to myself.

I began to walk toward the library.

As I reached the door, I happened to see Bradshaw drive away.

As she disappeared down the road, the blue-and-yellow car that had been idling by the front of the library suddenly pulled away from the curb and followed her.

I could just make out a man with dark glasses and a shaved head behind the wheel.

Chapter Five

"I'm so sorry you had another tough day at work," Rafaela said.

My sisters had insisted on taking me out—we were currently sitting in my favorite restaurant—Peter's Table.

"It was tough for you guys, too," I said. "That article was about all of us."

"Yes," Rafaela said. "But we didn't have graffiti spray-painted on our places of work."

"And we also weren't accosted by Andrew Wyatt and Bradshaw Tyndall," Alberta said. "I wish I'd been there. I would have taken a piece out of both of them."

We all paused as the waiter arrived with our food.

I had ordered the chicken pot pie. It wasn't the fanciest dish they made, but it was the very definition of comfort food, and that was exactly what I needed right now. The crust was light and flaky, the chicken was juicy and tender, and the vegetables were cooked to perfection. And the gravy inside was just heavenly.

Rafaela had ordered a turkey sandwich and a salad with walnuts, dried cranberries, and blue cheese. Alberta had ordered a steak and fries.

Everything smelled wonderful as it was set down in front of us.

Soon I had taken my first bite of the pot pie and followed that with a sip of iced tea.

Both were delicious—it was exactly what I needed.

"So I figured out why the name Charles Tyndall caused me such concern," Rafaela said.

Alberta looked up sharply. "And why is that?"

"It's nothing special," Rafaela said. "By that I mean it's nothing psychic—I don't have any special knowledge or anything. I haven't had any visions."

"Of course not," Alberta said. "None of us have visions. But you are very sensitive—you may have noticed something."

"No—it's nothing like that. I was just overcome by sympathy. The Tyndall family has had so much tragedy."

"What do you mean?" Alberta said. "The grandfather dying?"

Rafaela and I looked at each other.

"You don't remember?" I said. "Bradshaw and Geraldine's parents?"

"No."

Rafaela wrinkled her forehead. "It happened when you were studying for the bar."

"And that's when Dad was sick, too," I said.

"That's probably why you don't remember it," Rafaela said. "Or to be more accurate why you probably didn't hear about it at all—you were busy with other things."

"So what happened?" Alberta asked.

Rafaela thought back. "There was an accident, as I recall. A skiing accident in the Swiss Alps—an avalanche. Bradshaw and Geraldine's parents were killed—all four of them."

"Who's Geraldine?" Alberta said.

"That's right," Rafaela said. "You're a little older than us."

"I'm not that much older," Alberta said, ruffled.

"I just meant that you wouldn't have known her in school," Rafaela replied. "Geraldine was a year younger than Bradshaw, so I hardly knew her myself. Geraldine is Bradshaw's cousin. Her father and Bradshaw's father were brothers—Charles Tyndall's two sons."

"Oh, I see," Alberta said. "So both brothers and their wives were killed, leaving the two cousins as orphans."

"Yes."

"That's terrible," Alberta said.

"I agree."

"So what happened to the girls?" Alberta said. "Bradshaw, at least, doesn't seem to be doing so badly."

"Well, it didn't happen so long ago," Rafaela said. "So basically both Geraldine and Bradshaw were quite capable of taking care of themselves. And Charles, of course, was already deceased, and his sons had already received their inheritance, which was reportedly very large."

"So both girls inherited money from their fathers?"

"Yes—and in addition, Bradshaw received her grandfather's mansion. Her father was the older sibling, and her family was already living in it anyway. Geraldine, I believe, went to live with her mother's relatives in Annapolis. Bradshaw's mother didn't seem to have any family."

Alberta's face was sober. "That really is a tragedy. It's sad to think of Bradshaw rattling around in that big, old mansion alone."

She sighed. "And it begs the question, why would anyone pose as Charles Tyndall and send our professor friend all that information? That seems a bit hard on Bradshaw."

Rafaela nodded. "Everyone says Bradshaw was her grandfather's favorite. They were apparently very close."

She paused abruptly. "Unless it really was Charles Tyndall. Do you think—"

"No," Alberta said firmly. "Whoever heard of a ghost sending an email? I doubt they'd have the energy. Besides, I don't think Charles Tyndall would want to send an otherworldly message about us. He'd want to send a message about his own business—or send a message to Bradshaw if they were as close as you say."

"But there were those rumors," Rafaela interjected. "About Charles being a member of—"

"Charles Tyndall was never a member of the Crabtree Coven," Alberta said. "That was just a rumor floated by people who were jealous of his success. And none of us can see or communicate with ghosts, so we could hardly investigate that anyway."

"So what do we do?" I asked.

"About?" Alberta replied.

"About Professor Mike," I said. "About our symbol being splashed all over the papers. About this mysterious email correspondent who knows all about us and doesn't mind telling everybody our family history."

"I don't know that there's anything to be done about it," Alberta answered.

"What?" I said, stunned.

"Let's just be reasonable about this," Alberta said. "I'd still like to give Professor Mike a piece of my mind. And the same goes for our unnamed graffiti artist and everybody who's harassed you at the library. But in the long run, this may not be that big a deal. It may just all blow over."

Rafaela looked startled. "But this damages the symbol. This damages our ability to keep our powers secret."

"It may not be as bad as all that," Alberta said.

"I can't believe you're taking this so calmly," Rafaela replied. "People will start to *remember*. People will notice that my healing abilities are beyond what's normally possible. And then there's your work for the police. People will start to notice—"

"I've worked on two missing person cases," Alberta said. "And they didn't see me using my scrying abilities. They think I'm just a clever profiler."

Rafaela persisted. "But they *will* start to remember. Magic leaves a trace that people will notice. What about Chloe and her—"

She stopped and I looked up at her.

"Yes?" Alberta prompted. "Chloe and her what? Her amazing ability to grow vegetables? I think we're safe there."

"Hey," I said.

"I'm quite sure Chloe has abilities that are just as advanced as yours or mine," Rafaela said. "She just hasn't grown into them yet."

"And she never will if she doesn't become more disciplined. Imagine—using all four elements."

Alberta snorted.

"Hey," I said again.

"I'm sure Chloe is extremely talented," Rafaela said, throwing me a sympathetic glance. "And that's not the point anyway. The point is that all our powers are in danger of exposure."

Alberta waved a hand. "People will forget."

"What if they don't?"

"This is an enlightened age," Alberta said. "No one's going to care."

"What if they do?"

"Should we tell Mom?" I asked.

Both of my sisters looked at me.

"We shouldn't bother her," Alberta said at once.

"She needs to know," Rafaela said just as quickly.

Both our parents were down in Florida at the moment. After Dad's illness, they'd both taken early retirement, and they were currently deciding where they wanted to spend that retirement. Mom and Dad still had their house in Crabtree Bay, but they were spending an extended vacation in Florida to see if they might like the year-round warm weather better.

"Mom's got other things on her mind," Alberta said.

"This is something she needs to know," Rafaela said again. "We can't keep her in the dark."

"Good evening, ladies," said a new voice.

I looked up to see a man with dark hair and an olive complexion standing by our table. It was Peter Gambelli, the owner of the restaurant.

Peter was very social and often came out to greet his guests during the course of an evening, but this time it seemed to me as if there was something extra warm about his recognition of us.

He certainly seemed to be beaming.

"Welcome, ladies!" he exclaimed. "We're delighted to have three such lovely enchantresses with us tonight—if the local talk is to be believed."

Peter's tone was friendly, and he seemed to be genuinely glad that we were there. I didn't take offense at his words, and Rafaela and Alberta didn't seem to be offended, either. Alberta, in particular, seemed to be delighted to see our host.

Peter continued. "Me? I don't believe in such things. But I do believe that all women are at least a little magical. And I am lucky to be under your spell tonight."

He winked at us.

"Oh, Peter," Alberta said.

Rafaela and I exchanged a glance.

"Tonight, for you, dessert is on the house," Peter said. "What can I get for you ladies?"

Alberta glanced at me. "We were thinking of the strawberry shortcake."

Strawberry shortcake was one of my favorites, and Peter's Table made an excellent version of it.

"A wonderful choice," Peter said. "Local strawberries are in season right now, and they are superb."

He winked at us. "I will also send out some of my world-famous chocolate cake. It wouldn't hurt, I think, to have a little taste of both."

He disappeared into the kitchen.

I frowned. "What did he mean by 'local talk'?"

Alberta answered, but she seemed a little distracted.

"He probably just means that article in the paper."

Her gaze drifted over to the door of the kitchen.

Peter soon returned with two waiters, who set a strawberry shortcake and a chocolate cake down on the table and then disappeared.

Peter, however, lingered.

I ate a little of the strawberry shortcake, which was delicious, and I also ate a little of the chocolate cake, which was just as amazing—it was hard for me to tell which one was better.

But despite the wonderful meal and the equally wonderful dessert, something was weighing on my mind.

Rafaela, Alberta, and Peter were all engaged in conversation—and Peter seemed to be flirting a little extra hard with Alberta—so I figured they wouldn't miss me if I disappeared for a little while.

I excused myself and walked past the bar to the terrace in the back.

As I passed the bar, I thought one of the figures seated there looked familiar.

I told myself it was nothing and walked on.

Outside, the air was warm and muggy but not unpleasant, and I could hear crickets singing in the grass beyond the terrace. There were several tables with diners, but they were well spaced, and over by the wooden railing, I was far enough away not to disturb anyone.

No one even seemed to have noticed that I was out there.

I thought once more of the phrase Peter had used—'local talk.' I had a feeling that more was going on than just the newspaper article. A germ of an idea was growing in my mind—it seemed to me that someone was trying to start trouble. But what kind? I just wasn't sure. I wished I could pinpoint what was bothering me.

"Chloe?" said a voice.

The voice sounded uncertain, and I turned to see Professor Mike standing just behind me.

I felt a flash of anger, followed by the little flutter I felt every time I saw him.

How could someone be so good-looking and so irritating at the same time?

But there was something else in his face—he looked nervous and unsure of himself—and I felt my anger subsiding.

I sensed he wanted to talk, and for some reason, I wanted to listen.

"Chloe," Mike said. "I saw the graffiti this morning—I'm sorry."

Despite what he had done, I felt a rush of sympathy for him—he looked so sad.

"That's okay," I said. "It washed off. And the library's been spray-painted before—usually with worse words."

Mike shook his head. "It was more than that. There was graffiti all over town."

I was startled. "What?"

Mike looked sheepish. "I'd show you pictures, but I don't want to upset you."

"Thanks, I think."

"The thing is—it's all over social media," Mike said. "Mostly local people's pages and accounts. But everybody in town is buzzing about you and your sisters. I'm really sorry. I never expected this to blow up this way."

He looked at me. "Chloe, I'm sorry. I never meant to hurt you or your sisters."

I looked up into his dark eyes, and I saw a warmth there I hadn't expected to see.

Maybe Professor Mike wasn't so bad after all.

He ran a hand over his hair. "And the frustrating thing is that nobody seems to understand what I was trying to say. Everybody seems to believe that I was calling you and your sisters witches—when I was really only saying you *think* you're witches. No one understands the piece at all."

I stared at Mike. "But you're sorry you wrote it, right?"

He blinked. "No—I'm not sorry at all. I am sorry about the way people reacted to it—I never expected people to make a big deal about it the way they did—or for it to blow up the way it did. I guess I didn't take into account how narrow-minded small-town folk are."

"Narrow-minded?" I said. I'd felt, on more than one occasion, that Crabtree Bay was a little too gossipy and close-knit myself. But it was my home, and I didn't like to hear an outsider criticizing it. "There's nothing wrong with small towns."

Mike looked at my face.

"I'm sorry," he said again. "I didn't mean that. In fact, that's the opposite of the point I'm trying to get across in my work. Small-town people are no worse than big-city people are. They're actually equally superstitious. My point is that superstition can happen anywhere— even in this modern day and age when we think we're so enlightened."

Professor Mike was clearly warming to his topic, but I'd heard enough.

"So let me get this straight," I said. "You're sorry about the way people reacted. But you're not sorry about writing the piece in the paper?"

A smile quirked at the corners of Mike's mouth. "That's right— you never did answer my question the other day. But I think it's been answered by your behavior. You really do think you're a witch, don't you?"

"And you haven't answered my question," I said. "You're not sorry about writing the newspaper article, are you?"

Mike was silent for a moment.

"If I had it to do over again," he said at last, "I would do it differently. I would deliver my message in a different way—perhaps highlighting the scholarship aspect of it and downplaying the more sensational details. And I would definitely make my point stronger— that none of this superstition is real, but it still has a hold on the minds of otherwise rational people."

He paused. "But no. I'm not sorry about my article. I think it needed to be done."

"That's all I need to know," I said. I turned and left the terrace.

I hurried back to my table, and Rafaela and Alberta were now alone—Peter had left.

The two of them were laughing about something as I slipped back into my seat.

"So what did I miss?" I said.

"Where did you go?" Alberta said. "I never even saw you leave."

Rafaela shot a sly look at her. "Chloe told us where she was going. You were just too preoccupied to notice."

"I went out to the terrace," I said. "I just needed a little air."
Rafaela's phone buzzed then, and she picked it up.
She tapped on the screen and then frowned.
"What is it?" Alberta said.
"It's from Josie," Rafaela said. "She's a nurse I know."
She looked up at us. "Bradshaw Tyndall's been shot."

Chapter Six

That night I sat up in my room, staring at my phone.

It turned out that Bradshaw had been shot *at*—not shot.

A shot had been fired through the window at her while she sat in her car, and while the bullet hadn't touched her, she'd been badly scared.

The bullet had been found on the floor of the car.

There were lots of theories as to who had fired the shot and what the motive had been. The most common theory was that it had been an accident—that area gangs or drug dealers had gotten into an altercation and Bradshaw had simply been in the wrong place at the wrong time.

But I was worried all the same—and I did what I usually did when I was worried.

I called my mom.

Maura Everly Bartlett Delaney answered the phone on the first ring. My mother had actually been born Maura Marian Bartlett Everly, but had dropped her "middle name" and kept her father's last name when she married my dad. I could picture her now, her hair still naturally blond, her blue eyes wide with concern as she answered.

"Chloe? What's wrong?"

My mom drew her abilities from water, like Rafaela did, and she was intuitive when it came to her daughters' emotional states.

"I'm fine," I said. I wasn't quite sure where to start. I didn't know what I wanted to tell her—I just knew I wanted to hear her voice. "How are you and Dad?"

"Is that Chloe?"

I could hear Dad's voice in the background. I could picture him, too—his hair still mostly black with just a few silver hairs, his beard streaked with a few more. Richard Delaney was given to reading in the evenings, and I imagined him now with his black-rimmed glasses partially obscuring his dark eyes.

"Yes, dear, it's Chloe," Maura replied.

"Tell her hi," Richard called back.

"Your father says hello," Maura said to me.

"You guys are doing okay?" I said.

"Yes, honey. We're fine," she said. "Your dad's doing well. He does everything his doctor tells him." I could hear a smile in her voice now. "Well, almost everything."

"No one could exercise that much!" I heard him call out.

"So you guys are loving Florida?" I said.

"Florida is very nice," Maura replied. "But Maryland is nice, too. We're still undecided."

She paused, and I could picture her frowning.

"Seriously, honey. What's wrong?"

I wasn't sure what was troubling me the most, and I also wasn't sure what Alberta, Rafaela, and I had decided on at dinner—whether we would tell Mom about the symbol or not. There was sort of an unspoken agreement among the three of us that we wouldn't tell Mom and Dad certain serious things unless we all agreed on it.

But I was disturbed by something I couldn't quite place my finger on, and I found the words just tumbling out.

I told her about everything—the symbol, Professor Mike, the graffiti, and Bradshaw being shot at.

My mother listened patiently, and at the end of my tale there was just silence.

I knew she wasn't shocked or upset—she was just thinking everything over.

"It certainly has been a busy few days for you," she said at last.

"What do you think about the symbol?" I asked. "Do you think we're in danger?"

Maura sighed. "Things have changed a lot since the days when our ancestor created that symbol. I'm inclined to agree with Alberta. Being a witch just isn't a big deal any more—we're hardly the weirdest people out there. You can find much stranger things with even a casual search on the internet."

"I know," I said. "But things are different in a close-knit community like ours. Differences stand out—and there's been a lot of attention. Most people have been nice, but there's always that smaller group that's not nice. And in a small town, the not-nice people know where to find you."

"That's true," Maura said. "I'm in Florida, and you're in the middle of everything up there."

She paused. "The three of you might want to put your heads together. It might not be a bad idea to come up with a new protection spell."

"But what about the damage to the symbol?" I asked.

"I'm not worried about the symbol," Maura said. "I'm worried about you and your sisters."

She came up with some suggestions for protective measures we could take, and I jotted everything down.

Once she was sure I'd written down everything exactly, Maura returned to my list of troubles.

"Now why did you bring up Bradshaw Tyndall?" she asked. "Are you worried about her in general—the violence of it? Or do you think there's a connection to the other issue somehow?"

"That's just it," I said. "I just don't know. I don't know if it's one or the other or both. But I do feel something at the back of my mind— an idea growing."

"Growing?" Maura said quickly.

"Yes."

"That's important," Maura said. "Hang on to that. Don't let it disappear."

"Why?" I said.

Maura was thoughtful. "I always said your powers were unique. I think you may be far more talented than you realize."

Her tone changed and became teasing. "Now what about this Mike Fellowes? I sense you have very strong emotions in connection with him."

"He's the one who revealed our symbol," I said. "He's the one who splashed our history all over the local newspaper. Of course I have strong emotions in connection with him."

"That's not it. There's something more."

I hesitated. "He's not bad-looking."

I could hear my mother smiling. "Oh. You failed to mention that before."

"Mom!"

Luckily, I was twenty-three and well past the blushing stage. But I couldn't help shifting a little on the bed where I sat.

"He's horrible."

"Hmmm," Maura said—but she didn't elaborate.

She gave me a little more advice on protective maneuvers and then prepared to sign off.

"Sleep well, honey," Maura said. "And try not to worry too much."

"You tell her to call if she needs us," Richard said. Then he raised his voice. "We'll be on the next plane if you need us, Chloe. And don't be afraid to go to the police."

I had to smile. Dad called himself the "witch protector." I knew he'd be up here in a shot if we were in trouble.

"Thanks, Dad," I said.

After a couple more assurances from both of my parents, I eventually hung up.

I sat for a moment, and then I got up and walked over to the window. On the windowsill sat four pots with four flowers—each one represented a member of my family, and I had grown them with a special spell that I had created. There was a red rose for Alberta, a blue hydrangea for Rafaela, a yellow daffodil for my mom, and a dark purple iris for my dad. Each one was tied to their personal health and well-being, and as long as the plants were healthy, I knew that my loved ones were healthy, too.

As I looked at them now, I was relieved to see that their colors were bright, and they were thriving.

But as I continued to gaze at them, it seemed to me that the blue petals of Rafaela's hydrangea looked just the tiniest bit gray around the edges. I felt a flash of panic.

Then I glanced at my phone—it was getting too late for me to call her.

I looked back at the flower. It still looked a little grayish, but it occurred to me that it might just be a trick of the light—it was late and my eyes were tired.

I decided I would call her in the morning, and I went to sleep.

By the time I woke up the next morning, Alberta had already left for work, and I ate breakfast by myself as usual. As I ate, I mulled over what to say to Rafaela—I did want to find out if she was okay, but I didn't want to sound too panicky.

I was still thinking over what to say when I stepped out of the house and found the Wednesday edition of *The Morning Cider* waiting for me on the front step.

This time there were no headlines about beauty pageants or dog yoga—the front page was entirely taken up with news about Bradshaw Tyndall.

I read through it quickly, but there wasn't anything in the paper that I didn't know—Bradshaw had been shot at while she sat in her car, but she was basically unharmed.

I got in the car then and called Rafaela. She didn't answer, and I left a message.

Then I sent her a quick text.

I was sure she was all right—I'd glanced at her flower this morning, and it still looked a little gray—but it was otherwise perfectly healthy—it was hardly dying. But all the same, I wanted to hear from Rafaela just to reassure myself.

I pushed my worry away and put my phone in my purse.

Then I drove to work, and I was pleased to find that the library was still free of graffiti.

I collected an armful of books from the book drop, went in and said hello to Rita and Barry, and then went out to get the rest of the books and other items.

The library opened at nine-thirty the way it usually did, and our patrons, who were waiting outside, hurried in. I saw a lot of our morning regulars, and as everyone filed in, I saw that it was going to be a Joe day. He smiled at me and then went over to the graphic novel section.

Everything suddenly seemed to be back to normal—but I still felt like something somewhere was off.

I really hoped I was wrong.

The morning went smoothly, and by the afternoon I had forgotten about my earlier worries. Rafaela had texted me back that she was fine, and I felt a huge sense of relief.

The flower in my room must have been losing color for another reason—I resolved to check the soil when I got home.

I was just stepping around the circulation desk when Joe walked up, clutching a comic book. Rita was already approaching the desk to take over for a little while, but I was in a good mood, and I figured I'd linger and help Joe out.

"Would you like to check that out?" I said.

"No thanks," Joe said. "At least—not yet."

He glanced over his shoulder. "Do you mind if we talk for just a sec?"

I looked up at Joe. His normally good-natured face was clouded by worry.

"Sure," I said.

I stepped away from the desk, and Rita took my place.

Joe motioned me over to the stairwell that led down to the basement, and I followed him.

We were pretty far from most of the patrons there, so it was possible for us to talk a little louder.

"So how have you been doing?" Joe said.

I smiled. "It's been a little bumpy lately, but I'm in good shape today."

"Good," Joe said. He looked a little less worried.

"I want to thank you again," I said. "For helping me out the other day."

Joe's brow creased.

"That's actually what I want to talk to you about," he said.

"What do you mean?" I asked.

Joe glanced around and lowered his voice. "It's just that there's a suspicious character outside, and I was wondering if you would like me to go and talk to this particular individual."

"A suspicious character?" I said. "Is it Professor Mike again?"

"No—it's a female," Joe said. "But something about her just doesn't seem right. And she's been staring at the library since it opened this morning."

"Show me," I said.

Joe led me to the front of the library, and the two of us peered out the window together.

There was indeed a girl sitting on the sidewalk across the street, staring at the library. She seemed to be about my age, and she had long, dark hair and very pale skin. She also gave off a distinctly creepy vibe—even from across the street.

Joe was strong and athletic, but somehow I had a feeling this was something he couldn't handle—the girl looked like something more in my line.

"Thanks for bringing this to my attention," I said quietly. "I think you're right—I think there's something wrong here."

"You want me to go talk to her?" Joe asked.

"No thanks. I think I'd better take this one."

"Okay," Joe said. "But let me know if you need me. I'll watch from the window. Just raise your hand, and I'll come running right out."

"Thanks," I said.

I went to the door and stepped out of the library.

The day was cloudy but very hot and humid, and the gray sky above was somehow no relief from the brightness of the sun.

I crossed the street and came to stand next to the girl who was staring at the library.

She didn't look up as I approached. Instead, she continued to stare across the street, her pale, bare arms wrapped around her knees.

There was a strange sense of power—of energy—surging around the girl, and I hesitated to sit down next to her. Under other circumstances I would have done just that. Despite the anger I could feel swirling around the girl, she looked so small and forlorn that I felt sorry for her.

Maybe I was misreading her—maybe she just needed help.

"Hi," I said, trying to make my tone as friendly as possible. "I'm Chloe. I've heard you've been out here for a little while."

The girl turned dark, baleful eyes on me. "I know who you are."

Her tone didn't invite conversation.

I could see the girl's dark hair clinging damply to her face and neck.

"It's awfully hot out here," I said. "Would you like to come inside?"

The girl continued to stare up at me. I crouched down next to her—I didn't want her to have to stare into the glare that suffused the gray sky.

"What's your name?" I asked.

"Ariadne," the girl said. "Ariadne Frost."

Somehow the name seemed to suit her.

"So, Ariadne, what are you—"

"That information was *not* to be shared," she said hotly, interrupting me.

I could feel her anger even more strongly now—it crackled in the air.

"What information?" I said.

"The information in the newspaper," Ariadne said, her eyes blazing. "It was given in confidence—it was given in trust. It was *not* meant to be distributed to the masses."

"Is this about the article in *The Morning Cider*?" I asked. "The one that ran on Tuesday?"

"Yes," Ariadne said. "And now I—we—are in danger because of it."

"In danger?" I said. "You?"

My gaze dropped then, and I happened to see a single pearl on a chain around Ariadne's neck. The pearl and the fine gold chain were in stark contrast to the plainness of the sleeveless T-shirt and khaki shorts that she wore.

An item from that same newspaper article suddenly popped into my head. I remembered that it mentioned the three symbols of the Crabtree Coven—the crow, the pearl, and the eye—and it had also said that members of the coven had once worn a single pearl to show their allegiance to each other. I'd dismissed the detail as embroidery dreamed up by Professor Mike, but now I wondered if maybe the idea wasn't so fanciful after all.

"Do you think you're part of the Crabtree Coven?" I said.

Ariadne quickly wrapped her fingers around the pearl.

"Tell your friend—" she said.

"What friend?" I asked.

"The one who came to see you here."

"You mean Mike Fellowes?"

"Tell your friend that the information was not to be shared."

"He's not my friend," I said.

Ariadne went on as if I hadn't spoken, her dark eyes flashing.

"Tell your friend there will be consequences."

"Consequences?" I said. "What do you mean?"

But Ariadne simply stood and ran away.

Chapter Seven

Since Ariadne had taken herself off voluntarily, Joe's assistance hadn't been necessary.

But all the same, I felt troubled by our conversation.

Ariadne seemed to believe that she was a member of the Crabtree Coven and that she'd been exposed by Mike's article just as my sisters and I had been. That was impossible, of course, since the coven was now extinct—and my family would have known if they'd returned. But Ariadne did seem like a troubled girl who truly believed she'd been wronged. I would definitely tell my sisters about Ariadne tonight—but first I had someone else to see.

I was going to pay Professor Mike a visit.

Henrietta College was nearby—only six miles away—and when I went back into the library and returned to the circulation desk and my computer, I went straight to the college's website. I was soon able to discover that Professor Mike Fellowes had office hours this afternoon. There was also a phone number, but I figured it was better if I showed up unannounced.

I took my lunch hour soon after I returned from my break, and I asked Rita if it was okay if I happened to be a little late coming back.

Rita looked at me with concern, but she agreed readily.

I left the library and got in my car.

I drove quickly over to the college.

Henrietta College was nestled in a quiet parcel of land surrounded by fields and forests, and as I parked my car and walked across the campus, I couldn't help but admire its beauty. The buildings were graceful and made of red brick, and students sat in the shade of trees that were dotted all over the lawns. The lawns themselves were lush and green despite the heat of the summer—clearly Henrietta College did a good job taking care of its grounds.

I knew exactly which building Professor Mike was in, and I knew his office number—all that information had been on the school's website. As I approached the building, however, it occurred to me that it might be locked and require a key card to get in.

Luckily, I reached the door along with three students, and I went in with them.

Professor Mike's office was on the second floor.

I hurried up the stairs.

I saw that Mike's door was standing open, and I made myself pause for just a moment before I went in. My temper was simmering, but I reminded myself that it was best to be calm if I wanted answers.

I walked in.

Mike looked up as I entered, and I saw a look of happiness spread over his face—he was clearly glad to see me. And as his dark eyes looked into mine, I found I was having trouble breathing.

Calmness would have to wait for another time—I would have to get what I needed to say out before his good looks clouded my mind.

"Why didn't you tell me the truth?" I blurted out.

Mike looked at me, puzzled. "I'm sorry?"

I stepped farther into the room. "You told me that you received emails from someone pretending to be Charles Tyndall, but that's not what happened, is it?"

Mike stood up from his desk. "Would you like to have a seat?"

He looked concerned.

I glanced down at a chair. "I might as well."

Mike walked past me and closed the door. Then he sat down again. "What's this all about?"

55

Now that the effect of his handsome face had worn off, I felt my anger returning.

"Why did you tell me that whole ridiculous story?" I demanded.

"I'm still not sure what this is about," Mike said.

"When you first came to see me two days ago," I said, "you told me that you had learned about my family and our symbol from someone claiming to be Charles Tyndall."

"Yes."

"Then who is Ariadne Frost?" I said. I threw the words at him like an accusation.

Mike stared at me. "Who?"

"Ariadne Frost," I said. "She seems to think she's a member of the Crabtree Coven."

"I have no idea who that is," Mike said.

"Well, she seems to know you. She said she gave you information that wasn't to be shared. She said there will be consequences."

Mike shook his head. "I don't know anything about this. What I told you at the library when I was nearly accosted by your boyfriend is true—I received emails from someone claiming to be Charles Tyndall that led me to do my own research."

"Joe is not my boyfriend," I said firmly.

"He isn't?" Mike said.

"No."

Mike stared at me for a moment, and a smile spread over his face. For some reason, that annoyed me.

"Then who is Ariadne Frost?"

"I don't know," Mike said. "You met her—not me."

His smile grew broader, and that annoyed me still further.

"So let me get this straight," I said. "You've never met Ariadne Frost?"

"No."

"And she never gave you any information about me or my family?"

"No."

"Then why does she think she has?" I asked.

"I really couldn't say."

Mike got busy on his computer. "Here—let me show you one of the emails."

After a moment, he motioned me over, and he had me sit in his chair.

Mike leaned over me to scroll with the mouse.

"This is the first email I received," he said.

I looked at the screen in front of me and started to read.

"Hi, Professor. I have heard about your research. Here is some info you should know."

Below that were several long paragraphs with a lot of misspellings. The author of the email also had trouble distinguishing between the use of "its" and "it's"—and also "your" and "you're." It was signed "Charles Tyndall, Business Tycoon."

I sat back in the chair.

"He died a long time ago, and I never knew him," I said, "but this doesn't sound like Charles Tyndall."

Mike quirked an eyebrow at me. "Well, surely that a given now?"

"Yes," I said. "But weren't you suspicious from the beginning? Does this sound like the writing of a business tycoon to you?"

Mike shrugged. "Not every successful businessman is a great word stylist. You don't necessarily need to compose beautiful emails to be a leader in your industry. Besides—the information was good."

"Can I see another one?"

Mike leaned over me once again, and he clicked on a new email.

I read through this one also. It was much like the first—a simple preamble followed by several paragraphs full of information—and misspellings.

"Hmmm," I said.

"What is it?" Mike asked.

"It's like someone has cribbed information from a more knowledgeable person," I said. "Sort of like a kid copying from a book rather than doing his own work."

"Maybe that's what happened," Mike said. "Maybe the author of the email did get the information from someone else. Like I said, the information was still good. So what if they copied it?"

"I don't know," I said. "I just don't know."

Mike was still leaning over me. "But something bothers you about this?"

I could feel the idea in the back of my mind growing—taking a vague, tantalizing shape.

But that was hardly something I could tell Professor Mike.

I stood up suddenly, and I found myself standing very close to him. I also found that I was having trouble breathing again.

"Thank you," I said. "For showing me all of this."

"What's with the sudden formality?" Mike said.

"What do you mean?"

"You come in here, eyes blazing, demanding to know what's going on, and now you're all polite?"

I looked up at Mike. The smirk on his face was really irritating.

I scooted around him. "I—uh—have to go now. Thank you for your time."

I hurried toward the door.

"If you need to shout at me some more," Mike called after me, "you know where to find me."

I glanced back at him. He was still smirking.

I drove back to work and ate one of the granola bars I always kept stashed in my purse on the way. I actually arrived a little early, so I went down to the break room and got a bottle of water out of the refrigerator. I ate another granola bar and an apple.

Then I went back upstairs.

"Is everything all right?" Rita whispered as I returned to the circulation desk.

I looked into her warm, brown eyes.

"It is and it isn't," I said. "But I'm fine for now."

Rita gave my arm a squeeze, and we got back to work.

I had trouble concentrating the rest of the day, but thankfully my shift came to an end, and Emma, our page, and Stu, the other librarian, came to relieve us.

Truthfully, I didn't know what was bothering me. Some of it might have been Professor Mike and his know-it-all attitude. But part of it was something else—a feeling like something was coming.

I hurried home.

As I pulled up to Alberta's house, I noticed that Rafaela's car was parked at the curb. I slotted my car in behind hers and went inside.

I found Rafaela sitting on the couch, sipping a cup of tea. Her big, blue-green eyes looked troubled. Alberta was sitting in a chair next to her. She looked troubled, too, but the worry on her face was different—she seemed to be concerned about Rafaela.

They both looked up as I came in.

I set my purse down. "What's going on? Is everything okay?"

"Rafaela's house was broken into last night," Alberta said bluntly.

"What?" I sat down next to Rafaela.

"It's not a big deal," she said. "Really."

"But when I texted you this morning," I said, "you said everything was fine."

"It is," Rafaela said. "I don't want you to worry."

"Someone broke in through the sliding glass door," Alberta interjected. "I've been telling her that lock is too flimsy—they always are. She needs to get a new lock installed and also laminated glass. At the very least, she needs to set a block of wood down in the track."

"Stop," Rafaela said softly, with a glance at me. "You'll upset her."

I sighed. Rafaela and Alberta both tended to think of me as the baby of the family, and they also tended to keep things from me to protect me—although Rafaela was the worse of the two.

"So that's why you didn't tell me," I said. "You're trying to protect me again."

There was a sudden yowl from upstairs, and Sibyl ran down the stairs and through the living room. She moved so fast that all I saw was a black streak. She then galloped back up the stairs and was gone.

"Crazy cat," Alberta said.

"So what happened?" I said to Rafaela. "You weren't hurt, were you?"

She shook her head. "It was nothing—really. I'm fine."

"She never saw them," Alberta said. "She came down to find the lock busted and the door open. Then she found a bunch of her stuff was missing."

"What did they take?" I asked.

Rafaela frowned. "That's the thing—it really was nothing. Someone had gone through my desk and taken some papers and some photos—and a few trinkets. It was all personal stuff—stuff that was only valuable to me."

"You aren't missing any bank statements, are you?" I asked. "Or tax documents? Anything like that?"

"No," Rafaela said. "All my financial stuff is in good order—it's all still there. And my credit cards and driver's license are still in my wallet. My passport is still in my desk, too."

Rafaela's house was extremely neat and tidy—and everything had its place. I knew that she would know very quickly if anything important was missing.

"That's really strange," I said. "Did you go to the police?"

"That's exactly what I told her to do," Alberta said triumphantly.

I looked at Rafaela. "Does that mean you didn't go?"

She shrugged. "I can't go to the police. The missing stuff wasn't worth more than twenty dollars or so. It's not worth their time."

"They broke your door," I said. "They broke into your house. What if they come back again?"

"I told her that, too," Alberta said. "We should go to the station right now."

"We can't," Rafaela said. "They'll think we're bothering them over something trivial."

"They'll think nothing of the kind," Alberta said firmly. "And there may have been other break-ins in the neighborhood. The police may know exactly what's going on."

Rafaela stared at Alberta for a long moment. Then she turned to look at me.

"I agree with Alberta one hundred percent," I said. "You should go to the police. And you should have told me what was wrong this morning."

Rafaela looked at both of us again.

"All right," she said at last. "I'll go to the police. But I'll go in the morning. I'm too tired tonight."

Alberta nodded approvingly. "I'm not surprised you're tired. I'm sure you've been worrying all day. You have to take care of yourself, too, you know. And of course you'll stay with us tonight."

Rafaela smiled a little. "Now that you mention it, staying here would be a relief."

"That's settled, then." Alberta stood. "Now I'm going to fix the three of us some dinner."

Rafaela and I exchanged a glance. The fettucine alfredo the other night had been pretty good, but Alberta's cooking skills were always a little uncertain. I figured we might not be so lucky a second time, and I could tell Rafaela was thinking the same thing.

"How about I cook?" Rafaela said. "Think of it as payment for letting me crash here tonight."

"Sounds good to me," I said. "Rafaela could make that chicken you like so much."

"That's right. I could."

Alberta darted a suspicious glance first at Rafaela, then at me. Both of us kept our faces carefully neutral.

"All right," Alberta said after a moment's pause. "I do love that chicken."

There was a sudden yowl from overhead, as Sibyl chose that moment to voice her opinion.

Rafaela giggled. "Sounds like Sibyl likes my chicken, too."

"Crazy cat," Alberta said.

Chapter Eight

I was awakened in the morning by a soft snuffling sound in my ear. I opened my eyes and saw Sibyl sitting right by my face, her orange eyes staring right into mine.

I sat up quickly. "Sibyl, what are you doing?"

I glanced across the room to my door. I could see that it was standing open just wide enough to admit a cat.

Alberta was fanatical about the locks on the front and back doors, but the latches on a lot of the interior doors were pretty weak, and Sibyl could open many of them if she was determined enough.

And apparently this morning she was determined enough.

She meowed softly, and I was grateful it wasn't one of her yowls. I glanced at her. Sibyl was a smart cat—did she understand that it was early morning and her humans preferred it to be quiet? Maybe she just wanted breakfast, and it wasn't an attack of the crazies.

She meowed again, and I glanced at the clock by my bed.

"It's four a.m.," I said to Sibyl. "And today is my day off. Surely Alberta doesn't feed you this early in the morning?"

Not only was it four a.m., I'd also had trouble sleeping during the night. The sky had kept lighting up with silent flashes—heat lightning—and the sudden bursts of dazzling light had kept me awake. The lightning had eventually given way to actual rain—quiet, steady, with no hint of lightning—and I'd been able to fall asleep.

But by that point the damage had been done, and most of the night had worn away.

Sibyl remained silent and sat quietly for several moments. I closed my eyes and tried to go back to sleep. But she continued to sit right next to me, and I opened my eyes.

She was still staring at me.

"All right," I said.

I sat up, and Sibyl jumped off the bed and hurried to the door.

I followed her.

We walked out into the hall, but instead of turning toward the stairs, Sibyl turned toward the bedroom where Rafaela was sleeping.

She began running her paws over the corner of the door without her claws out. Eventually, I heard the door click as the lock disengaged, and she then began to push on the door with her head and paws. After a few moments, the door swung open just a little, and Sibyl slipped inside.

"So that's how you do it," I murmured to myself.

I went to the door and peered inside. Sibyl was sitting on the floor by Rafaela's bed, staring back at me, her amber eyes bright.

"Come on, Sibyl," I whispered. "Come out of there."

But Sibyl didn't move.

"Come on out," I said. "You'll wake Rafaela."

She continued to sit where she was.

"Crazy cat," I muttered.

I went back to my room and almost climbed into bed again. But something made me turn on the light and check Rafaela's flower. The blue hydrangea was still a little gray around the edges, but it didn't seem any worse than before.

I turned out the light and got back in bed.

Sleep eluded me, however, and I was still wide-awake when Alberta's alarm went off at five.

I heard her get up, and shortly afterward, Rafaela got up also. They bustled around for a little while, and then they both went downstairs. Soon I could hear them clattering around in the kitchen.

I sighed and decided to get up myself.

I went downstairs and found Alberta and Rafaela at the little table in the kitchen eating fluffy omelets most likely whipped up by Rafaela.

It smelled heavenly, but I was in no mood for food just yet.

"Would you like an omelet?" Rafaela asked as I made my appearance.

"No thanks," I said. "I need coffee first."

Alberta looked at me in surprise. "To what do we owe this honor? I believe it's the first time since you arrived that I've actually seen you in the morning before I've left."

"Sibyl woke me up," I said. "I couldn't go back to sleep."

I glanced over at Rafaela. Sibyl was sitting on the floor next to her chair staring up at her.

I got busy with the coffee maker, and I glanced back at Sibyl.

She was staring at Rafaela steadily.

Rafaela glanced down at the cat.

"Do you like eggs?" she asked in a singsong voice.

She looked up at Alberta. "Does Sibyl like eggs?"

"I don't know," Alberta said. "She's never been that interested in them before."

She addressed Sibyl. "You've got a fresh bowl of crunchies, baby. Don't you want your crunchies?"

Sibyl didn't turn to look at her. Instead, she simply continued to stare up at Rafaela.

The coffee maker did its work, and soon the kitchen was filled with the aroma of percolating coffee.

I poured a mug out for myself and then inhaled gratefully.

"Would you guys like a cup?"

"No thanks," Alberta said. "I'm trying to cut back."

"I've got my tea already," Rafaela said.

I fixed my coffee with cream and sugar and then sat down at the table.

I took several long sips, and then I looked at my sisters.

"Wait. Are you guys going to the police station this morning? Were you going to go without me?"

Rafaela looked up at me, and then she glanced at Alberta.

"I guess so," Rafaela said. "It wasn't really a plan or anything to exclude you. We just figured you wouldn't be up."

Sibyl suddenly made a chirrup sound and ran from the room. I could hear her galloping up the stairs.

A moment later, the doorbell rang.

Alberta turned in her chair. "Are either of you expecting anyone?"

Rafaela and I both replied in the negative.

The doorbell rang again.

Alberta got up, frowning. "I'll see who it is."

She left the kitchen, and I heard the front door open.

"Oh!" I heard her exclaim. "You're here already!"

Rafaela and I exchanged a puzzled glance.

"Girls!" Alberta called out. "The police are here already!"

We both got up and hurried to the door.

There was indeed a uniformed police officer standing outside on the front step.

"I presume you're here about the break-in at my sister's house?" Alberta said.

The police officer was a young, blond man with a good-natured countenance.

He turned wide, puzzled eyes on Alberta. "Break-in, ma'am?"

"Yes," Alberta said. "The break-in at Rafaela's house yesterday. I assume there were other break-ins in her neighborhood?"

The police officer glanced at Rafaela and me. "So your sister is here?"

"Yes."

"Are both of these ladies your sisters?"

"Yes."

The young officer puffed out his cheeks. "Do you mind if we start again, ma'am? We seem to have gotten a little off track."

Alberta blinked. "Yes, certainly."

"I'm Officer Tyler Gil," the police officer said. "Are you Alberta Bartlett?"

"Yes, I am," Alberta said.

"And these two ladies are your sisters, Rafaela and Chloe Bartlett?"

"Yes."

Officer Gil's face became politely neutral. "Would you three ladies mind coming down to the station with me for a little chat?"

"What?" Alberta said. "Why? Is this about the break-in at Rafaela's house?"

"I'm not aware of any break-in," Officer Gil said carefully.

"It's something else?" Alberta demanded.

"Possibly," Officer Gil said. "We just want to talk."

Alberta looked around at Rafaela and me.

"Ordinarily, I'd say we needed an experienced criminal defense attorney to accompany us. But since Rafaela is the victim here, I'd say we're okay to go to the station. What do you guys think?"

Rafaela's big, blue-green eyes looked troubled, but she nodded her assent.

"Chloe? What about you?" Alberta asked.

"Sure," I said. "If it'll help clear things up."

"All right, then," Alberta said, turning to Officer Gil. "We'll go with you. I should warn you, however, that I'm an attorney myself. I'm a tax attorney, but I'm still an attorney."

"Is that so?" Officer Gil said pleasantly. "If you ladies would like to accompany me, my car is just outside."

"Do you mind if we drive ourselves?" Alberta asked. Her tone was a little officious.

"By all means," the officer said. "This is just a chat."

He stepped back, and the three of us grabbed our purses and then stepped out of the house.

Alberta made a big show of locking the door.

Then the officer walked down to his squad car, and Alberta waved us to the garage.

"I'll drive us over," she said.

"Do you recognize Officer Gil?" Rafaela whispered to Alberta.

"No. Why would I?"

"I was just wondering if you recognized him from any of the missing person cases you worked on."

"No," Alberta replied, opening the garage. "That was the police in Annapolis. I don't know the people at the local precinct at all."

We all got in her car.

Officer Gil waited for us as Alberta backed down the driveway, and then we all drove over to the police station.

Once at the station, we parked near Officer Gil's car, and he ushered us inside.

We entered a small lobby, where a woman sat behind what I presumed was bulletproof glass, and Officer Gil gave the woman a smile and a brief wave.

Then he led us through a green metal door into a concrete hallway.

"Just down here," he said.

Officer Gil led us into a room filled with low-walled cubicles. He led us over to a desk, and a woman with rich brown skin and curly black hair looked up and smiled at us.

"Which one of you is Chloe?" Officer Gil asked.

Feeling slightly foolish, I raised my hand.

"This is Detective Mia Coleman," the officer said. "You'll be going with her."

"You're separating us?" I said.

"Just for the moment." His smile was reassuring.

Detective Coleman stood up and shook my hand, and Officer Gil led my sisters away.

"You're Chloe Bartlett?" the detective said.

"Yes."

She smiled. "Would you follow me, please?"

Detective Coleman led me to a small room with a table and three chairs that was lit with a sickly fluorescent glow. She waved me to a seat and then closed the door and sat down opposite me.

"But where are my manners?" she said suddenly. "May I offer you a cup of coffee? Some tea? It is early in the morning."

"No thanks," I said. "Detective—"

She smiled. "Please call me Mia."

"Mia," I said. "What's going on here? Is this about my sister's house being broken into?"

Mia's smile never wavered, but she became careful, just as Officer Gil had done.

"I'm not aware of any break-in," she said.

She'd brought a folder with her, and she opened it and slid a piece of paper toward me.

I glanced at it—it was a photograph of our symbol.

I drew in my breath sharply. Even though I'd seen our symbol in public twice now, it was still a shock to see it presented to me by a stranger.

"Do you recognize that?" Mia asked.

I resisted the urge to look up at her, and I continued to stare down at the photo. I knew she'd heard me gasp, and I knew the symbol and my family's story had been splashed all over the local newspaper. There would be no point in my denying that I knew what it was. And yet, I still had to be careful about what I said—I didn't want to sound crazy, and I still had no idea why I was here.

"Yes," I said. "I recognize it."

"Can you tell me about it?" Mia asked.

I continued to stare at the photo. In the photo, the symbol was drawn in black on a white sheet of paper, and the paper had been crumpled and then smoothed out.

I wondered why the detective was showing me a photo and not the crumpled piece of paper itself.

I frowned. "Where did this come from? Is this evidence of some kind?"

Mia simply smiled at me pleasantly. "Why don't you just tell me a little about it?"

"It's a symbol that's important to my family."

"Does it mean anything?"

"It's for protection," I said.

Mia tapped on the photo. "You believe this symbol protects you?"

"Yes."

"Does it mean anything else?"

"No."

"Is it gang-related?" Mia asked.

I looked up at her then, startled. "No."

"Does it have anything to do with revenge?"

"No," I said.

"But it is something you and your family like to keep secret?"

"Yes."

Mia watched me for a moment, and then she took another photo from the folder and slid it toward me.

"Do you recognize this symbol?"

I stared at the photograph. A symbol with a lot of squiggles and curlicues was drawn in black paint on a tan-colored surface. The tan surface had a bit of a curve to it.

"What is that?" I asked.

"I was hoping you could tell me," Mia said.

I continued to stare at the photo, but I couldn't make sense of the curlicues or the tan object it was painted on.

"I've never seen it before," I said. "I don't know what this is."

Mia took the two photos away and then slid two more over to me.

"Do you recognize these two young ladies?"

I looked at the photos. Both featured young blond women in their early twenties, and superficially they were a bit alike. One I knew. The other I didn't.

"This one is Bradshaw Tyndall," I said. "I don't know the other one."

"Are you sure?" Mia said. "You haven't seen her around town? Maybe at a party or a friend's house?"

"No," I said.

"Tell me about Bradshaw. How do you feel about her?"

"I don't really feel anything about her."

"No? No jealousy? I understand she's seeing your former boyfriend."

"No jealousy," I said firmly.

"How about drugs?" Mia asked suddenly. "Do you like to party?"

"What?" I said. "No."

"Come on. A young girl like you? You must like to go out and have a little fun. Do you know any places where you can get some good stuff?"

"No," I said.

Mia smiled at me. "You won't get into trouble. I'm just looking for information."

"No," I said firmly. "No drugs."

Mia nodded.

"Are you familiar with firearms?" she asked briskly.

"I know they exist," I said.

"Do you own one?"

"No."

"Do you have friends who own them?"

"No," I said.

"Have you ever fired one?"

"No."

"Can you tell me what you did yesterday?" Mia asked, switching topics suddenly. "Starting in the morning and coming up to this morning?"

"I got up, I went to work, I came home and had dinner," I said. "Then I went to bed."

"Is that all?"

"Yes," I said shortly.

"What about your sisters?" Mia asked. "Do you have any idea what their days were like?"

"As far as I know, their days were similar."

"How about the evening?" Mia asked. "Do you know what they did?"

70

"We were all together," I said. "We all had dinner at my sister Alberta's house, and then we all spent the night there."

Mia's eyebrows rose. "You were all together?"

"Yes."

"All night?"

"Yes."

"What was the occasion? Slumber party?"

"No," I said. "My sister Rafaela's house was broken into. She was worried about staying in her home alone."

"Did she report the break-in?"

"No. We were trying to get her to report it. Eventually we got her to agree to do it this morning."

"I see," Mia said. "So you were all at your sister Alberta's house all of last night?"

"Yes."

"But you said you went home last night."

"I did," I said. "I'm staying at Alberta's house right now. I moved back to town a few months ago, and I don't have an apartment of my own yet."

"I see," Mia said again.

She took back the pictures of the two blond girls and stared at them for a moment. Then she put them back in the folder and closed it.

Then she looked at me for a moment.

"Is there anything you'd like to tell me?" she asked. "Anything that's weighing on your mind?"

"No," I said.

Mia reached into a pocket of her suit jacket and pulled out a card. She slid it across to me.

"This is my card. Feel free to call me if anything occurs to you that you'd like me to know."

I took the card. "About what? I still don't know why I'm here."

Mia smiled and stood. "The situation is ongoing."

She held out a hand. "If you would follow me, please."

We left the small room, and Mia showed me to another small room with several tables and chairs and a long counter. Officer Gil was waiting inside.

"Officer Gil will see to you now," Mia said. "Thank you for your time, Ms. Bartlett."

Officer Gil took my driver's license and made a photocopy. Then he took my fingerprints. He said I didn't have to have that done, but I didn't see any reason to refuse, and I agreed without hesitation.

After everything was done, I was reunited with my sisters in the lobby.

Rafaela was looking worried. Alberta was looking grim.

We walked outside in silence, and none of us said anything until we were in the car.

"Did they tell you guys anything?" I asked as I settled in the back seat.

Rafaela shook her head.

"Did they show you the symbol?" Alberta asked, glancing at me in the rearview mirror.

"You mean our symbol?" I said. "Yes. They showed it to me."

"No," Alberta said. "Not ours. The other one."

"The one with all the squiggles?" I said. "It was painted on something tan?"

"Yes—that's the one. Do you know what it is?"

"No," I said. "Do you?"

"Yes," Alberta said grimly. "It's the Sleeping Beauty Curse."

Chapter Nine

We learned a lot of information in rapid succession.

Texts flew back and forth among friends and co-workers.

We learned that a girl named Lisa Stroup had been found unconscious at Bradshaw Tyndall's house yesterday. We learned that she'd been wearing Bradshaw's clothes, and she was found clutching a piece of paper with our symbol on it.

Lisa apparently had been working as domestic help for Bradshaw, cleaning the house in the afternoons. Lisa appeared to be unharmed and in good health—she just wouldn't wake up. The police believed she'd been given a drug of some kind.

Bradshaw had returned to the house later that night and had discovered the young cleaning woman.

Bradshaw herself had then been shot—for real this time—by an unseen intruder who had fled. She'd been shot in the arm but was otherwise unhurt, and she'd been discharged from the hospital in the early morning.

Bradshaw was said to be furious, and apparently she also believed that I was responsible for her being shot.

As we sat in Alberta's living room, Rafaela turned big, worried eyes on her.

"What did Bradshaw say about the assailant exactly?" she said. "Were there any details?"

Alberta, who seemed to have the most knowledgeable social network, was busily texting a friend. She waited a moment and then looked up at us.

"She said she couldn't see the person who attacked her—she just saw a shadow moving."

"Oh," Rafaela said. She seemed disappointed.

"What's wrong?" Alberta asked.

"I was just hoping the intruder was very tall or obviously a man."

"Why?"

Rafaela glanced at me. "I was hoping we could rule out Chloe right away as a suspect."

"I imagine even Bradshaw would notice something like that," Alberta replied. "I think it's pretty clear that she didn't see who it was."

"Then it's ridiculous for her to suspect Chloe," Rafaela said.

"Of course it is," Alberta said. "But she's upset and scared right now—she doesn't really know what she's saying. It'll blow over soon."

Rafaela frowned again.

"You don't think so?" Alberta said.

Rafaela looked at me once more, and I could see concern and worry in her eyes.

"It's just that the detective who questioned me kept asking about you and Andrew," she said to me. "She seemed to think you were really jealous and you wanted Andrew back."

"Was it Detective Mia Coleman?" I said.

"I believe that was her name—yes."

"She mostly asked me about drugs," I said. "But I'm not surprised to hear she hammered at you on the jealousy angle. She did seem to be pretty certain I was in on it somehow."

Rafaela looked even more troubled.

"Don't worry," I said. "Everything will be fine."

I glanced up at Alberta, hoping to change the subject. "How about you? Did you talk to Detective Mia?"

"No," Alberta replied. "I spoke to a male detective—and he wasn't bad-looking, either."

She paused.

"Did you two both agree to be fingerprinted?"

"Yes," I said.

Rafaela simply nodded.

"I did, too," Alberta said. "We probably shouldn't have. But I suppose it can't hurt anything."

"Unless—" Rafaela said. She stopped abruptly.

She turned to me. "Chloe, I have a feeling somebody's got it in for you."

"What do you mean?" I said.

She shook her head. "I don't know. I just wish Bradshaw hadn't seen only a shadow."

"That reminds me," I said suddenly. "I forgot to tell you guys I met somebody strange yesterday."

"Strange how?" Alberta asked.

"I met a girl at the library," I said. "She said her name was Ariadne Frost. She said a friend of mine had given away secrets. And she was wearing a single pearl."

Alberta's eyebrows rose. "Oh."

"She also said there would be consequences."

"Oh," Alberta said again.

"What?" Rafaela said.

"The Crabtree Coven," Alberta said. "Professor Mike's article said the members used to wear a single pearl."

"But that's impossible," Rafaela said. "We'd know if they were active again."

"I know," Alberta replied. "I'm just telling you what the article said."

She turned to me.

"Did you mention it to the police?"

"No," I said. "I was so irritated that I didn't even think of it. I also went to confront Professor Mike about Ariadne—I didn't mention that, either."

"And how did that visit go?" Alberta asked.

"Mike said he had no idea who she was."

"Interesting," Alberta said.

"I think we need to call Mom," Rafaela said abruptly. "We need someone more powerful and experienced here."

"Why?" Alberta said. "It'll only upset her. And nothing's happened to us. Nobody was charged with anything."

"But something supernatural is going on," Rafaela said. "I can feel it."

"You don't know that."

"Bradshaw said she saw a shadow," Rafaela said.

"I'm sure she did," Alberta replied. "It was dark, and she couldn't see who it was. There's no reason to believe it wasn't an ordinary person."

"The Crabtree Coven keeps popping up," Rafaela said.

Alberta waved a hand. "Rumors. Just rumors."

"What about the Sleeping Beauty Curse?" Rafaela said. "You mentioned that yourself."

"Yes, what about the curse?" I asked.

Alberta had brought it up and then refused to say another word about it.

"It's nothing," Alberta said. "I'm sure it's just a tattoo."

"Tattoo?" I said. "Who said anything about a tattoo?"

"No one," Alberta said. "I just threw that out as an example."

"An example of what?" I said. "You know something about it, don't you?"

"No, I do not."

She said the words very firmly, but she glanced furtively at her phone.

"I knew it!" I said.

Alberta looked up at me. "What?"

I turned to Rafaela. "She texted Mom already. She just doesn't want us to know."

"Alberta," Rafaela said. "Are you trying to keep us in the dark?"

"She is," I said. "She's playing big sister to both of us this time. She's worried, and she wants to consult Mom without the two of us knowing about it."

"You might as well tell us what you know," Rafaela said. "We'll find out soon enough."

Alberta sighed. "I'm hardly an expert in curses. That's why I wanted to talk to Mom before I said anything to you guys."

"Out with it," Rafaela said.

Alberta glanced at her phone. "Hey, look at the time. You know what? I should really be getting to the office."

"You called your office just like I did," Rafaela said. "I heard you. We all have the day off now."

"We really should get to work with those protective measures Mom gave us," Alberta said. "We neglected them and look what happened. We need to start setting things up before anything else strange occurs."

"We have time," I said. "A few more minutes isn't going to make a difference."

"Alberta, please," Rafaela said. "Just tell us."

"Fine," Alberta said at last. "But I really don't know much."

She stared at us as if she hoped we would accept her plea of ignorance.

We stared back.

Alberta sighed.

"The Sleeping Beauty Curse is basically a curse of compulsion," she said at last. "The victim falls into a deep sleep, but all metabolic functions—except for breathing—stop. The person under the curse doesn't need to eat or drink, and all aging processes will stop."

"That last part doesn't sound so bad," Rafaela said.

"The problem is," Alberta said, "that the person under the curse is basically a prisoner. The person who cast the curse can command the victim to do things, to say things, and the victim must obey—all while remaining in a dream-like trance."

"So the victim is conscious?" I asked.

"Sort of," Alberta replied. "The victim only responds to the voice of the person who cast the spell. No other voices can get through."

"So," Rafaela said, "what if the person who cast the spell ordered the victim to walk to the edge of a cliff and jump off?"

"Then the victim would do just that," Alberta said. "It's really horrible."

"How is the curse cast?" I asked.

Alberta's forehead wrinkled in thought. "I believe there's an incantation and a ritual. And there's also a rune that's necessary."

"A rune," I said quickly. "That's what that symbol was with all the curlicues?"

"Yes."

"So what was the tan object the rune was painted on?" I asked.

"That was an arm," Alberta said.

"I get it now," Rafaela said. "I couldn't figure out what was in that picture before. The rune was painted on Lisa Stroup to complete the curse."

"Yes," Alberta said.

"How did you know about it?" Rafaela asked.

"I studied runes once. They're a bit old-fashioned and hard to use correctly. So I gave up on them eventually. I remembered that one because of the name. I remember thinking it was a shame to give a pretty, fairy-tale name to something so awful."

I was puzzled. "But why would someone put a Sleeping Beauty Curse on Bradshaw Tyndall's cleaning lady?"

"I have no idea," Alberta said. "But at least she's safe at the moment. She's sleeping peacefully at the hospital right now—no one will be able to get to her there. There are cameras and security all over the place."

"How is the curse broken?" Rafaela asked.

"That I don't know," Alberta replied. "I need to learn more about it if we're going to free her. I imagine it can't be easy."

"Why didn't you want us to know?" Rafaela said.

Alberta sighed. "Because if this really is the Sleeping Beauty Curse, then that means someone in town is performing magic—someone we don't know about. And we should have known. It means our wards aren't working properly. And anyone at all could be in this town."

We were all silent for a moment.

"What did Mom say?" I asked.

Alberta shook her head. "I haven't heard from her yet."

"Well, there's no use in hiding from a problem," Rafaela said. "Is there anything here we can use? Do you have any of your old books on runes?"

"I might," Alberta said. "But I don't know how much good they'll be. I don't know much about curses. None of us do—we never needed to. This town was always safe. We could focus on positive things instead—healing, growing, helping. We didn't need to know about defense."

She paused. "I don't know about you guys, but I'm tired. I could use a little rest—do you guys want to stay in this afternoon and watch a movie? I'll make us lunch."

An impish smile lit up Rafaela's face. "Sure. Then you can tell us about this good-looking cop you talked to."

"Maybe it would be a better idea to go out," Alberta said.

I caught Rafaela's eye.

"Oh, I see," I said. "You want to go out to Peter's Table. Maybe see Peter again?"

"Never mind," Alberta said. "Let's not go anywhere or do anything."

I glanced at her—she really did look tired. Maybe all the worrying about the Sleeping Beauty Curse had made this harder on her than it had been on us.

"You know," I said. "How about I do the cooking for lunch this time? You cooked for us Monday night, and Rafaela cooked last night. It's my turn."

Rafaela and Alberta exchanged a glance.

"Hey," I said. "What's that look about? I'm not a bad cook."

"No—" Rafaela said.

"It's not that you can't cook," Alberta said. "It's just that you cook the same things over and over again. Your repertoire is a little limited."

"What?" I said.

Alberta gave me a level look. "Be honest. You were thinking of making grilled cheese sandwiches just now, weren't you?"

I *did* like grilled cheese sandwiches—I loved them, in fact. But I'd actually been thinking of something else.

"For your information," I said with dignity, "I was thinking of making quesadillas."

"Which are basically grilled cheese sandwiches," Alberta said.

"They are not," I replied. "They're made with flour tortillas, and then I throw in some vegetables and maybe a little shredded chicken."

"And?" Alberta prompted. "I think you're leaving the main ingredient out."

"And cheese," I said.

"Exactly," Alberta replied.

"Fine," I said. "I'll go to the grocery store and pick out something else, and Rafaela can come with me as a consultant. And you can stay here, Alberta, and rest. Or do some baking—you haven't done any baking in about three days, and I know how that relaxes you."

A light went on in Alberta's eyes. "I have been wanting to make cinnamon rolls. But that takes some extra time. You need about two hours to let the dough rise."

"That's perfect," I said. "You can get started on that, and we'll leave you to work in peace for a little while."

"Sounds good to me," Rafaela said. "I've got a few things in mind."

"All right," Alberta said, already heading toward the kitchen. "I'll see you guys a little later."

Rafaela smiled at me. "Looks like you found just the right thing."

The two of us went outside and got in my car. The nearest supermarket was only a mile away, and soon we were in the store, walking up and down the aisles.

"So I know you said you had something in mind," I said, glancing around for Rafaela. "What were you thinking of?"

There were three women in the aisle up ahead of us. They were standing in a cluster and whispering, and one of them looked back at me. I looked up at her, and the three of them quickly moved on.

"I was thinking of fish," Rafaela said. She didn't seem to have noticed the women.

I wrinkled my nose. "What kind of fish? Salmon?"

"Oh, come on, fussy," Rafaela said. "Fish isn't so bad—you just need to know how to choose a good piece. Let's go over to the counter."

We walked to the fish counter, and we settled on mahi-mahi. Rafaela claimed that it was light and not too fishy at all, and we could make fish tacos—that way I would still get to use my tortillas.

We picked up some fresh tomatoes and an avocado, and then we headed to the checkout.

As we waited in line, a voice floated over to me.

"Nothing but jealousy," I heard someone say.

"And walking around town like she's done nothing wrong," said another voice.

I glanced around and saw the same group of women I'd seen before in a nearby line.

Rafaela looked over at me.

I knew she'd heard them this time.

More snippets of conversation floated over to us.

"—trying to get her out of the way."

"—wants him all to herself."

The women eventually made it through the line and headed for the exit. One of them threw a baleful glance over at me as she left.

Rafaela placed a hand on my arm. "Don't listen to them. We'll get you through this. No one who really knows you could believe for thirty seconds that you shot Bradshaw."

I appreciated the reassurance, but I couldn't help thinking about what she'd said earlier in the day.

Somebody's got it in for you.

Chapter Ten

Rafaela stayed over at Alberta's house again that night, and in the morning, we all had breakfast together. I got up a little earlier than usual, and Alberta waited a little longer before going into the office—she didn't leave at the crack of dawn like she usually did.

There were no fluffy omelets this morning—Alberta had indeed made her cinnamon rolls yesterday, and she warmed them up for us in the morning.

The kitchen was soon full of the heavenly scent of cinnamon and sugar, and the buttery roll melted in my mouth as I drank my coffee.

"Alberta," I murmured, "you really are a wonderful baker."

"Thanks," she said. She gave me a worried glance. "Did you sleep okay last night?"

Sibyl had spent a good portion of the night running up and down the stairs. She was a small cat, but somehow she managed to make a lot of noise, and no amount of coaxing with food or toys was able to calm her down. Her galloping, however, had eventually fallen into a steady rhythm, and once I was used to the sound, I fell asleep.

Sibyl was nowhere to be found this morning.

"I slept well," I said. "How about you?"

"Just fine," Alberta said. "After I learned how to tune Sibyl out. I don't know what's going on with that cat lately."

I glanced over at Rafaela. She looked perfectly healthy, but her flower had been a little grayer this morning.

"Are you all right, Raf?" I said.

Rafaela turned startled blue-green eyes on me. "Yes, of course—I'm fine. You're the one we have to worry about."

She and Alberta exchanged a glance. I knew they'd been talking to their friends about the general mood in the town. Apparently quite a few people believed that I was responsible for the attacks on Bradshaw—and for what had happened to Lisa Stroup. No one knew about the Sleeping Beauty Curse, of course, except for us, but a rumor was floating around that I had placed a "spell" on her.

Friends had been texting me with words of encouragement, but they—like my sisters—were trying to keep the full extent of the rumors from me.

Unfortunately, I was able to gather quite enough information on my own—I knew what people were saying about me.

I looked up to see both Alberta and Rafaela staring at me with concern.

"Have another cinnamon roll, Chloe," Alberta said.

"I've already had one," I said.

"You could use another," Alberta replied. "I can tell."

I smiled a little to myself. Alberta was definitely a "feeder"—whenever someone was troubled, she brought out the baked goods.

"Well, if you insist," I said.

"More coffee?" Rafaela said. "I'll get you some more coffee."

She got up without waiting for an answer and patted me on the shoulder.

"So I know why Mom didn't text me back yesterday," Alberta said.

"Why not?" Rafaela said.

"Hurricane," Alberta replied. "Mom and Dad had to evacuate."

"What?" I said.

"Hurricane Demelza?" Rafaela asked.

"That's the one," Alberta replied.

Rafaela returned to the table and set a cup of coffee in front of me. "But I thought Hurricane Demelza was headed out to sea."

"It was," Alberta said. "Apparently it changed its mind and turned inland."

"Where are they?" I said. "Are they okay? Why didn't they come up here?"

"They can hardly fly up here in a hurricane," Rafaela said gently.

"I know," I said. "But they can drive. I assume they drove to wherever they are now."

"They're fine," Alberta said to me in her soothing, big-sister voice. "They're staying with friends who are outside of the evacuation zone. They didn't want to go too far because of Maisie and Tibi. You know they don't like to travel—and they're already nervous as it is because of the storm."

Maisie and Tibi were our parents' pets—Maisie was a Russian Blue cat and Tibi, short for Tiberius, was a Yorkshire terrier. And Alberta was right—neither one of them liked to travel much. That was one of the reasons Mom and Dad had chosen to make their stay in Florida a long one—they didn't want to have to move their fur babies back and forth too much while they were deciding where they wanted to live.

"They're really okay?" Rafaela asked.

"They really are," Alberta said. "And Mom texted me back about the rune. She said she thinks I'm right. From what I described, she believes someone has indeed cast the Sleeping Beauty Curse on Lisa Stroup."

"So what do we do?" I asked. "How can we break the curse?"

Alberta began to fiddle with one of her earrings. It was emerald green—just like her eyes.

"It's not going to be easy. It turns out there's more than one reason it's called the Sleeping Beauty Curse. It doesn't just place the victim into an ageless, dream-like trance. It also has to be broken by a kiss."

"A kiss from whom?" I asked.

"From the person who cast the curse."

"Oh," Rafaela said. "You're right. That's not going to be easy."

85

"Is that the only way?" I said.

"Mom's not sure," Alberta said. "She doesn't have access to her usual sources at the moment. But she's going to keep looking and see if she can find another solution. If there's another way to break the curse, she'll let us know right away."

"Does she know about everything?" Rafaela asked, with a side-glance at me. "Does Dad?"

"They do," Alberta said. "And they did want to come up here. They were torn between their two sets of kids—the furry ones and the non-furry ones. But I told them we'd be okay, and we'd take care of Chloe."

I nodded. "They should definitely stay where they and the pets are safe. They don't need to come up here for us—or for me."

I sighed to myself. Alberta and Rafaela were worried about me, but I was really worried about Rafaela.

An idea was still growing in the back of my mind—something was taking shape. And somehow, hazily, I could see Rafaela in the middle of it.

"So what we need to do at this point," I said, "is find out who placed a curse on Lisa Stroup. Then we can work on the kiss part and how to save her."

"I think you're right," Alberta said. "We need to find out who cast the curse. And we also need to find out who's been shooting at Bradshaw. The next time someone shoots at her, she might not be so lucky."

"Do you think it's the same person?" Rafaela asked.

"I'm inclined to," Alberta said. "Although at this point, I don't want to assume anything. I don't really see what the connection could be between them—other than the fact that Lisa works for Bradshaw."

Something tugged at my memory.

"Didn't somebody say—"

I stopped. I'd had something for a moment, but then I lost it.

"Didn't somebody say what?" Alberta asked.

"I'm not sure," I said. "I hope it'll come back to me."

Rafaela rose. "Well, I should be getting to work. And you two need to go, too."

Rafaela left the house first, and then Alberta and I walked out together.

Alberta clicked her tongue in irritation as she glanced down at the front step.

"I wonder if Rafaela saw this."

"What?" I said.

She stooped down and picked up the latest edition of *The Morning Cider*.

She held it out to me.

I could see a big, bold headline.

Bradshaw had been shot at again.

Alberta sighed. "I expect we'll be getting another visit from the police."

We both got into our cars and drove to work.

I was just getting out of my car when someone who was standing in the shade of a nearby tree suddenly rushed toward me.

I felt a flash of panic.

I'd already closed the car door, so I turned my back to the car and braced myself against it. Then I got ready to strike out with the heel of my palm toward the nose of my attacker.

I felt a rush of adrenaline surge through me.

But my onrushing assailant suddenly stopped and stood before me.

It was Bradshaw Tyndall.

She was wearing white jean shorts which once again showed off her long, tanned legs. She was wearing a tank top, and her blond hair was perfectly smooth and frizz-free despite the heat and humidity of the morning.

For my part, I could feel beads of sweat running down my back and neck. Seeing someone rushing toward me had done nothing to help me stay calm and collected.

"Bradshaw," I said, "you nearly gave me a heart attack."

Bradshaw was staring at me balefully.

"I nearly gave you a heart attack?" she sputtered. "You've been trying to kill me!"

"I haven't—"

"Stop it!" Bradshaw screamed. "Leave me alone!"

Her voice echoed down the quiet street, and I felt sweat running down my back again.

I happened to notice then that she had a cast on her lower arm. I'd vaguely noticed something white on her arm before when she'd run up to me, but somehow I'd thought it was part of her outfit—a fashionable wrist band or something like that.

"You got shot in the forearm?" I said.

I was puzzled. For some reason, I'd assumed she'd been shot in the upper arm.

"Oh," Bradshaw said. "You didn't know where you'd shot me? I'm so sorry for you."

"No, it's not that," I said. I realized that I'd been assuming someone had been aiming for her heart and had missed. But I could hardly tell Bradshaw that.

"I'm sorry you got shot," I said. "I really am. But I didn't do it."

Bradshaw was fuming. "Sorry I got shot? Or sorry you missed?"

"Bradshaw—"

"You're a lousy shot, by the way," she said. "Three times and you still can't kill me."

"Bradshaw—"

"No. Stop it. I mean it. You're pathetic and jealous. I can't believe you'd kill me just to get Andrew back."

I ignored the Andrew comment. "Where did the latest one happen?"

Bradshaw stared at me. "What are you talking about?"

"Where were you the third time someone shot at you?"

"Like you don't know."

"I don't."

"I'm not telling you anything," Bradshaw said. "And anyway, you tried to kill me four times—not just three."

"But you just said—"

"You shot at me three times," Bradshaw said. "But the other attempt was when you cast that little witchy spell on Lisa."

"What?" I said.

Bradshaw looked smug. "You thought she was me. I knew that little creep was trying on my clothes when I wasn't around. She was wearing my clothes, and she'd been trying for ages to get her dishwater hair to look like mine. You saw her messing around in my stuff, and you thought she was me."

She smiled. "I bet you were pretty shocked when you saw me walking around just fine."

"Lisa used to try on your clothes?" I said. Something tugged at my memory.

"She did it all the time," Bradshaw said. "I would come home and find stuff out of place in my closet. I think she used to put on my makeup, too. But it doesn't matter now—she got what she deserved for being creepy."

"That's what I was trying to remember before!" I exclaimed. "Lisa was wearing your clothes. That attack wasn't meant for her—it was meant for you."

"I know," Bradshaw said. "I just said that."

She stared at me like I'd lost my mind.

"So then the curse wasn't—" I began.

I stopped myself.

Bradshaw gave me a superior smile. "Oh, I know all about your little spell—everyone does."

I chose my next words carefully.

"What makes you think what happened to Lisa was a spell?" I asked.

"You'll find out," Bradshaw said smugly. "It's all over town."

She suddenly leaned closer. "So like I said—"

"Hey, Chloe!" called a voice. "Are you okay?"

I looked up to see Joe Osgood walking down the sidewalk toward us.

"Leave me alone," Bradshaw hissed. Then she hurried off to her car.

Joe jogged up to me. His good-natured blue eyes were filled with concern.

"Is everything all right?" he asked. "Was Bradshaw giving you a hard time?"

I watched as Bradshaw hopped in her Jeep and sped off.

"Yes, thanks, Joe," I said. "Everything is okay."

As Bradshaw disappeared around a corner, another car suddenly started up and went after her. I was startled to see that it was the same blue car with the yellow lightning bolt that had followed Bradshaw after her first angry visit to the library. Inside, I could just make out a man in a sleeveless T-shirt and dark glasses. His head appeared to be shaved.

Somehow he looked familiar.

"Can you see the guy in that car?" I asked Joe. "Do you recognize him?"

Joe looked where I was pointing. He squinted a little.

"Oh yeah," he said. "I know that guy—that's Chris Young."

"Chris Young," I murmured. It sounded like a name I should recognize.

"Yeah," Joe said. "He's Bradshaw's ex-boyfriend. She dated him before Andrew."

"Oh," I said. I remembered now—it had been a while since I'd last seen him. "Their relationship was a little while ago."

"That's right," Joe said. "He's been mooning after Bradshaw for ages—trying to get back with her."

Comprehension dawned on his face.

"He's the one!" Joe shouted.

"I'm sorry?" I said.

"Everyone's blaming you. But it's really him."

"Are you saying—"

"Bradshaw came here because she thinks you shot her, didn't she?" Joe said.

"Yes," I said.

"And of course she does—everybody thinks you're guilty."

"Thanks," I said.

"But it's really Chris," Joe said excitedly. "He's mad because he can't get her back."

"You really think so?" I said. "That seems a little—"

Joe turned suddenly. "I'm going to go after him."

"What?" I said. "Joe, don't—"

But he was already sprinting off to his car.

He jumped in and took off.

"Joe, wait!" I shouted at him as he zoomed past.

But he was already gone—I was too late to stop him.

Chapter Eleven

A half an hour later, Joe walked into the library and came up to me at the circulation desk.

"I don't know," he said. "This is tricky."

I was still clutching the piece of paper I'd found taped on the front door. I'd had other things to do, of course, but every time my hands were free, I picked up the sheet of paper again.

I couldn't seem to let it go.

I looked up at Joe. He didn't seem too ruffled after his chase after Chris Young and Bradshaw—he only seemed puzzled.

I was relieved. I'd considered calling the police after he zoomed off—but then I hadn't known what to tell them. I could tell them that someone I knew was chasing two other people, and that there might be trouble—but then again, there might not be.

From the looks of Joe, I'd made the right decision—he appeared to be completely unharmed.

"So what's tricky?" I said. "Is everything okay?"

Joe stared back at me with a genuine sense of befuddlement in his clear blue eyes.

"I'm fine," he said. "I'm just not sure what I saw."

"What happened?" I asked.

"Well, nothing really," Joe said. "Bradshaw drove really fast to her house, and Chris drove really fast after her. They both got out of their cars, and they seemed to be arguing for a while. Then they seemed to get a little quieter, and eventually, Bradshaw went into her house, and Chris drove away."

"Nobody got hurt?"

"No."

"Did they see you?" I asked.

Joe shook his head. "No."

"So everything's okay, then?"

"That's the thing," Joe said. "Bradshaw seemed really nervous around Chris—just the way she moved, you know? Her body language. I'd definitely say Chris is stalking her."

He paused, and his smooth forehead crinkled in thought.

"But then she's being weird, too."

"What do you mean?" I said.

Joe glanced at me. "It's just—Bradshaw believes you're trying to kill her, right? Everybody else certainly does."

"Yes, she does—and thanks for bringing that up."

"No," Joe said. "I'm not trying to be funny. It's just that the whole situation is so weird. Bradshaw can't be that scared of you, or else she wouldn't have come here. What if you had a gun with you? I wouldn't confront somebody who was trying to kill me—and I'm a big guy."

Joe's words gave me pause—what he said made sense. I suddenly thought again of the fact that Bradshaw had been shot in the forearm. It reminded me of something—but what, I couldn't quite recall.

"You're right," I said slowly. "I wouldn't confront someone who was trying to kill me, either."

Joe glanced down at my hands. "What have you got there?"

I looked at the folded-up piece of paper I was clutching.

I handed it to him.

He unfolded it and read aloud. "Lisa Stroup, Victim of Witch."

He didn't read any further, but he didn't need to. I already knew what it said. The sheet of paper—a flyer, really—went on to claim in very colorful language that a witch had cast a spell on Lisa and that if she wasn't rescued soon, she would die. The flyer also said that the only way to save Lisa was to bring the witch to justice—and it implied heavily that the identity of the witch was well-known.

"Well," Joe said after a moment. "I know you didn't do this. And I know you didn't try to kill Bradshaw."

"Thanks," I said.

Joe's faith in me really made me feel a lot better. Before Joe had come in, a few patrons had let me know that these flyers were all over town—they were taped on the doors of offices and restaurants, and some had even been left on the windshields of cars.

My patrons—like Joe—had let me know that they didn't believe a word of it. But I'd continued to obsess over the flyer, and I'd been working myself into a state over it.

His kind comments had come just in time.

Joe continued to peruse the flyer.

"You know, this person doesn't know how to spell," he said. "They can't tell the difference between 'your' and 'you're.' "

"That's true," I said with approval. I'd noticed that, but the realization hadn't really pushed through the haze of emotion before.

Joe looked up at me. "I know you think I'm a meathead, but I know a few things."

"You're not a meathead," I said. "I've never thought that about you."

He smiled. "Thanks."

"Thanks for looking out for me," I said. "And I'm glad you didn't get hurt this morning running after Chris like you did. You should take care of yourself."

His smile grew a little broader. "Yeah, I'll do that." He glanced at his watch. "I'd better get going—work, you know. Text me if you need anything."

"I will," I said. "Thanks."

I couldn't help watching Joe as he walked out of the library—he really wasn't bad-looking.

I glanced up to see Mrs. Ludlow glaring at me.

"Shhh!" she hissed.

At lunchtime, I went outside with my insulated lunch bag and prepared to sit in the shade of a tree on the back lawn. I didn't always bring my lunch—hence the stash I kept in my purse and the refrigerator—but Rafaela had kindly packed one for me, and I was looking forward to seeing what she made me.

The afternoon was very hot and humid, but the air-conditioning in the library had been on high, and I was happy to have an opportunity to warm up a little.

As I headed toward my favorite lunch spot, I happened to see a tall figure waiting in the shade of a different tree.

"Oh no, not again," I said to myself.

I could see that the waiting figure was Andrew—and he was standing by the same tree that had sheltered Bradshaw Tyndall earlier in the day.

I was about to get ambushed again.

Andrew rushed up to me, his dark hair curling in the humidity, his handsome face a mask of sorrow.

"Please, please, Chloe," he said. "Please stop doing this."

I could see that there were tears standing in his striking green eyes, and I resisted the urge to roll my own.

"Please, Chloe," he said. "I'm begging you."

He took my hand and dropped down to one knee.

"Please. Leave Bradshaw alone."

A woman jogged by then in bright pink shorts and a black sports bra, the sun glistening off her damp, tanned skin. She slowed down as she saw us, and I could see white earbuds in her ears. She probably couldn't hear what Andrew was saying, and she stared at us curiously. There was a slight smile on her face.

I glanced down at Andrew kneeling and holding my hand, and I wondered if the woman thought he was proposing.

I gave her a weak smile, and she jogged on.

"Andrew," I hissed. "Get up."

He stood. "Chloe, I mean it. I understand that you lost a lot when you lost me, and you've never been able to get over that. But this has to stop. Please leave Bradshaw alone—if for no other reason than that it would make me happy. Let me have good memories of you—not terrible ones."

I had a very strong desire to do him bodily harm. While I fought the urge off, Andrew took my hand again.

"Besides, Chloe," he said. "You have nothing to worry about where Bradshaw is concerned. Nothing at all."

"That's great," I said. "I'm not concerned."

"I can see that you don't understand." Andrew heaved a great sigh, and he threw both of his arms up in an exaggerated gesture.

As he brought his arms back down, I thought I saw something on his upper arm, just under his white T-shirt sleeve.

He fixed me with a piercing stare. "Chloe, I don't want to give you false hope. I want you to understand in no uncertain terms that I'm taken. I'm with someone. Do you understand?"

"Yes, I understand," I said. "And I don't care."

He went on as if I hadn't said anything. "I'm not necessarily with Bradshaw anymore."

"So Bradshaw was right," I said. "She said you were sneaking around on her."

Andrew brought his hands up and ran them through his hair in frustration. "You're just not understanding this. You keep focusing on Bradshaw, and I'm trying to tell you that you have nothing to worry about there."

He brought his hands down once more, and I thought I glimpsed something under his sleeve again.

"What's that on your arm?" I said. "Is that a tattoo? Is that a letter 'G'?"

Andrew suddenly went white under his tan. "No—no, it isn't. You didn't see anything."

An older man with white hair and an uncertain, shuffling gait went by us on the sidewalk then, pushing a grocery cart in front of him. He stared at us for a moment and then continued on his way.

Andrew waited until the man had passed by, and then he went on in a hurry, his words tumbling over each other.

"Chloe, promise me you won't do anything rash," he said. "Promise me you won't hurt her. You think with Bradshaw out of the picture you'll have a chance. But you really don't. My heart belongs to another."

"I'm really fine with that," I said.

Andrew went down on his knees again. "Chloe, don't. Throw the gun away—throw it in the lake. No one else needs to get hurt. No one needs to die. Just throw it in the lake—that'll wash the fingerprints off. No one ever needs to know it was you. I won't tell anyone—I promise."

"I don't think you can usually get good fingerprints off a gun anyway," I said. "At least not from the grip—or the handle—or whatever it's called. It has an uneven surface—it's not good for getting a clean print."

"Oh Chloe!" Andrew wailed. "How can you be so cold? Please, please don't hurt her. Please get rid of the gun."

He got up suddenly and ran away, sobbing.

I could feel eyes on me then, and I looked up.

The man with the grocery cart was standing on the corner.

He was staring at me steadily.

I sighed and went into the library. I was no longer in the mood for lunch.

My troubles weren't over, however. About an hour later, I was in the stacks shelving books when there was a soft rustle of cloth behind me.

I turned to see Detective Mia. Her manner was stiff and formal, and there was an intensity in her dark eyes that I hadn't seen before.

She looked like the cat who had caught the mouse.

I put the book I was shelving into its proper place and prepared for a difficult interview.

"Is this about what was in the paper this morning?" I asked. "Or is this about the scene with Andrew?"

"Andrew?" Mia said blankly.

"I guess this is about the paper, then," I said. I'd been sitting on a step stool, and I stood up.

"And what was in the paper?" Mia said.

"Truthfully, I don't know," I replied. "My sister mentioned it to me, but I didn't see it myself."

I'd meant to look up the article about Bradshaw when I'd arrived at work, but actually seeing Bradshaw herself had put that out of my mind.

"Well, while you're being truthful," Mia said, "how about you come down to the station with me for another little chat?"

I glanced behind me at the cart full of books I had to put away. I glanced beyond them to the shelves—I was right by 364.1—Crimes and Offenses in the Dewey Decimal system. My eyes dropped just a little lower, and I was looking at our true crime section. A memory stirred, and I had a feeling that there was a book in that section I needed to look at.

I couldn't quite remember what it was, though.

"If you're worried about your work," Mia said, interrupting my reverie, "I've already talked to your boss. She said it's okay for you to come with me."

"Sure," I said. "Just let me get my purse."

A few minutes later, Detective Mia and I were walking out of the library, and Rita looked up from the circulation desk. She gave me a wave, and I could see sympathy in her kind, brown eyes.

We rode in silence over to the station, and once inside, Mia stopped by her desk to pick up a folder and a recorder. Then we went back to the same small, bare room with the fluorescent lights that I had been in before.

We sat down at a table across from one another.

"So, Chloe," Mia said. "I'd like to continue our conversation from the other day."

She paused with her hand over her slim, black voice recorder. "Do you mind if I record this?"

"Go ahead," I said.

She tapped on the small, red "record" button and then opened the folder in front of her. She took out a small notepad and flipped through several pages of handwritten notes. She paused and read something. Then she looked up at me.

"It appears you left something out of our interview the other day," Mia said. "Any particular reason why?"

"I left something out?" I said, momentarily puzzled. Then it came back to me. "Oh—you mean when I talked to Ariadne and Mike."

"Ariadne?" Mia said.

"Yes—I talked to her first. She's the reason I went to see Mike in the first place."

"I see." Mia jotted down a brief note on her notepad. "We'll get to her in just a moment. Now you admit that you went to see Mike Fellowes, a professor at Henrietta College, on Wednesday."

"Yes," I said.

"And you concealed that fact from me previously. You didn't just go to work and then go home."

"I didn't conceal it," I said. "I just didn't think of it."

"And why didn't you think of it?"

"I was irritated," I said. "I was angry, even. I just wasn't thinking clearly."

Mia looked up at me. "And you're thinking clearly now?"

"Yes," I said firmly.

"What was your conversation with Professor Fellowes about?"

"How did you find out about it?" I asked.

Mia simply smiled at me politely and waited for me to go on.

I sighed. Since I figured she wanted to hear mostly about Mike, I told her briefly that Ariadne had accused Mike of "giving away secrets." And then I told her about how I had confronted Mike. I went over the emails he'd received, his research and the newspaper article, and his claim that he didn't know who had sent the emails.

"So he showed the emails to you?" Mia asked.

"Yes," I said.

"And you were angry with him that he had spread rumors about your family based on these emails?"

"I was at first," I said. "But there's no point in being angry any longer. Everything's out in the open now."

"By 'everything' you mean your family's so-called magical abilities?"

"Yes," I said. The slight edge of sarcasm in Mia's voice wasn't lost on me.

"Now tell me about Ariadne," she said.

I told her quickly how Ariadne had waited outside the library, had accused Mike, and had muttered warnings of consequences. Under questioning, I admitted that I believed Ariadne was a member of the Crabtree Coven.

"So let me get this straight," Mia said. "A young woman you've never met appears out of nowhere and issues threats over these emails and their revelations—threats that are directed against Professor Fellowes."

"I wouldn't say threats exactly," I said.

" 'There will be consequences' sounds like a threat to me," Mia replied. "And you say she's a member of the—"

She glanced down at her notes. "Crabtree Coven?"

"I don't know that for certain," I said. "It was just a guess. She was wearing a single pearl as they are said to have done."

Mia smiled broadly. "Interesting, isn't it, that a new magical threat shows up just in time."

She leaned forward. "Would it interest you to know that we traced the IP address of the emails that were sent to the professor? 'IP' stands for 'internet protocol,' in case you were wondering."

"You did?" I said. "That's wonderful. Where did they come from?"

Mia was watching me carefully. "They came from your library."

"What?" I said, startled.

"They came from that little bank of ten computers you have for library patrons," Mia said. "Someone sat down at those computers and sent all of those emails to Professor Fellowes."

"But that would mean the person who did it has a library card."

"Or the person is an employee."

Mia was staring at me steadily. "Chloe, would you say you would do anything for your sister?"

"Which one?" I said, though the question was really irrelevant—I would do anything for either one of them.

"Rafaela."

"Of course I'd do anything for her," I said.

"Would she do anything for you?"

"What?" I said. "What do you—"

I stopped and Mia looked around.

There was suddenly a sound of shouting in the hallway, followed by several loud pops.

The lights went out for just a moment and then flickered back on weakly.

Mia stood up. The shouting grew louder.

"Stay here," she said. "I'll be right back."

She rushed out of the room, closing the door behind her.

I sat still for several moments, listening to the commotion outside.

Then I glanced at Mia's notebook.

I was just leaning forward to take a look when the door burst open and Mia came back in.

I looked around. The shouting in the hallway had stopped.

Mia walked over and scooped up her things.

"I think we had a pretty good chat today," she said quickly. "I don't need anything further from you. I'll take you back to your place of employment now."

"What's going on?" I said. "What happened out there?"

Mia gave me her broad smile. "Nothing you need to worry about. If you'll follow me, please."

She drove me back to the library, and I spent the rest of the day thinking about my missed opportunity.

I really wished I'd been able to get a look at that notepad.

As I drove home, I wondered idly if Alberta might be able to use her powers to get us a peek.

I was still thinking about it as I walked into the house.

Luckily, Alberta and Rafaela were sitting on the couch in the living room.

"Alberta, I was just—"

I stopped when I saw Rafaela. She was sitting with her head bowed and her eyes downcast. She looked like a wilting flower.

Alberta had her arm around her, comforting her, and I quickly sat down at her other side.

"Rafaela, what's wrong?" I said.

She raised her big, blue-green eyes to mine. There were tears standing in them.

"I was just with the police," she said. "They think I did it. They think I cursed Lisa and shot Bradshaw."

"What?" I said. "That's crazy."

"It isn't," Rafaela said. "They just found my fingerprints on that little slip of paper."

Chapter Twelve

"That's it," Alberta said. "No more cooperating with the police."

We were all seated at the kitchen table with mugs of tea. I'd forgone my usual coffee in place of the chamomile the other two were having. Drinking something soothing like chamomile seemed like a better idea than consuming a ton of caffeine.

I needed something calming right now.

And so did Alberta. I'd just finished telling her and Rafaela about my conversation with Detective Mia, and Alberta's green eyes were flashing fire. Even her red hair seemed to be giving off sparks.

"So from what I can tell," I said, "Mia believes that I sent those emails to Professor Mike. And she thinks Rafaela cursed Lisa and shot Bradshaw—I guess on my behalf. I think that's what she was getting at with the 'would-you-do-anything-for-your-sister' stuff."

Alberta was still fuming. "From now on, if any of us gets called in to talk to the police, we'll have an attorney present—a proper criminal defense attorney—not me. It's what we should have done from the beginning."

Rafaela turned troubled eyes on Alberta. "But won't that make us look guilty?"

"Not at all," Alberta said. "It'll make us look smart. I didn't insist on it in the beginning because I knew we were innocent. But I felt a little funny doing it—I should know by now to always follow my instincts."

"Did the police contact you today?" I asked Alberta.

She shook her head. "No. Nothing. Not even a phone call. I guess Detective Mia wants to focus on the two of you—get one of you to crack and start talking."

Alberta got up and came back with the container of cinnamon buns she had made the other day. She distributed these to us and then sat down again.

She went on as if the interruption had never happened.

"And that's the thing, isn't it?" she said. "Detective Mia is trying to trick you—trying to surprise you into giving something away. That's why she's telling you things she shouldn't. She shouldn't have told you, Rafaela, about the fingerprints, and she shouldn't have told Chloe about the IP address. She only did that to try to provoke a reaction— and she did *that* because they have no evidence."

Alberta bit into a cinnamon roll. "No—that's not enough. Lisa could have picked up that piece of paper with the symbol on it at any time. And they have no evidence at all linking you to the shootings with Bradshaw. They need some evidence—a witness ideally—that places you at the house on that night. And of course, there are no witnesses because you were here with us."

"I didn't know you could get fingerprints from paper," I said. "And I thought I was fairly knowledgeable. I always think of them being on doorknobs and drinking glasses—things like that."

"You can get fingerprints from a lot of surfaces," Alberta replied. "But you're right—surfaces like glass and metal are the easiest to lift fingerprints from. Surfaces like paper are a little more involved, but they're still very possible, and they're done all the time. Other things like fabrics or rough or textured surfaces—like the checkered grip of a handgun—are extremely tough to lift prints from."

"So they really could have Rafaela's prints on that piece of paper?" I said.

"It's entirely possible," Alberta said. "In fact, I'm sure they do. It's the only reason they're focusing on her instead of you now."

"It must have been from the break-in," Rafaela said with a soft sigh. She didn't seem to be taking things well, and every moment she seemed to droop more and more.

Alberta shot a worried glance over at her. "I think you're right about that. Whoever broke into your house and stole a few little odds and ends stole them on purpose. The thief was looking to plant something of yours at the scene with Lisa in order to point to you. And I think the piece of paper with the symbol was chosen purposefully—it would point to you—to us—faster than anything else would. Especially after all the publicity about it in the newspaper."

I looked up sharply. "Do you think they're related? The break-in and the emails? Do you think the same person who sent the emails also broke into Rafaela's house to get something to incriminate her?"

Alberta was fuming again. "I think it's a very strong possibility. Somebody's trying to set Rafaela up."

We both looked over at her, and she gave us a wan smile in return. I could only imagine how hard this must have been on her—to hear that her fingerprints had been found at a crime scene, and know that she was a suspect must be taking a terrible toll.

"It's okay," she said softly. "The part about the police, I mean. It's a pretty logical conclusion on their part."

"It's not okay," I said. "We've been telling them about the break-in, and they haven't been listening so far. We'll have to get that through to Detective Mia. Rafaela's things were stolen and someone planted that piece of paper."

"No good," Alberta said. "As you said, we've brought it up before and no one's shown any interest. We didn't report it at the time, and they probably think we made it up."

"But the broken door," I said.

"We could have done that ourselves," Alberta replied. "Those locks are always flimsy. And nothing valuable was taken."

She sighed.

"You mentioned the curse earlier," she said to me. "Do you think the police believe in the curse? Does Detective Mia believe that Lisa is under a spell?"

"I don't think so," I said. "I just said 'curse' because I know what it is. I'm pretty sure Mia still thinks some kind of drug was used. She didn't mention the curse, but she was pretty skeptical about the subject of magic in general. I don't think she believed me about my meeting Ariadne at all—I think she thinks I made it up."

"Well, I'm sorry Detective Mia doesn't believe you," Alberta said. She was starting to calm down. "But it's probably better that she doesn't believe in the curse. I imagine this case has been pretty frustrating for her, and that's why she's zeroed in on the two of you."

She became brisk. "So, Rafaela, you are absolutely staying here tonight. And I know it's Friday, but I, for one, am not really in the mood to go out. How about we just order some Chinese takeout and watch movies?"

"I could use some fried rice and egg drop soup," I said.

We both looked over at Rafaela.

"Sounds good," she said quietly.

So we ordered Chinese food and sat down to watch some of our favorite movies. The night wore on, and eventually, Rafaela fell asleep curled up in a corner of the couch.

"I was hoping she'd fall asleep," Alberta said softly.

"Me, too," I said.

Alberta got up and draped a light blanket over her.

"I've been wanting to talk to you," I said.

"I know," Alberta replied. "I could tell. Let's go up to my office."

We left the TV on quietly and tiptoed up the stairs.

Alberta's office was a really tiny bedroom with a desk, a laptop, and two chairs, and we went inside and closed the door.

"So how are Mom and Dad?" I asked as I sat down.

I was perfectly capable of calling or texting them myself, but somehow Alberta had been elected as our ambassador on this particular occasion—possibly because she seemed the most clearheaded at the moment.

"They're both good," Alberta said, seating herself behind her desk. "The hurricane has passed, and they'll be heading back to their place in the morning."

She paused. "They wanted to come right up and leave Maisie and Tibi at a kennel, but I told them to stay down there and take care of things."

I nodded. "I agree—it's best for them to stay down there. I only wanted them to come up here earlier because I thought it might be safer for them. But at the moment, they're much safer where they are. It's a terrible time for a hurricane, though."

"No time is good for a hurricane," Alberta replied. "But I know what you mean."

"Speaking of cats and dogs," I said. "Where's Sibyl? I haven't seen her since I got home."

"Oh Sibyl." Alberta sighed. "She's wedged herself under the sink in the hall bathroom."

I frowned. "You mean she's in the cabinet under the sink?"

"No. There's a little panel under the cabinet. Somehow she's managed to find a space behind the panel, and she's squished herself into it. She refuses to come out."

"Is she trapped?" I asked, alarmed. "Should we call a vet? Or maybe a carpenter?"

"No, she's fine," Alberta said. "She's just acting crazy as usual these days."

She gave me a sharp glance.

"So what's this all about?"

"Well—"

"You want me to use my scrying power, don't you?"

"Yes," I said. "How did you know?"

"I gathered as much when you were talking about Detective Mia's notebook and how much you wanted to get a look at it."

"Yes, that's it," I said. "That's exactly what I was hoping you could take a look at. We have to know what evidence they have—maybe it'll help us to figure out who's really behind this."

Alberta shook her head. "I don't know."

"But we have to save our sister," I protested. "Someone's trying to frame her."

"It's not that," Alberta said. "I agree with you on that. We have to save her. But I don't think scrying will do any good in this case."

"Why not?"

"Because scrying is an art—it's divination. It deals with impressions—and yes—sometimes I can see physical objects like pieces of paper. But in this case, it's not going to do us a lot of good."

"But the folder—"

"Probably doesn't have much of anything in it," Alberta said. "Police officers don't keep files in paper any more than you guys keep records in a card catalog. No one keeps information on paper anymore. Everything's electronic."

"But there *was* a folder," I said. I was starting to get really frustrated. Alberta could be really stubborn at times—and this appeared to be one of those times.

"I know," Alberta said. "I saw the folder, too, back when we were all interviewed the first time. I just don't think there's much in it—I saw a few photos, from what I recall, which she showed to us freely. I think the folder's a dead end. And like I said, the real information is all electronic. And that's very hard to get at with scrying."

I gave Alberta a level look. "Why are you being so stubborn? Why won't you at least try?"

Alberta stared back at me, and I could see sympathy in her eyes.

"Because you're all wrapped up in this," she said. "You think looking in the folder is going to solve everything and get Rafaela out of danger immediately. But that's not going to happen. Scrying doesn't work that way. Nothing works that way. There are no easy answers."

"But there was a notepad, too," I said. "I told you that. Mia wrote notes and everything. We could—"

I stopped. I studied Alberta's face.

"I get it," I said. "You were planning to do the scrying all along. You just wanted to get me out of the way first." I looked around the office. "You never do your scrying in here. You always said it was too cramped to allow the impressions to flow."

I paused. "You were going to wait until after I went to bed, weren't you?"

Alberta's expression grew very innocent. "Why, Chloe."

Then her natural aversion to dissembling reasserted itself—she always liked to tell people the absolute truth. Her face went very red.

"Yes. I was going to do it after you went to sleep."

"Oh Alberta," I said. "Please let me sit with you when you do it. Please, please, please? I'll even make the mugwort tea. And I promise I'll be quiet."

Alberta sighed. "Fine. You can sit with me. But you really do have to be quiet."

"Thank you, thank you, thank you!" I said. I jumped up to make the tea.

"Little sisters," Alberta muttered as I hurried out of the room.

Soon we were sitting in Alberta's bedroom in front of her vanity. She'd draped a cloth over the regular mirror that sat there, and she'd set up her much smaller black mirror on the table top in front of it. The black mirror was draped in a black cloth for protection, and our two cups of tea sat just in front of it, filling the air with the sage-like scent of mugwort.

We both drank the tea—it promoted calmness as well as second sight and higher forms of awareness. These were all things Alberta would need when using the mirror for divination.

"Okay," Alberta said as we set our empty cups down. "I'm going to focus on Detective Mia—her thoughts and impressions. It's really much better to focus on a person rather than an object like a notebook. And these are the three questions I'm going to focus on while I'm using the black mirror. Tell me what you think of them."

I listened attentively.

"One. What does Mia know about the gun that shot Bradshaw Tyndall? Two. What does Mia know about the house where Bradshaw was shot? Three. What does Mia know about the night Lisa Stroup was cursed?"

"Those are all good," I said. "You should also ask it where Bradshaw was the last time she was shot at."

Alberta looked exasperated. "I'm not really asking the mirror anything—you know that, right? Besides, I already know where Bradshaw was shot at this last time—it was at her house. It was in the paper this morning."

"I know that about the mirror," I said, stung. "Poor choice of words. And those are all good questions—they should be enough."

Alberta quickly swept the cups away and got out a candle in an antique holder and a lighter. She glanced at me.

"You should probably scooch back a little. We don't want your reflection in the mirror."

I moved my chair back, and Alberta frowned at me.

"You should scooch back a little more."

I sighed and did as she asked. I could tell she was still a little irritated with me.

Once I had moved back a sufficient amount, Alberta lit the candle. Then she rose and turned out the lights and shut the door.

Her bedroom was plunged into gloom. The only light in the room came from the tiny flame that rose solemnly from the candle.

Alberta sat down again, and I could see her face bathed in the soft light from the candle.

She took the black cloth off the mirror and set it aside. The mirror, which had a simple metal frame, was supported by a rosewood stand. The face of the mirror itself was black, and now that the cover was off, I could see the flame from the candle reflected in its inky depths.

"Please remember to stay quiet," Alberta murmured. She moved her chair back and angled it a little. I knew it was important for her not to see her own reflection in the mirror—that would affect the images she saw.

Then Alberta stared steadily into the mirror, and her face took on a look of peaceful concentration.

The scrying had begun.

Alberta was silent for the most part, but from time to time, she murmured softly to herself. The room was quiet also, and while I watched Alberta intently at first, trying to figure out what the little changes in her expression meant, eventually my attention wandered.

After what felt like hours, I found myself drifting off.

"I knew it!" Alberta said suddenly.

My eyes snapped open. "What? What's going on?"

Alberta's face was triumphant in the candlelight. "The police and Detective Mia really have nothing to go on. They have no evidence other than the fingerprints on the paper and the fact that that same slip of paper has our symbol on it."

I was disappointed. "That's all? You didn't learn anything else?"

Alberta's eyes were shining, reflecting the flame from the candle.

"On the contrary—I learned two very valuable things. First, the police found nothing at Bradshaw's house—no signs of a break-in. There were no signs of forced entry at any of the doors or windows, and there were no footprints on the lawn—or in the house."

I thought back. "It was raining that night."

"Yes," Alberta said excitedly.

"There's a big paved drive up to Bradshaw's house," I said slowly. "So anyone could have walked up the drive and not left footprints on the lawn. But if there are no damp spots in the house, then that means the shooter must have been in the house all along."

"That's a very strong possibility," Alberta said approvingly. "Although it's also possible that the shooter took off his or her shoes and put them in a bag so as not to leave any wet spots or prints on the floor. It's also possible that the spots simply dried. But the shooter *could* have been in the house all long—and then there's the fact that there was no forced entry."

"So that's another sign that the shooter could have been inside the house," I said. "At the very least it means the shooter had a key."

Alberta nodded approvingly again. "Yes—that's very possible. The shooter could have had a key and tiptoed in. It's also possible that the door was unlocked. Though after the first time Bradshaw was shot at, I'd hope that she'd have the good sense to lock the door."

"What about fingerprints?" I asked.

Alberta shrugged. "There are dozens of them in the house. Bradshaw has a lot of parties, so it's impossible to say when any of the prints were laid down. On this particular night, however, she says she was alone."

"So you said you learned two things—was that the second one? That Bradshaw was alone?"

"No," Alberta said, and her excitement returned. "The second thing I learned was about the projectiles that were fired at Bradshaw. All of them, including the one in her arm, were .54 caliber balls."

"Balls?" I said. "Not bullets?"

"Nope. They were balls fired from a Revolutionary War-era, single-shot, muzzle-loading flintlock pistol."

"A Revolutionary War-era pistol?" I said.

"Yes," Alberta replied in triumph.

I was puzzled. "Where would somebody get something like that?"

"Well, until recently," Alberta said, "there was one in Bradshaw's house."

Chapter Thirteen

"Good morning, sleepyhead."

I walked into Rafaela's room and placed a cup of cranberry tea on the table by her bed.

She was just stirring, and she looked content and well rested—her appearance was in stark contrast to the flower in my room. The once-blue hydrangea had lost all its color and was now drooping.

Rafaela sat up, and I sat down on the edge of her bed.

Sunlight was streaming into the room, and Rafaela glanced around. "What time is it?"

"Later than your usual time," I said. "We let you sleep. We figured you needed it."

Rafaela was typically an early riser—even on the weekends. She liked to get up early and get in a workout—usually yoga.

Sibyl walked into the room then, her black coat glossy in the sunshine, and I reached down to pet her—I was glad to see that she was no longer hiding under the bathroom cabinet.

But she eluded my hand and jumped on the bed.

She did a complete circuit of the bed, avoiding both of us entirely, and then jumped off the bed and left the room.

"That was interesting," Rafaela said. She took a sip of the cranberry tea and peered at me over the rim of the cup.

"You two were scrying without me, weren't you?"

"Alberta actually did the scrying," I said. "I was just there to send out positive and helpful vibes."

Rafaela gave me a sly smile. "Now who's being the protective sister?"

Even though she was smiling, I could feel a sense of weariness stealing over her again—the sense of peace sleep had given her had disappeared now that she was awake.

"We weren't going to keep it from you," I said. "We just wanted to let you sleep."

"That was sweet of you," Rafaela said.

"Alberta's making pancakes, if you're interested," I said.

Rafaela smiled. "I'm always interested in pancakes."

Sibyl returned to the room and jumped on the bed. She made another circuit, avoiding both of us again, and then jumped down and left the room once more.

"What was that about?" Rafaela said.

"No idea," I said.

"Well, go on and scoot now so I can get dressed," Rafaela said. "I'll see you down there."

Soon the downstairs was filled with the buttery scent of pancakes cooking in a cast iron skillet, and I set the table while Alberta worked in the kitchen.

Sibyl could be seen walking around on the couch in the living room, making a complete trip around the cushions, the back, and both arms before jumping down and then starting all over again.

"Crazy cat," Alberta muttered.

But I wasn't paying much attention to Sibyl—at the moment my mind was taken up with deciding what kind of topping to have on my pancakes.

I wasn't sure if I was in the mood for maple syrup or jam.

Rafaela soon came down to join us, and I did what I always did.

I decided to have both.

"There she goes again," Alberta said with a significant glance at Rafaela.

I had divided my little stack of pancakes in two, cutting them all right down the middle. I'd poured syrup carefully over one stack, and now I was spreading strawberry jam on the other half.

"What I don't understand," Alberta said, "is why you don't just make two little stacks? Why do you always make one stack and then cut it down the middle?"

"It tastes better that way," I said, spearing a little stack of pancake triangles coated in syrup. The triangles did indeed taste heavenly and the syrup was rich and sweet—Alberta always bought the good stuff.

"You're as crazy as my cat over there," Alberta said.

We were seated in the dining room, and I glanced behind me. Sibyl was still making her circuits of the couch.

"Chloe should eat her pancakes any way she likes," Rafaela said benevolently.

I glanced at her plate—Rafaela had spread a thin layer of butter and strawberry jam on each pancake like she always did. She never touched the syrup.

Alberta, on the other hand, loved maple syrup, and she poured it liberally over her stack of pancakes. She enjoyed jam sometimes, too, and she'd even been known to put peanut butter on her pancakes from time to time.

I then moved on to my jam pancakes and cut a stack of triangles from them. The strawberry jam was delicious also—Alberta always bought hers from a local business.

"And what's with the switching?" Alberta said, watching me. "Why can't you just pick a flavor and stick with it till you finish it?"

"I like the differences," I said. "I like switching between the dark syrup and the tart jam."

"Alberta, Chloe can eat her pancakes any way she likes," Rafaela said with a pointed look over a glass of milk.

"Mom didn't like it, either," Alberta said. "She said it drove her crazy."

Rafaela sighed. "Why don't you two tell me what you learned about in your scrying session last night?"

Alberta went through everything she had discovered and ended up by telling her about the flintlock pistol.

"Bradshaw owned a pistol from the Revolutionary War?" Rafaela said in surprise. "Somehow that doesn't seem like her."

"I imagine it was an heirloom," Alberta said.

"Yes—it was," I said suddenly. "At least—I wouldn't be surprised if it was. She used to be in all those parades, remember?"

Bradshaw was a member of the Daughters of the American Revolution—a group you could only get into by being a direct descendant of a soldier who had fought in the Revolutionary War. She had ridden every year for a number of years in an open-air carriage in our annual Patriot's Parade, dressed up in a red, white, and blue outfit in celebration of her heritage. Her much shyer cousin, Geraldine, could have ridden beside her but had chosen not to. Bradshaw had been a little ham in those days, waving enthusiastically at the crowd and participating in every local parade and pageant she could find. Everybody had said back then that Bradshaw was destined to be a famous actress. But after appearing in a few local plays, she had quit, and her local stardom had faded away.

"I remember that," Rafaela said. "She wore that Betsy Ross costume one time, didn't she?"

"Yes, she did," I said.

"That's right," Alberta said. "She was in the DAR. So that explains the pistol."

"So why is that significant?" Rafaela asked. "You mentioned the pistol as if it explains something."

"It shows that the person who shot her wasn't just a visitor to her house—or an intruder," Alberta replied. "It was someone who knew the house—and Bradshaw—well."

"Well, that goes with the other evidence, doesn't it?" Rafaela said. "The lack of footprints and no sign of forced entry—"

She broke off suddenly, as if something had just occurred to her.

"Yes, it does," Alberta said. "But either of those two things could have been accomplished by a clever criminal. The antique pistol, however, and its bullets had to have been used by someone who had intimate knowledge of the household. From what I divined, the gun was displayed but not loaded, and the bullets—balls, really—were kept somewhere else."

"Where is the pistol now?" I said. "Were you able to see that?"

"It's missing," Alberta replied. "Wherever it is, it's not in the hands of the police."

Rafaela had grown pensive, and she looked over at Alberta. "It's not only a clever criminal that could leave no footprints and not have to break anything to get in."

"I know," Alberta said with a trace of asperity. "That's my whole point. Whoever it was likely knew Bradshaw well, and she let the person in, and then that same person possibly hid and jumped out later. Or maybe the person had a key and simply let themselves in."

Rafaela continued to look worried. "There's another possibility."

"Which is?"

"It could have been something supernatural," Rafaela said quietly. "A spell to unlock the door." She paused. "Or someone could even have conjured something—a spirit or an entity—and sent it to the house."

She shivered and glanced at me.

"Now don't go upsetting yourself," Alberta said. "I've never heard of any kind of entity or presence that can cast a curse. And I've certainly never heard of one that can fire a gun."

"A poltergeist—"

"No," Alberta replied firmly. "Not even a poltergeist. And you know as well as I do that true hauntings are rare—extremely rare."

Rafaela sighed gently. "So it's someone well acquainted with the house."

"Yes," Alberta said.

"But surely the police have thought of all of this?" Rafaela said. "They must have realized that the available physical evidence points to someone with access to the house."

"I'm sure they have." It was Alberta's turn to sigh.

"Then why are they focusing on us?" The worried look had returned to Rafaela's face, and she glanced at me again.

"Because the available physical evidence is largely a negative," Alberta said. "They have no useful prints except for yours, and no evidence that anyone was in the house except for Bradshaw—and Lisa. And Lisa is currently under a curse, which is something they don't understand or believe in. They have no idea how to investigate something supernatural—they're really in the dark here. They're doing the best they can with what they have."

"And that brings me back to my earlier point," Rafaela said with just a touch of stubbornness. "Since what happened to Lisa is supernatural in origin, we can't rule out the involvement of the supernatural in the attacks on Bradshaw."

Alberta and Rafaela were staring at each other as if an argument was going to break out at any minute, and I jumped in quickly.

"What happens to Lisa?" I blurted out.

Both of my sisters turned to look at me.

"What was that?" Alberta said.

"What happens to Lisa?" I said again. "Have you heard anything else from Mom? What happens if we aren't able to break the curse?"

Alberta's face grew sober. "Mom did find out a little more. It turns out that the victim will eventually die if the curse isn't lifted."

"How long does Lisa have?" Rafaela asked.

"That depends on the skill of the person who cast the curse," Alberta replied. "Someone very skilled could potentially cast a curse that could sustain the victim for hundreds of years—just like in *Sleeping Beauty*. But someone else might only be able to cast a curse that sustains the victim for a few months, or even a few weeks. The problem is that strength is needed to sustain the 'life-support' aspect of the curse—the element that maintains the suspended animation part. Without enough magic to support the body's processes, they're going to stop. And ordinary medical intervention won't do any good. No nutrition or hydration will be able to break through."

"Has Mom found any other way to break the curse?" Rafaela asked.

"No," Alberta said. "A kiss from the one who cursed her is still the only way she knows about."

"So we have to find who did this," I said. "We have to find out who cursed Lisa if we want to save her and Bradshaw—and you, Rafaela. Are we all in agreement?"

"Yes," Alberta said promptly. "We don't know for sure that the same person is responsible for the attacks on Lisa and Bradshaw, and for framing Rafaela, but it's not a bad place to start from. We can be reasonably certain that one person has done all three things. But we should keep an open mind. If anything comes up that contradicts our working theory, we shouldn't be afraid to look at it."

"Works for me," I said. "Raf? What do you think?"

Rafaela gave me one of the long looks that she'd been giving me ever since this discussion had started.

"Yes," she said. "I agree. We need to find out who's behind this, and I think we can assume one person is responsible for everything. Three lives are at stake here."

"So where do we start?" Alberta said.

"We need to look for magic and motive," I said. "We need to figure out who has the ability to cast a curse, and who might have a reason to kill Bradshaw."

"Just Bradshaw?" Rafaela interjected. "What about someone who might be after Lisa?"

"No—Chloe's right," Alberta replied. "Lisa was in Bradshaw's house and dressed in Bradshaw's clothes when the curse was cast on her. She also has similar height, weight, and coloring. It's reasonable to assume that the person who cast the curse thought he or she was casting it on Bradshaw. We can definitely start from there—always keeping in mind that if something pops up that contradicts that premise that we can't ignore it. We look at everything."

"All right," Rafaela said. "As long as we don't rule it out completely."

"So back to my question," Alberta said. "Where do we start?"

"Chris Young," I said.

"Who?" Alberta said.

"Chris Young," I replied. "He's Bradshaw's ex. He's been following her around, trying to get back with her."

"How do you know about this?" Rafaela asked.

"I didn't tell you guys this?" I said. "Maybe I didn't. On the two occasions Bradshaw came to confront me at the library, she was followed by a guy in a car as she drove away. I knew the guy looked familiar, but I couldn't place him. Then Joe told me Chris's name, and I remembered him. And then Joe followed Chris and Bradshaw to see what happened."

Rafaela was incredulous. "He followed them?"

"Yes—and then he came back and reported to me. He said Chris caught up with Bradshaw, and they seemed to be arguing. Joe said Chris definitely seemed like a stalker."

"What does Joe do all day anyway?" Alberta asked. "How does he have so much time to hang around the library and chase after people?"

I frowned in thought. "I think he's a social media influencer. He takes pictures of himself with various products—mostly sports and health related—and then he posts them and gets lots of likes and attention."

"And that's a job?" Alberta said. "You know I don't pay much attention to social media. Is he sort of like a model?"

"I guess that's exactly what he is," I said. "Companies pay him for posing with their products—sort of like a sponsorship. He has a lot of subscribers, so there's a pretty steady demand for his services. That's how he has so much time. He can pretty much make his own schedule."

"Okay," Alberta said. "So you and Joe think Chris Young might be stalking Bradshaw?"

"Yes," I said.

"Why would he be shooting at her?" Alberta said. "If he wants to get back with her?"

"Maybe he's trying to scare her," I said. "Maybe he thinks that will make her feel like he can protect her or something. And you did say that the Sleeping Beauty Curse is a curse of compulsion. Could he use that to order her to get back together with him?"

"Yes, he could," Alberta replied. "That's a good point. What about the magic part? Does he have the ability to do something like that?"

"I don't know," I said. "That's what I have to find out."

"And that's really what's important here, isn't it?" Alberta said. "It's no use searching for a motive if the suspect doesn't have the ability to cast curses."

"I know," I replied in irritation. "That's what I said a few moments ago. We need someone who has a motive and someone who has magical ability."

"So who fits that description?"

"Ariadne Frost is a possibility," I said.

"She's the one who might be a member of the Crabtree Coven?" Rafaela asked.

"That's the one."

"And what would her motive be?" Alberta said.

"I don't know," I said. "She did say there would be 'consequences' for the revelations in *The Morning Cider*. Maybe since Charles Tyndall is mentioned in the article, she blames Bradshaw. I guess I'll have to find out."

"That's two potential suspects," Alberta said. "Is there anyone else?"

"I've been thinking," I said slowly. "Since Bradshaw is known to be wealthy—she has that big house and everything—maybe we could look at good, old-fashioned money as a motive. Who inherits if something happens to Bradshaw?"

Alberta nodded. "It's always a good idea to stick with the basics. Who does inherit? Do you have any idea?"

"No," I said. "I don't know who would inherit her house and her money. The only relative I know of hers is Geraldine."

Rafaela looked startled. "You really think Geraldine would kill her cousin for her money?"

"I would hope not," I said. "But we have to consider everything."

"But Geraldine's in Annapolis," Rafaela protested.

"It's not that far away," Alberta said, "and it's not like she can't drive here. Besides, she would know Bradshaw's house well, and she might also have a key."

She turned to me. "Any reason to believe she has any magic?"

"I don't know anything about that," I said. "I'll—"

Alberta interrupted me. "Before you say you'll have to find out, I'm taking this one. I'll look into who might benefit financially from Bradshaw's death. And I'll also get with Mom and see if any of the protections she has in place can help us pinpoint an unknown magic worker in the area."

"But shouldn't those protections have alerted us earlier?" Rafaela said.

Alberta was grim. "They should have, but they didn't. Maybe we can tweak them a little and find something out."

She looked at Rafaela and me. "Any other suspects?"

I thought about the people in town. "No one else comes to mind."

"I can't think of anyone," Rafaela said with a little glance at me.

"All right, then," Alberta said. "We have a lot to do. We'd better get to work."

"What about me?" Rafaela said. "I don't have anything to look into."

Alberta and I exchanged a glance.

"Since you're the police's major suspect," Alberta said, "maybe you should just take it easy. Relax here at my house."

I nodded. "You need to take care of yourself. You look like you could use a little rest."

I took a good look at Rafaela—she did indeed look as though she could use a long vacation. She was looking careworn and rundown—there were dark circles under her blue-green eyes.

"Okay. You two go off and do your sleuthing," she said. "But promise me you'll be very, very careful."

"We'll be careful," Alberta said. "Don't worry about that. You just look out for yourself."

She stood and began to clear the table.

As I got up to clear away my dishes, Rafaela stood and wrapped me in a hug.

"I know you're worried about me," she said in a low voice. "But I'm more worried about you. I've still got a terrible feeling that someone is after you."

Chapter Fourteen

I went up to my room to get ready to go out. As I walked in, I went straight to my family of flowerpots. As I had feared, Rafaela's hydrangea wasn't looking any better. In fact, it was actually looking worse—it was definitely drooping more, and the petals, which had gone completely gray, were now starting to fall off.

I sighed and touched the flower gently. Rafaela was such a sweet person that even though she herself was in great emotional distress, all she could do was think of others—and more specifically, worry about me. It was true that I'd been questioned by the police, too, but she was the one they were truly focusing on. And someone had broken into her house and stolen her things so they could be planted to incriminate her.

Someone was after Rafaela, and I had to stop whoever it was—before things got worse.

I was soon ready to go out—but then I realized that I didn't know where to find Chris Young or Ariadne Frost. I got out my phone and started to do a little research online.

I didn't find out much about Chris—but I did eventually find a few photos of Ariadne. I squinted at the background—I knew just where she was.

I went to my purse then and rummaged through it until I found Professor Mike's card. I realized that, not too long ago, I would have been angry—I would have assumed that Mike had purposefully deceived me. But now that I didn't automatically get angry every time I thought about Mike, I was able to look at the situation more rationally.

From the pictures, it appeared that Ariadne was a student at Henrietta College.

Mike had said that he didn't know her—and I realized it was very possible that that was true. There were fifteen hundred students at the school, and I couldn't imagine that they would all take his classes. And it was also possible that he did know her by sight and didn't actually know her name.

And now that I knew that the emails from Charles Tyndall had actually been sent to Mike from my own library, I knew that if Ariadne had sent them, Mike very likely had no knowledge of it. I couldn't remember ever having seen Ariadne at the library—apart from the day she'd come to talk to me—but she certainly could have come in on a day when I was out. I figured I would call Mike and see if he wouldn't mind looking at a picture of Ariadne, and then he could tell me if he'd seen her around campus.

Maybe he'd know where I might find her.

I sat for a moment, looking at Mike's cell number on his card, and I felt a little flutter of happiness at the thought of calling him.

I told myself I was being ridiculous, and I quickly typed in his number.

Mike answered after two rings, and I wondered if he could see my name on the caller ID or just the number.

"Hello?"

"Hi, Mike," I said. "It's Chloe Bartlett."

"Oh hey, Chloe," he said. He sounded pleased, and I could picture his brown eyes lighting up.

I could feel myself smiling at the thought, and I quickly told myself to focus.

"So, Mike," I said. "I was wondering if we could meet up some time. I have a few more questions that I'd like to ask you."

"Uh, sure," he said. "Is anything wrong?"

He sounded concerned.

"No, nothing's wrong," I said. "I just thought you might be able to help me identify someone."

"I'd be happy to try," Mike replied. "When did you want to meet up?"

"Ideally, the sooner, the better. I know it's the weekend, so you may have plans."

"Well, I'm at the school at the moment. You could swing by right now if you wanted to."

"That's great," I said. "I'll be right over. Where are you?"

"I'm in my office." Mike's voice took on a teasing quality. "I know you know where that is."

I chose to ignore that last part. "See you soon."

I hung up and hurried downstairs.

I stopped in the living room to check my purse just to make sure I had everything I needed—including the length of cord I'd knotted last night for protection. I could hear Alberta and Rafaela rattling around in the kitchen, and as I looked up from my bag, I could see Sibyl still making a circuit of the couch, covering the back, the seat, and both arms.

I walked over to her, and she paused, allowing me to pet her sleek black fur. She closed her amber eyes as I scratched the soft fur under her chin, and she began to purr just a little.

Then she went back to walking around the sofa.

"You're going to wear yourself out," I murmured to Sibyl. "Not to mention the hole you're going to wear in the couch."

I went outside and drove over to Henrietta College.

Since it was Saturday, there were a lot of empty parking spaces, and I had no trouble finding a spot near Mike's building. The morning was already very warm, and the blazing sun overhead promised another hot day. There was a haze in the air, however, that hinted that clouds weren't far off and offered a vague chance of rain.

As I walked up to Mike's building, I thought that a little rain wouldn't be a bad thing—it might give us a nice, cool evening for a change.

Mike's door was open, and I found him sitting behind his desk. He looked up expectantly as I approached, and he smiled when he saw it was me.

I felt an answering flutter in my heart, and I noticed once again just how good-looking he was.

He jumped up from his desk.

"Hey, Chloe." He pulled out a chair for me, and I sat down.

I glanced around a little nervously—I remembered how I had stormed into this same office the other day, and now I was about to broach the same topic again.

Mike leaned against the edge of his desk.

"What's up?"

I looked up at him.

"Sorry about the way I barged in here before," I said. "I shouldn't have accused you like that."

I saw a suspicious-looking twinkle light up Mike's dark eyes. He was definitely amused.

"That's all right," he said. "I—"

He stopped suddenly, and I thought I saw a slight flush creep up his face.

"I was going to kid you about that," Mike said. "But then I realized that I've been—"

He stopped again. "But this isn't about me. You said you wanted my help identifying someone?"

I hadn't expected Mike to be so solicitous, and I was momentarily thrown off.

"I—yes," I said. I opened my purse to get my phone, and I had to rummage around to find it.

"Here it is," I murmured to myself.

I found the picture of Ariadne Frost on my phone, and I stood up to show it to Mike.

"I asked you something a little like this before," I said, holding out my phone. "Do you recognize this girl?"

Mike took the phone and looked at the picture. In the image, Ariadne Frost stared back at the camera, her dark eyes squinting in the sunlight, her dark hair looking just a little purple in the bright sunshine. The cheery caption under the photo proclaimed, "Back for the summer session!!!" And Ariadne was tagged along with a number of other people. A Henrietta College building was clearly visible in the background.

Mike nodded. "Yes, I know her. That's Tina Chandler. She's taking a Master's in English. She's in the one graduate-level class I teach."

He frowned. "What's this about?"

"Tina Chandler?" I said, puzzled. "She said her name was Ariadne Frost. And Ariadne Frost was tagged in this post. There's no mention of a Tina."

Mike looked at my phone again. "You're right. I don't see Tina listed here. Maybe Ariadne is the name she goes by online."

He gave me a little smirk. "That's not a crime."

"I know," I said. "But if you recall, when I came in here the other day demanding to know why you hadn't told me the truth, the person I was asking about was Ariadne Frost—or rather, Tina Chandler."

Mike's smirk deepened. "I remember the day—and that name—well. You were in fine form."

This time I didn't mind that he was teasing me—but I had a point to get across.

"Okay, good," I said. "You remember that. So my point is that Ariadne and Tina are the same person. And Tina Chandler—your student—is the one who accused you of giving out information that you should have kept secret."

Mike frowned once more. "Are you sure about that?"

"Yes," I said. "The girl in this photo was very angry about the newspaper article and everything it gave away. She said the information wasn't to be shared. And that there would be consequences."

Mike shook his head. "Tina never said anything like that to me."

He paused. "Did she say she sent the emails?"

"No, she didn't," I replied. "I've since learned that the emails were sent from my library. I haven't seen her there before, but I'm not there all the time."

Mike gave me back my phone and went to his desk.

He took a sheet of paper out of a file in a drawer and handed it to me.

I looked it over. It was the flyer from a day ago saying that the witch in town needed to be brought to justice.

I eyed Mike suspiciously. "Why do you have this?"

He gave me a bemused look. "I didn't put these all over town if that's what you're thinking. I found them all over campus, and I kept one to study. Notice anything interesting about that flyer?"

I felt a wave of anxiety wash over me as I perused the flyer once again. I knew its contents very well.

"Yes," I said. "The person who wrote this flyer made the same spelling mistakes as the person who sent you those emails."

"Exactly," Mike said. "I'd bet good money that the same person wrote the flyers and the emails."

I handed the flyer back to him. "What's your point?"

"My point is that Tina Chandler is a student in my class. I've read papers she's turned in, and she writes very well. I don't think she composed the emails or the flyer."

"She could have used poor spelling on purpose," I said.

Mike shook his head. "I don't think so. I get the impression that the person who wrote the emails was trying to sound smart—and not quite making it. Besides, it wouldn't make any sense for Tina to have written the emails and the flyer—didn't you say she was upset about everything being made public?"

"Yes, I did," I said. "But she did say the information had been given to you in confidence, and there would be consequences for everything being published. Did the emails say anything about keeping the information secret?"

"No, they didn't say anything like that," Mike replied. "In fact, the author of the emails explicitly stated a desire to help with my research. I got the impression I was being encouraged to publish the information."

He paused. "What exactly are you accusing Tina of?"

"I'm not accusing her of anything," I said. "I'm just trying to figure out what's going on. The police believe my sister cursed Lisa Stroup and shot Bradshaw Tyndall, and I'm just trying to clear her name. And I'm also hoping to save Lisa and Bradshaw from the real culprit. Whoever it is is still out there."

"I heard about your sister," Mike said softly. "That her fingerprints had been found at the scene."

I looked up at him. There was concern in his dark eyes.

"That's not quite true," I said. "Though I'm not surprised that the rumor mill has got it wrong. Lisa was found clutching a piece of paper that had my sister's fingerprints on it. Rafaela's house was broken into just before the attack on Lisa and Bradshaw—we think that's how the culprit got the slip of paper."

"That's the piece of paper with your family's famous symbol on it?"

"Yes." Somehow I felt a great sense of relief telling all of this to Mike—it was good to talk to someone outside the family.

A smile quirked at the corners of his mouth. "And do the police really believe that your sister Rafaela cursed Lisa?"

"I don't think so," I replied. "I think they think she was drugged. The symbol is really only important to the police because it points to my sister."

"And what about you?" Mike asked, watching me. "Do you believe Lisa was cursed—or drugged?"

He continued to watch me, and I looked away.

Mike went on. "So you're here playing the amateur sleuth? You think you'll save your sister and the other ladies, too?"

I looked at him again. His tone had become brisk, but I could hear a teasing undercurrent in it.

"Are you making fun of me?" I asked.

Mike smiled for real then. "No, not at all. I'm interested."

"In?"

"In you. You're not at all the way I thought you'd be."

"What do you mean?" I said.

Mike took a deep breath. "When I first decided to go down to the library and confront you, I had an image in my mind of the kind of person you'd be. I thought you'd be airheaded and silly—that you'd be playacting at being a witch. But instead I find out that you're much more complex than I ever imagined. And now you're taking it on yourself to ferret out a would-be killer and save three people in the process."

"I'm not doing it alone," I said. "My sister Alberta is helping."

Mike smiled again. "Would you like to go for a walk?"

"Why?"

"I'd like to learn more about this—about you. And I'd like to help you if I can."

Mike paused and looked down at his shoes. Then he looked up at me.

"There's also something I'd like to tell you."

"What?" I said.

Again the smile, though this time it looked a little shy.

"You'll have to come with me to find out."

Chapter Fifteen

"What's that?" Mike said.

I glanced down at my purse and then back up at him. The late morning was already getting hot, and the haziness that threatened rain still hung in the air. I'd agreed to go on that walk with Mike, and we'd ambled along in companionable silence in the heat. It felt strangely good to walk beside him, and I was very curious about what he had to tell me.

But neither of us had felt the need to rush into conversation, and we were currently walking slowly through campus.

From time to time, Mike would point out a building or school landmark.

But this time he was interested in me.

I looked down at the black cord he was looking at. I had attached it to my purse last night, after carefully tying knots into it. It was cord magic, and the black color indicated that it was for protection and repelling negativity. I'd actually tied it onto a little silver charm that my mother had given me long ago when I was still in school. The charm just said "Chloe," and it had a clip that enabled it to be hooked onto a backpack or a purse. The charm itself didn't have any power—all the power was in the cord—but it gave me a good way to attach the cord to the purse. And I just liked looking at it—it made me feel safe.

"It's just a piece of cord," I said.

Mike continued to look at it. "But it has knots in it, and it looks deliberate. I'm sure you did it for a reason—women always have reasons for the things they attach to their purses."

"You'll think it's silly."

"No, I won't."

I knew exactly how he felt about the whole witch business, but I plunged ahead anyway.

"It's called cord magic," I said. "Some people believe that if you tie knots into a cord while thinking about something you want to happen and saying a spell, that it will lock your intention and your power into the knots. As you release the knots, what you want will come true. And black is a protective color. If you want to keep anything safe from harm, you should cover it in black."

"Some people believe that?" Mike said. "What about you? What do you believe?"

I remained silent.

"Chloe," Mike said softly. "I have to know. Do you believe you're a witch?"

I stopped walking. I suddenly felt like I couldn't breathe.

"Is that what you wanted to say to me?" I said after a moment. "Is that why we came out on this walk?"

"No," Mike said. "There's something else that I want to tell you. But I need to know. I've asked you before, but you haven't answered. What do you believe about yourself, Chloe? Do you believe you're a witch?"

I looked up into his dark eyes, and this time I didn't see amusement or scorn or disbelief—just honest interest.

I decided to trust him.

"Yes," I said at last. "I'm a witch."

I watched Mike's face—but he didn't laugh or even react at all. He just continued to look at me with the same patient, open expression.

After a moment, he looked down.

"Then that makes this even worse," he said.

"What?" I said.

"I'm sorry," Mike said. "And I'm not just sorry about the local storm that has erupted over my newspaper piece—although I'm sorry about that, too. But what I'm really sorry about is sharing your family's story without asking—without consulting you first. That was something private, and it belongs to you. And I'm even sorrier now that I finally understand that you're not just playacting. You have a genuine belief, and I exposed it to everybody. I'm sorry about that."

I stared at Mike. I was stunned.

"You're—"

"Sorry," he said. "I really mean it this time."

"I don't know what to say," I said.

"You don't have to say anything."

We started walking again.

"Thank you," I said after a moment.

Mike simply nodded.

"So does this mean that you believe in witches?" I asked.

Mike looked over at me. "I can't quite get my head around that. Let's just say that I believe that you believe. But I can't honestly say that I believe your black cord is going to protect you from much of anything."

"Fair enough," I said. I smiled. "Does this mean we're friends?"

It was Mike's turn to look startled. "Friends?"

He nearly choked on the word, and I couldn't help noticing that a faint flush had crept up his face.

"Of course we're friends," he said. "Why wouldn't we be?"

He cleared his throat several times and then went on in a hurry.

"And I meant what I said before. I want to help you."

"That's really sweet of you," I said.

"What do you need me to do?" Mike asked.

I thought for a moment. "I'm not really sure."

Mike gave me a sidelong glance.

"Do you actually know what you're doing?" he said with something of a return of his old teasing manner. "Do you have a plan?"

"Not exactly."

"I thought not."

His tone was still teasing, but there was a difference this time. His whole attitude was much friendlier—there was an undercurrent of warmth now.

We had walked on a little ways, and I stopped suddenly and looked around. We had left the campus, and we were now walking along a sidewalk through a well-tended neighborhood.

"Wait," I said. "Where are we going? You never did tell me where we were headed."

"I thought maybe we'd go to Salty Sweet," Mike said. "It's an ice cream parlor. It's a little out of the way, and only students go there. I thought it might be a good place to talk."

"Ice cream?" I said. "Isn't it a little early for that? It isn't even time for lunch yet."

Mike glanced at his watch. "It's eleven forty. Lunchtime isn't that far off."

He grinned, surprising me. "Besides, any time is good for ice cream."

We soon drew in sight of a little shopping center, and I could see Salty Sweet up ahead of us—it was a cheerful shop with a pink-and-white awning and ice cream cones in all colors of the rainbow painted on the big front windows.

We went inside.

The door had only just closed behind us when there was a happy shriek, and three small children ran past us.

I looked up at Mike. "I thought you said only students came here. Or has Henrietta College now opened up a preschool?"

I couldn't help teasing him a little—he'd done it to me so many times that I had to return the favor.

Mike looked a little sheepish. "Well, not *only* students. I just meant a lot of students—and also locals—but not locals from over your way in Crabtree Bay. We're almost in New Weybridge now, and most of the customers are from there."

I couldn't resist teasing him a little further.

"I get it," I said. "You brought me to some place out of the way so no one would see you with a witch."

"No," Mike said. "I brought you to Salty Sweet because the ice cream is far superior to what you have in Crabtree Bay. You guys think you're better than us because your town's a little bigger, but all you've got in Crabtree Bay are big chain-store ice cream parlors. This place has wonderful ice cream that they make right here in the shop. All fresh ingredients. And nothing was shipped in from a hundred miles away."

"You've got us there," I said. "We can't claim that we make our own ice cream."

I glanced around. The interior was pink and white like the awning outside, and the walls were decorated with Norman Rockwell-type prints. There was a long line in front of us, and the menu boards overhead listed about twenty flavors—and there were also sandwiches and omelets available. Servers with red-and-white hats scooped ice cream from tubs guarded by glass and placed it into cones and paper cups. The savory scent of eggs wafted in from the back, and a waitress went by with a little tray of breakfast sandwiches.

I glanced up at the choices overhead.

"What are you going to get?" I asked.

"Me?" Mike grinned. "Rocky road. And I might get some extra chocolate sprinkles. What about you?"

"I still think it's a little early for ice cream," I said. "But I might try a scoop of one of the sorbets—in a cup."

Mike feigned shock. "It's never too early for ice cream. And I can't believe you don't want a cone."

I made a face. "I don't think cones go too well with sorbet."

"Maybe you're right." Mike glanced around. "Why don't you go find a seat, and I'll get our ice cream. Then we can talk about your sleuthing and what comes next."

I looked up at him. "Are you sure? I don't want to leave you to wait in this line by yourself."

Mike waved it off. "It would be my pleasure. What kind of sorbet did you want?"

I smiled. "Surprise me."

He grinned. "Oh, I will. You can be sure about that."

I glanced around the room. Parents and children seemed to occupy every one of the little round tables. For an out-of-the-way place, it was certainly packed.

"A lot of kids here today," Mike observed. "The students must be sleeping in this morning."

He pointed. "There's more seating in the back."

I looked where he indicated, and I saw that there was a corner to a nearby wall and the room continued beyond it.

"Thanks," I said. "See you soon."

I walked away, and I tried not to look back to see if he was watching me.

On the other side of the corner, there were red booths as well as tables, and the crowd was much sparser.

I was surveying the room and trying to decide if I wanted a table or a booth when I spotted a girl who looked familiar.

She had short dark hair and pale skin, and she was wearing a gray polo shirt and white jean shorts along with white tennis shoes.

She glanced at me, and I realized that I was looking at Geraldine Tyndall.

She was seated at one of the booths, and her companion, a dark-haired male, had his back to me. When she continued to stare, the man turned to look at me, and I found myself staring into the brilliant green eyes of Andrew Wyatt.

I groaned inwardly.

Andrew was instantly on his feet.

"Oh no!" he cried. "She's found us!"

Andrew came toward me, and I skirted around several tables to avoid him. Doing so brought me closer to Geraldine, and I could see that she and Andrew were probably just about ready to leave. There were two empty sundae glasses and two empty plates on the table, and a big silver purse sat next to them. And lying next to the purse was a card with Andrew's face on the front.

I remembered with a certain sense of embarrassment that Andrew had given me a card like that once long ago. He'd had the cards made himself, and they featured his headshot on the front in black and white, which did nothing to diminish the unique charisma of his eyes—somehow they actually seemed more intense due to the lack of color. I wondered if these were the same cards, or if he'd had new ones made since we'd been together.

I shuddered as I remembered what had been inside—Andrew had copied the lyrics from a popular song in calligraphy—which hadn't been so bad. But he had also pressed a kiss in green lipstick just below the lyrics—the lipstick had come from a play he'd been appearing in back then as an elf or a fairy or something.

At the time, I'd been charmed by the kiss—but now I didn't remember it so fondly.

I wondered if he'd planted a kiss inside Geraldine's card, too.

"Chloe!" Andrew cried. "Chloe! Stay away from her!"

Andrew had continued to chase me, and I realized that moving toward Geraldine was exactly the wrong way to go.

I hurriedly scooted past Geraldine and tried to make it to the corner, but Andrew suddenly lunged for me and cut off my escape.

I stood for a moment, trapped, and then Andrew suddenly fell to his knees and wrapped his arms around me.

"Oh please, Chloe!" he wailed. "Please don't hurt Geraldine!"

I glanced around. Several mothers and their children were staring at us.

"Andrew, let me go," I said.

I tried to pull free, but my hands were trapped under his encircling arms.

He looked up at me, and his eyes were misty. I thought I could see tears forming in them.

"Please—I love her," he said. "Don't kill her. I told you you had nothing to worry about with Bradshaw—and now you know. Please leave her alone—stop this vendetta you've got going. And leave *us* alone. We just want to be allowed to share our love in peace. Please, Chloe, don't turn your deadly gaze Geraldine's way."

For his part, Andrew actually did turn to look at Geraldine.

"Run, Geraldine, run!" he cried. "I told you she'd come for us."

I looked over at Geraldine. She was sitting frozen, fear and uncertainty reflected in her dark eyes.

A waitress came around the corner and stopped when she saw our little tableau.

Geraldine hastily waved her over, and the waitress gave her a little black book with a credit card in it. Geraldine quickly signed a little white slip, and then she swept her things into her purse.

Mike came hurrying around the corner next.

"Chloe?" he said. "Is everything okay?"

He then saw Andrew with his arms wrapped around me, and he started toward us.

"Let her go!"

Andrew quickly released me and jumped back.

He ran toward Geraldine and grabbed her hand.

"Come on," he said. "They're both crazy."

The two of them ran out of the ice cream parlor, and Mike moved to go after them, but I held him back.

"Just let them go," I said. "It's better if they just leave."

Mike turned back toward me. "Are you okay?"

"I'm fine," I said. "Just a little rattled."

"What was going on?" Mike asked. "Who was that guy?"

"That was my ex-boyfriend," I said.

Chapter Sixteen

"Are you doing all right?" Mike asked softly.

I looked over at him. The two of us were walking along the sidewalk back to Henrietta College, and Mike had gotten a to-go box for our ice cream. There were several cone-sized slots, and his rocky road cone nestled into one of them. My sorbet sat in one of the larger, cup-sized slots.

"You know, I didn't even know they made those things," I said, gesturing to the box.

Mike continued to look at me patiently, and eventually I answered him.

"Yes, I'm all right," I said. I smiled. "Our ice cream's going to melt in this heat."

"Would you like it now?" Mike asked. "I wasn't sure if you still wanted it."

"Sure. Now would be good. I could use a little sugar as a pick-me-up."

Mike handed over my sorbet and a spoon. It was definitely melting fast, but I scooped up a bit of the bright fuchsia sorbet and tasted it. It was cold and tangy and sweet—and good.

"That's delicious," I said. "What is it?"

"What do you think it is?" Mike asked.

"I don't know," I said. "It's a little bit like kiwi—but also a bit like a pear. And it's sweet."

"It's dragon fruit."

"Dragon fruit?" I said. "I didn't see that on the menu."

"They have a secret menu that you have to ask for specially," Mike said. "I told you I'd surprise you."

"Yes, you did," I said softly. "In more ways than one."

Mike began to work on his rocky road cone, which was in danger of spilling onto his hand.

"So that was your ex-boyfriend?" he said.

"Yes—Andrew and I dated in high school. I was much younger, and he was very handsome."

Mike chuckled. "It must have been about a million years ago."

"It was only five," I said. "But things are different now. You can see what he's like. I wouldn't fall for someone like that again."

"He does seem a little theatrical," Mike said.

He glanced at me furtively. "I gather Joe is different? Good-looking but maybe not so high-maintenance?"

"Joe?" I said, momentarily puzzled.

"Joe. He's possibly your current boyfriend? I saw him that day at the library."

"Oh no," I said. "Joe's a wonderful person, and he's always been very nice to me. But we aren't dating—I thought I told you that."

Mike looked up at me, and his face suddenly lit up.

"You did. I just wanted to double-check. So you're definitely not dating him?"

"No."

"You're sure?"

"Yes," I said. "I think know when I'm dating someone. And I'm not dating Joe."

"Oh," Mike said.

He seemed to be working hard to suppress a smile.

"Something funny about that?" I asked.

"No—no, not at all. I'm just—"

Mike stopped.

"We never did get a chance to talk about what you're going to do next," he said. "And how I can help."

"Well, I'm still not sure where to begin, except to start interviewing people," I said. I glanced up at Mike. "I don't suppose you could get me a meeting with Ariadne—or Tina—or whatever her name is."

Mike shook his head. "No. I think that would be highly inappropriate. And I don't really see how she could be involved in this anyway."

"She accused you of betraying a confidence," I said. "She said you gave away information that was meant to remain secret. Aren't you at least a little curious?"

"No," Mike said. "Tina's never said anything to me. Maybe she just got confused."

"She didn't sound confused to me."

Mike sighed. "I'm not going to harass my students."

We had reached the campus once again, and Mike glanced over at his building. Then he glanced down at my now-empty sorbet cup.

"Would you like to come in for some water?" he asked. "I've got some in the fridge."

"Sure," I said. "Thanks."

We went into Mike's building, and he led me to a little kitchenette. There was a white table with orange plastic chairs, and I sat down while Mike went to the refrigerator.

"Would you like still or sparkling?" he said.

"How about sparkling," I replied.

"Sparkling it is." He took two small green bottles out of the refrigerator and placed them on the table along with two cups.

I drank the water, relishing the coolness and the bubbles. "Thanks."

"Speaking of harassment," Mike said.

I was puzzled. "Were we speaking of harassment?"

"I'd mentioned it just before we came in here," Mike said. "And I realize that I need to apologize once again."

"For what?"

Mike looked rueful. "For that little scene in the library when we first met. Seeing Andrew acting like an idiot in the ice cream parlor made me realize that that's what I looked like, too. I'm sorry about that ambush. I never should have gone after you in public like that."

I thought back to that day and how mortifying it had been. "That's okay." I smiled as I remembered the look Mike had had on his face. "You were certainly full of righteous fervor."

Mike hung his head. "I thought I was doing the right thing—but I wasn't. Can you forgive me?"

"You're forgiven," I said.

"Thank you." Mike took a restoring swig of water, and then he took a deep breath.

"So you said you'll start 'interviewing people'? Who's first?"

"I thought I'd try Chris Young," I said. "He's Bradshaw's ex-boyfriend, and he seems to be stalking her."

Mike frowned. "That sounds kind of dangerous."

"And then there's Geraldine Tyndall," I said. "We just saw her in the ice cream parlor. She's Bradshaw's cousin, and I want to find out if she might inherit Bradshaw's money. My sister Alberta is really supposed to be investigating her, but now that I know she's in town, I might try to talk to her myself."

"Is Geraldine the girl we saw with Andrew?"

"Yes."

Mike shook his head. "I don't think that sounds like a good idea, either."

"I have to try," I said.

"Well, you have my number. Call me if you need anything. And if Chris or Andrew comes after you, please call the police, too."

"I will." I looked up at Mike. "Thanks for this."

"For what?"

"Thanks for this morning—it was nice. Not the Andrew part—but the rest."

"Just the tonic you needed?" Mike said.

"Yes," I said. "Spending time with a friend."

Mike cleared his throat.

"A shot in the arm," he said croakily.

"Yes," I said. Something tugged at my mind when he said that. I stood up and put my purse over my shoulder. Then I put my glass bottle and my paper cup in a nearby recycling bin.

Mike stood up also.

"Where are you going right now?" he said.

I frowned a little in thought. "I thought I might do a little reading."

"Oh," Mike said. "It's getting on toward lunchtime. I thought maybe you might be heading somewhere for lunch."

"No," I said abstractedly. "There's something I need to check into. And the sorbet should last me a little while."

I realized I was being a little impolite, and I made an effort to focus on Mike. "Thanks again for everything."

"Don't worry about it. I owe you a little something at least for making you a public spectacle."

I smiled at him and then left the room.

I hurried out of the building and ran down to my car.

I had suddenly remembered what I had wanted to see in the true crime section at the library.

I drove over quickly.

Stu was standing at the circulation desk when I walked in.

"Hi, Chloe," he said. Stu was our other librarian, and he was good-natured and a little vague—his mind always seemed to be on books. He had a shiny, bald pate on top and a ring of white at the back and sides, and he had black, plastic glasses that were always sliding down his nose. He was wearing a short-sleeve Oxford shirt and a pair of jeans with a belt. Several pens nestled in a pocket protector in his front shirt pocket.

"What are you doing here?" he said with a smile. "You're supposed to be off today."

"I just came in to do some reading," I said.

Stu beamed at me. "Marvelous. You really do have the reading bug. I keep telling you you have the makings of a great librarian."

"Thanks, Stu," I said. Ordinarily, I would have stopped to chat a little, but today I really needed to get to that true crime section.

I hurried through the stacks.

The book I was looking for was on a lower shelf, and I sat down on a gray, metal step stool and reached for it.

It was a book about a woman—Nancy DeVault—who had killed her husband. After a few minutes of skimming, I found the section I was looking for.

I read it over several times—the facts were just what I remembered. I took out a few more books that looked similar, and then I grabbed a book on fingerprints and biological evidence—I was still curious about how fingerprints could be obtained from paper.

Then I went to an empty study carrel and started reading. When I finally looked up, several hours had passed. I put the books back on the shelves, and then I turned to the computers—I spent another two hours doing research online. My internet research was much quicker, and I began to see that there was a pattern emerging in the crimes I was looking up.

The idea that had begun to grow in my mind was definitely taking root—and a form was beginning to appear.

I logged off the computer and decided to call it a day. I glanced up at the big clock overhead—it was nearly five thirty anyway—the library closed early on Saturdays. Then I went up to the circulation desk to say goodbye to Stu.

"Have a good night, Stu," I said.

He smiled when he saw me. "I was just about to lock up. If you'll wait a moment, I'll walk out with you."

"Sure," I said. I set my purse down on a nearby table and glanced around—the library was pretty much deserted, which wasn't unusual for a Saturday evening in the summer. Emily, our page, was just returning an empty cart to the desk, and the few stragglers left in the building grumbled when Stu turned out the lights, but shuffled out obediently.

Emily and Stu looked around the library but didn't find anybody hiding in the dark. Since we didn't collect any fines in the summer, there wasn't any money to count or lock away.

Stu ushered us all out through the front doors, and then he locked them and gave them a firm rattle.

Then all three of us walked down to the street.

It was Stu's custom to make sure that everyone made it to their car safely, so all three of us walked to Emily's car, and Stu and I waited on the sidewalk as she settled in and drove off.

Then Stu walked me to my car.

"I hope you don't mind if I ask—" Stu began as I unlocked my door.

He didn't continue.

"Ask what?" I said.

I looked up at him. The pleasant, vague smile he'd been wearing before had been replaced by a mild frown.

"It's just that I heard there was some trouble," he said. "Something about you and your sisters. I was just wondering if you were okay?"

I felt a rush of affection for Stu—it was just like him to be unaware of gossip and to have only the vaguest notion of what was going on.

"We're all right," I said gently. "I was accused of something I didn't do, and then my sister Rafaela was accused after me. But we're going to fix everything—it's going to work out. Thanks for asking."

Stu yawned then and quickly put a hand over his mouth.

"I do apologize," he said. "I don't mean to give you the idea that I'm not interested in what you're saying. I'm very interested. I'm just a little tired."

"You've had a long day," I said. "Saturdays are always a little tough."

Stu stifled another yawn. "It's not that. It's just that I've had trouble sleeping lately. Drag racing, you know."

I was startled. "Drag racing? When did you get into that?"

Stu chuckled. "I don't mean me. No, there's a group—I hesitate to call them a gang—but a group that comes out to my street in the wee hours and races. Their cars are terribly loud. They race three or four times and then leave. It used to be just the occasional event on the weekends—but it's been happening more and more often lately. They've even started doing it on weeknights."

"That's terrible," I said. "And really dangerous—somebody could get hurt. Have you called the police?"

Stu sighed. "I have. And our local police force is excellent—I really believe that. They're fine people. But alas, there is a lack of evidence. They haven't been able to catch anyone at it."

"But surely if it's every night, there must be some evidence."

"You would think so. But as I mentioned there are only three or four races, and then everyone disappears. And every time the police wait for them—I believe that's called a 'stakeout'—the drivers don't show up. I suppose they must be getting advance notice that the police will be there somehow."

Stu frowned. "There's one car that's present nearly every time—although it wasn't there last night. It's a blue car with yellow lightning bolts down the side."

I drew in my breath sharply.

Stu eyed me keenly. "You've seen it?"

"Yes," I said.

"Then you've seen one of the perpetrators—though maybe that word is too strong a term. Perhaps I should just say 'driver.' As I say, the car is almost always present—I even copied the license plate number down and gave that to the police, but I'm afraid there's not much they can do with that—it's not really evidence. Anybody can write down a license plate number and accuse someone of a crime."

Stu paused.

"I did see that same blue-and-yellow car parked over at a mechanics shop several times—the one over on First Street. I almost went in to see if I could find the driver, but then I realized that might not be the ideal way to proceed."

He smiled at me. "What I really ought to do is film one of these late-night races with my phone—but I can never seem to get it working in time. And then, of course, they always disappear so quickly. I keep hoping that one of my neighbors will catch them on video, but there are a lot of retirees on my street—none of us seem to be so good with technology."

"They'll get caught," I said. "It's only a matter of time."

"I'm sure you're right," Stu replied. "And so far no harm done— just a few senior citizens losing some sleep. And mind you, I can see why they chose our street—it's nice and straight and level. Not much in the way of obstacles. It really is an ideal raceway."

He stopped abruptly. "But I've been going on about myself, and I meant to find out how you and your sisters were doing."

"That's all right," I said. "My sisters and I are okay, and I hope having someone listen helped a bit."

Stu smiled his vague smile. "It did. It's always nice to have someone truly sympathetic as a listener—listening, you know, is an important part of this job."

His smile grew a little brighter.

"We'll make a librarian of you yet."

Chapter Seventeen

I drove home, and I was aware that my stomach was beginning to grumble.

I hadn't stopped at any time in the afternoon to get something to eat.

As I walked into the house, I was enveloped by the most delicious aromas, and my stomach began to growl even louder.

Alberta came out to greet me.

"How did everything go?" she said.

"I think it went pretty well," I replied. "I didn't find out much today, but I do have a few places I can start now."

I glanced over at the couch. "I see Sibyl has finally stopped her marching routine."

"Yes, she did." Alberta frowned just a little. "She stopped walking around shortly after you left. She's been sleeping ever since then in her cat bed."

"That's great," I said. "Finally, Sibyl is acting normal."

Alberta shook her head. "There's nothing normal about that. I bought the bed for her three years ago when she was a kitten—and it was quite expensive. She's never gone anywhere near it. This is actually the weirdest thing she's done yet."

She sighed. "Crazy cat."

I was just setting my purse down when Alberta grabbed my hand.

"Before you settle in," she said, "let me show you something."

She led me to the door, and as she opened it, I was hit by a blast of the early evening heat.

"I just walked in," I protested. "I was really enjoying the air-conditioning."

"It'll only take a moment, you big baby," Alberta replied. "I just want to show you the new protective runes."

She pointed to the doorjamb, and I could see that a tiny wooden plaque with even tinier runes had been attached to it.

"I got some advice from Mom on the runes," she said.

"They look good," I said. "How's she doing? How's Dad?"

"They're both doing well," Alberta said, shooing me back inside and closing the door. "I'll tell you more in a little bit."

I glanced at her face then—the little frown that had set in earlier was still there.

"What's wrong?" I said.

Alberta waved a hand. "It's just that this day isn't working out the way I thought it would."

She crossed quickly to her phone.

"And still no text," she said.

"Were you expecting one?"

"Sort of," she said. It seemed to me that she looked disappointed.

There was a loud clattering sound from the kitchen, and I looked around.

"Was that Rafaela?"

"Yes," Alberta said. "I told her she did *not* have to make dinner—I was very emphatic on that point. But I think it makes her feel better."

"What's wrong with Rafaela?" I asked.

"I have an idea what might be bothering her," Alberta said, "but she hasn't said much of anything. Maybe eating something will help her calm down a little."

"Well, it smells divine in here. What is she making?"

"French onion soup," Alberta replied. "And beef tips with rice. I also made an apple pie."

"I love Rafaela's french onion soup," I said, inhaling deeply. "And your apple pie, too. And Rafaela makes the best rice—so light and fluffy. Why didn't you want her to cook?"

Alberta glanced at her phone again. "It's just that I thought—"

She stopped. Her phone buzzed, and I could see that she'd just received a text. She quickly read it.

Her face fell.

"Nothing," she said at last. "It's not important."

"But what was—"

"It's not important," she said again. "Let's go see if Rafaela needs any help in the kitchen."

But Rafaela waved us away, and Alberta and I ended up setting the dining room table and sitting down at it.

"I can't believe how much use this table has been getting," Alberta murmured. "I just wish it were under other circumstances."

Rafaela soon came out with the french onion soup in ramekins, and she set one at each of our places. I admired the beautiful, bubbly covering of cheese that spilled over the edge of the white ramekins ever so slightly, and my stomach gave a loud growl.

"I skipped lunch today," I said to Rafaela, and she gave me a wan smile.

She soon returned with the beef tips and rice, and we all broke the cheesy crust on the top of our french onion soup.

"So who wants to go first?" Alberta asked. "Who wants to tell us how their day went?"

I glanced over at Rafaela. She was staring down at her soup steadily, and she didn't seem to have heard Alberta.

"Raf?" I said softly.

Alberta also glanced over at Rafaela. "It's okay. I'll go first. I spoke to Mom, and she and Dad are doing well. The storm, as you know, has passed, and they were able to go back to their rental home. The house is in good shape—they were very lucky, and there was no flooding. They lost a few shingles off the roof, though, and a utility shed with some lawn ornaments and deck furniture has blown away. But other than that, everything is fine, and both Tibi and Maisie are doing well—though they're still a little freaked out."

She took a deep breath. "And then there's what Mom found out."

Rafaela and I both looked at her.

"She has four rune stones set around Crabtree Bay," Alberta said. "She asked me to check on them to see if they had been tampered with or altered in any way. Luckily, they can't be moved—they've been spelled in place—but they were painted over with blue paint, and then burlap sacks had been placed over them. And new rune stones had been placed next to them."

Rafaela looked shocked. "Someone defaced Mom's rune stones? The ones that protect the town?"

"Yes," Alberta said. "And they also alert us whenever magic that is not performed by us is practiced within the town limits."

"So that's why we didn't know that a curse had been placed on Lisa Stroup," Rafaela said.

"Yes."

"Who placed the new stones?" I asked.

"I have no idea," Alberta said. "But I removed them."

"You removed them?" Rafaela blinked.

"Yes—I put them in the burlap sacks, and I—"

Rafaela interrupted. "You didn't bring them here, did you?"

"No," Alberta said in exasperation. "I buried them under a tree near a lake outside city limits—but first I took pictures of them and sent them to Mom. And I also cleaned up our rune stones and sent pictures of those to Mom. She said the paint shouldn't really affect them too much—the real issue was the other stones, which were dampening their effectiveness."

"Are they working again?" I asked.

"Mom thinks they are," Alberta replied. "She can't be one hundred percent sure from a distance, but she has her own rune stone that is tied to the originals through connective magic—sort of like the plants you have for us. We're all connected to the original rune stones, too, so if any magic not cast by us is performed in Crabtree Bay, we'll know—our fingertips will start tingling."

"I haven't felt that in ages," Rafaela said.

"Neither have I," I said. "I think I was a kid the last time that happened."

"That's because no one aside from us has performed any magic in this town in a long time," Alberta said. "Either that, or those competing runes have been active for a lot longer than we realized."

Rafaela looked pensive. "Then that means that the Crabtree Coven really could be operating here in town. In fact, they may even be the ones who set up those other runes."

"Yes," Alberta said.

The three of us sat in silence for a moment. I glanced over at Rafaela—she seemed to be sinking further into gloom.

"What else did you learn?" I said to Alberta quickly. "About Bradshaw and who inherits if she dies?"

Alberta looked up at me. "Well, that's a funny thing. I didn't learn nearly as much as I'd hoped, but what I did learn is confusing."

"What do you mean?"

"First of all," Alberta said, "I wasn't able to get a look at Charles Tyndall's will, which isn't surprising. I'm sure it's on file at the county clerk's office, but since this is Saturday, the office is naturally closed—I'll have to go over there on Monday. I'd like to take a look at the will to see what Bradshaw and Geraldine's parents actually received. And then I'd like to look at *their* parents' wills to see what they received—that might give me an idea of their current financial situation. But I have also spoken to a few people who might know a thing or two, and what I've heard puzzles me. I'm not really sure who—"

She stopped.

"I'm not really sure," she concluded.

"I don't suppose you could just ask Bradshaw's attorney?" I said.

Alberta shook her head. "No proper attorney would tell me anything, not even after a few drinks. And I'm sure Bradshaw has a financial advisor, too. If they told me anything, they should be fired immediately."

"Could you try scrying again?" I said.

"I could," Alberta said, but her tone was reluctant.

"What's wrong?" I said.

"It's just that I feel like this is kind of a gray area. We're only supposed to use our powers to help."

"And you are helping," I said.

Alberta sighed. "I feel like this is a little more like prying. There may be a money motive in the attacks on Bradshaw, and there may not. When I did the scrying before, I knew there was information about our situation in Detective Mia's possession. This situation is different. I don't know for a fact that divining information through scrying will get us what we need. And, on the practical side, I'm not really sure who or what to focus on. I'm not sure where the information we need resides."

"You could start with Charles Tyndall's will," I said.

"And I can also look it up on Monday," Alberta replied. "There's no need for scrying."

"Well, speaking of people who might inherit," I said, "I saw Geraldine today."

Alberta looked at me in surprise. "You saw her here in Crabtree Bay?"

"I saw her over at an ice cream parlor in New Weybridge," I said. "But it was close enough. She's certainly not in Annapolis."

"I knew she was here," Rafaela said quietly.

We both looked over at her.

"You did?" I said.

She nodded. "I heard Bradshaw asked Geraldine to come stay with her—she just arrived last night. Bradshaw doesn't have any other family, and she wanted someone she trusted to be around and help look out for her."

"I'm not sure if she should be trusting Geraldine," I said.

I told both of them quickly about my visit to Professor Mike, and then I told them about our visit to the ice cream parlor—and about the show that Andrew had put on.

Alberta stared at me. "So Andrew is cheating on Bradshaw with Geraldine?"

"Yes," I said. "Bradshaw said she knew he was sneaking around with someone. Although Andrew made it sound like they were actually broken up—he told me I didn't have to 'worry about' Bradshaw. So I'm not really sure what their relationship status is at the moment."

"I'm sorry you had to go through that," Rafaela said. "It sounds like Andrew was really horrible."

"You should have kicked him in the stomach when he grabbed you like that," Alberta said. "Or somewhere a little lower."

"I got through it," I said. "And Mike was a big help."

Alberta and Rafaela exchanged a glance. Alberta grinned then, and Rafaela gave a small, conspiratorial smile.

"What?" I said.

"Nothing," Alberta said. "It just seems like you and Professor Mike are getting along pretty well these days."

"We're not—" I said. "I'm not—"

I stopped. Rafaela was looking a little happier than I had seen her in a while, and I decided it wasn't worth protesting—and I wasn't sure what I was protesting anyway. Mike and I *were* getting along better than we had at first.

"It wasn't like it was a date," I said at last. "Mike was just being nice."

Alberta and Rafaela exchanged another glance.

For my part, I glanced over at Rafaela—she seemed to have relaxed a little bit, and I really wanted to know what was going on with her.

"Raf," I said softly. "How are you doing? We haven't heard very much about what you did today."

Rafaela's face immediately fell into somber lines again.

"I told Alberta a little," she murmured quietly.

"Just talk to us," I said. "Getting it all out could really help. And you know we want to listen."

Alberta nodded. "You take so much on yourself. I'm sure you're worried about burdening us with whatever happened, but you don't need to be worried. We can handle it."

Rafaela sighed—a soft, gentle sound.

"I went to see Lisa Stroup at the hospital today," she said.

"You told me that," Alberta said. "What happened?"

"I went to her room," Rafaela said haltingly. "She was propped up in bed, and the TV was on."

She paused. "She looked for all the world like she was watching it—but she wasn't. She was just staring straight ahead. I spoke to her, but she didn't respond."

Rafaela shook her head. "She's still in there—I know she is. But she's trapped. She's trapped inside her own body, and she can't move or speak until someone gives her an order. Whoever did this to her has complete control over her. They can order her to do anything—and she has to do it. Who would do something like that to another human being? How could someone cast a curse like that?"

Rafaela closed her eyes. I knew that she could very genuinely sense other people's pain, and I wondered if she was reliving what she had felt from Lisa right now.

I reached out to take her hand, and Rafaela grasped mine tightly.

"It's okay to feel what you're feeling," I said. "It's what makes you strong."

Alberta's solution was more practical.

"I'll warm up some apple pie," she said. "And a little vanilla ice cream probably wouldn't hurt."

Chapter Eighteen

Even though it was Saturday, all three of us went to bed early.

And the next morning, Alberta and I were both up early—that wasn't unusual for her, but it was for me. And Rafaela slept in again, which wasn't like her. We'd all decided that it was best if Rafaela stayed with Alberta and me until everything was over.

So far, it didn't look like that would be any time soon.

Usually, I had to work on Sundays, but Rita had very kindly given me the day off. So Alberta and I sat at the breakfast table and worried about our sister.

I was sipping my coffee and waiting for my toast to pop up. Alberta was fussing with half a grapefruit.

"I really should get some proper grapefruit spoons," she said.

There was a loud click, and I realized my toast had popped up. We were sitting in the dining room, and I went into the kitchen.

"Would you like me to make you some toast?" I said, as I removed two slices from the toaster.

The bread had been baked by Alberta herself, and I spread some of the Irish butter she always bought over the golden brown toast. It smelled wonderful as the butter melted and soaked in.

"No thanks," Alberta said as I returned to the table. "For some reason I'm not in the mood for carbs this morning. I'm just going to have the grapefruit and some plain yogurt."

"There are carbs in grapefruit," I said.

"Not those kind of carbs," Alberta said. "I meant no bready carbs."

"I see," I said. I paused. "That's not like you. You're usually the queen of bready carbs."

Alberta sighed. "I know. I'm just not in the mood for comfort food. I'm in the mood for action food."

"Yogurt and grapefruit is action food?" I said.

"It's simple and healthy," Alberta replied. "And there's lots of protein in the yogurt."

She sighed again. "I just wish I knew what to do for Rafaela."

"We'll fix this," I said.

"But that'll take time," Alberta replied. "I wish we could make her feel better *now*."

She looked up at me.

"You know, there was something I left out yesterday when I told you guys about Mom."

"What?" I said. "Why?"

"I just felt like it might upset Rafaela further."

"What is it?" I said. "What happened?"

"After I cleared away those competing rune stones," Alberta said, "Mom ran some kind of diagnostic. With her rune stones, charts, and some kind of cell phone app, she was able to go back over the last few weeks to see if any spells not originated by us were cast in our area."

I blinked. "There's an app that does that?"

"I don't think that's what the app does exactly. But Mom had a tech-savvy friend modify it, and she uses it in combination with a bunch of other things, like I said. Anyway, the point is that she discovered at least two definite uses of outsider magic that occurred in Crabtree Bay. One happened the night the spell was cast on Lisa."

"That makes sense," I said.

"And the other was on Friday at around four in the afternoon. She thinks it was some type of 'forget' spell, and she said it was very clumsy—it probably caused some kind of strange reaction in the immediate area."

"Can she tell who cast them?" I asked quickly.

"No," Alberta replied. "She just knows it wasn't us. Do you remember anything strange happening on Friday around that time?"

I thought for a moment. "Nothing springs to mind. But it wouldn't necessarily have been a big event, would it?"

"No—it could have been something very quiet that had no witnesses."

"Why didn't you want to tell Rafaela?" I asked.

"Because Mom isn't sure that those were the only two events," Alberta said. "Those are just the only two that she was able to uncover evidence of. There may have been more spells cast that she doesn't know about."

"That is pretty disturbing," I said.

"And while I'm disclosing things," Alberta said, "I should also mention something Rafaela didn't tell you. She went out with some friends for lunch yesterday, and while she was out, she overheard some people talking about her. They called her a murderer. She was really hurt."

"I know what that feels like," I murmured. "That's awful. I wish she didn't have to go through this."

"And she's still convinced that this is somehow about you," Alberta said.

I thought back to the wilting, once-blue flower in my room—my connective magic seemed to disagree.

Somehow the thought of the wilting flower stirred my mind, and an image of Geraldine suddenly popped into my head.

"Did I mention that Andrew got a tattoo of the letter 'G'?" I said. "I realize now that it must be for 'Geraldine.' "

"Wait, what?" Alberta said. "What's with the switch in topic?"

"I don't know," I said. "I just suddenly remembered it. I first saw it back when he harassed me outside the library—I didn't know what it was then. But after seeing him with Geraldine I understand it now. They must be together for real."

"If anyone else had gotten a tattoo like that," Alberta said, "I would have said that was sweet. But since it's him, I think it's ridiculous. Besides, it's not going to last. He's always chasing after half the girls in town."

There was a knock on the door then, and Alberta looked around, surprised.

"I wonder who that could be?"

She hurried to the door.

The door didn't have a peephole, so Alberta opened it cautiously.

Suddenly, she flung it wide.

"Peter!" she exclaimed.

I got up then and walked to the door—our visitor was a dark-haired man with an olive complexion and a big, beaming smile.

It was Peter—from Peter's Table.

His smile faded a little as he took in Alberta's expression.

"You look surprised," he said. "Have I come at a bad time? Did you not get my text this morning?"

Alberta seemed to light up as she looked at him—she was clearly happy to see him.

"Oh no—that's okay," she said. "I haven't seen your text yet—my phone's upstairs. But I'm glad you're here."

She glanced down at the big, white bags that Peter was carrying. "Have you brought something for me?"

"Yes," Peter said. "I brought breakfast for you and your lovely sisters."

He sniffed delicately at the air. "But I think I am catching the aroma of toast in the air. Have you eaten already?"

Alberta waved a dismissive hand. "No—that was nothing. Please come in. Your breakfast will be far better than any piece of toast."

The smile returned to Peter's face, and Alberta and I stood back so he could enter the house.

"What happened to your action food?" I murmured as Alberta shut the door.

"Never you mind," she said.

We led Peter to the kitchen, and he shooed us out.

Alberta and I sat down at the dining room table, and we watched him through the open doorway.

He began to bustle around with his bags.

"The true test of a chef is whether or not he or she can make eggs—and more specifically—whether he or she can make an omelet."

Peter pulled out a carton of eggs and flashed us a white smile.

"I make an excellent omelet."

Soon he was chopping herbs and melting butter in a skillet he had brought with him. I noticed with interest that he had brought some Gruyère cheese.

As he worked, I heard water running overhead.

It sounded like Rafaela was getting up for the day.

I glanced over at Alberta to see if she'd noticed—but she was watching Peter with a rapt expression on her face.

I suddenly realized what she'd been so upset about last night.

"I get it," I said, grinning at her.

She looked over at me. "You get what?"

"Peter was supposed to come over last night, wasn't he?" I said. "That's why you kept checking your texts. And that's why you told Rafaela she didn't need to cook."

"Yes," Alberta said. "Now shush." She made a swift little cutting gesture with her hand.

"That's awfully nice of him to come over," I replied. I couldn't resist teasing her. "It's not every chef that makes house calls."

"Peter just wanted to be nice," Alberta said, darting a glance into the kitchen. "He knows things have been difficult for us lately, and he just wanted to cheer us up."

"Us?" I said. "Or you?"

Fire flashed in Alberta's eyes.

"Shhh!" she hissed.

Then she darted another glance over at Peter, but he seemed to be absorbed in his work.

He glanced over his shoulder at us.

"Would either of you ladies like cheese?"

"I would. Absolutely," I said.

"None for me, thanks," Alberta said. She smiled at him.

I thought I could see a rosy flush creeping up her cheeks.

"You're blushing," I said.

"No, I'm not," Alberta hissed back.

"Yes, you are."

"Be quiet," Alberta whispered. "He's going to hear you."

But Peter appeared to be completely wrapped up in his cooking. He plated one omelet and then got to work on the next one.

Soon he had plated both omelets, and he was depositing them on the table in front of us.

"Cheese for you, Miss Chloe," he said. "And no cheese for you, Miss Alberta."

He winked at her, and Alberta—whose color had gone down—seemed to be blushing a little again.

"Are you going to join us?" Alberta asked, fluttering her eyelashes a little.

"That is very kind of you," Peter said. "But what of Miss Rafaela? I can hardly serve myself when I haven't served her yet."

"I'm here," Rafaela said softly.

I turned to see her walking into the dining room. Her hair was still a little damp—I thought I'd heard a hair dryer running shortly after I'd heard her running the water.

She must have realized that we had a guest and hurried to get ready.

"Good morning, Miss Rafaela," Peter said, beaming at her. "I hope you didn't interrupt your beauty sleep to come down to see me."

"No—not at all," Rafaela said. "It was about time for me to be up anyway."

Peter rushed to pull out a chair for her, and Alberta shot her an irritated look.

It seemed to me that Alberta was just a bit jealous of the attention Rafaela was receiving from Peter.

"And you, Miss Rafaela," he said as she was seated. "May I make you an omelet, also?"

"Please." She smiled wanly.

Peter stepped into the kitchen.

He returned a moment later with three glasses filled with juice, which he had produced from one of his voluminous bags.

"Grapefruit juice with just a touch of mineral water," he said, as he set a glass down in front of each of us. "The grapefruit pairs well with the omelet, but I think it's a touch too strong straight. The mineral water makes it a little less acidic and easier on the digestion."

Alberta pushed her own, half-eaten grapefruit to the side.

"Please go ahead and eat," Rafaela said. Her voice was low, and I could hear an attempt at cheerfulness in it. "There's no need to wait for me."

"Yes, please do go ahead, ladies," Peter called from the kitchen. "I know you would like to be polite and wait for your sister, but the omelet really is best eaten fresh from the pan. And I will have hers ready in just a few moments."

He got to work, and then he glanced over his shoulder at Rafaela.

"And now I will ask you the same question I asked your sisters. Cheese or no cheese?"

He gave her a wink.

"With cheese, please," Rafaela said quietly.

Alberta, who had been eating her omelet, froze with the fork halfway to her mouth. She was glaring at Rafaela.

I gave her a kick under the table.

She transferred her angry gaze to me.

"Cut it out," I whispered. "Peter isn't interested in Rafaela. And just look at her face."

We both looked over at her.

Peter had turned back to his skillet, and Rafaela was looking down at the table as she sipped at her juice.

She was clearly worried about something.

"They're not flirting," I whispered.

"Okay. I see that," Alberta hissed back. "You know how I get sometimes."

"Yes, I do," I said.

"Just be quiet, or they'll hear us," Alberta said.

I glanced at Peter and Rafaela—Peter was entirely focused on his next omelet, and Rafaela was absorbed in her own thoughts.

"I think you're safe," I said.

Alberta glared at me again.

Soon Peter had another omelet on the table for Rafaela, and he turned back to the kitchen to make one for himself.

Alberta and I had both finished our omelets by the time Peter made it to the table, but he and Rafaela ate theirs, and Peter and Alberta carried on a lively conversation. Rafaela mostly sat quietly with her eyes fixed on the table, and I wondered what was going on with her. I knew, of course, that she had plenty to worry about already, so it was really no surprise that she was distracted this morning.

But it seemed to me that her worry was somehow deeper this morning.

I wondered once again what was troubling her.

Breakfast eventually wound down, and Peter got up to start packing away his things.

As Peter washed his dishes and pans, Alberta thanked him profusely and helped to dry his dishes as he finished them.

Once he was done, Peter stood in the entrance to the kitchen and bowed to us.

"Thank you, ladies, for having me in your home today," he said. "I only hope that I have done a little with my cooking to cheer you up and make your day brighter."

"It was wonderful, Peter," Alberta said. "Thank you so much."

Peter bowed again. "And thank you, my dear, for letting me come over this morning after I had to do a horrible, horrible thing last night and cancel. I am truly sorry. Such a thing will never happen again."

Alberta waved a hand. "That's all right. I'm sure you were busy."

"No—it's not all right," Peter said. "I made a commitment to you, and it's important to me to honor my commitments. I would never, never have disappointed you like that if there hadn't been an emergency at the restaurant."

"I figured it had to be something like that," Alberta said. "I wasn't disappointed at all."

"That's kind of you to say," Peter said. His face suddenly darkened. "It was that boy—he came to me, begging for a job—said he needed the money. So I was good to him. I said to myself, 'Peter, you will show this boy a kindness and help him to get back on his feet.' And then I gave him a job as a delivery boy. And then what does he do? He doesn't show up for Saturday night delivery service. I have many customers who are counting on me, and the boy is not there. I had to do all the deliveries myself—I couldn't disappoint my customers. And in the process, I ended up disappointing you."

Peter shook his head. "That boy. Thinks he's a model. He'd better never darken my door again."

Peter looked over at Alberta. "But I'm sorry. I'm sorry to show you my temper. I place a high value on trust, and I want you to be able to trust me, also. That's very important to me. Please say you accept my apology."

"Oh, Peter," Alberta said. "I accept it with all my heart."

Peter and Alberta exchanged a few more heartfelt sentiments, and we all walked him to the door.

Then Peter was off back to the restaurant.

As the door closed behind him, Alberta sighed softly.

"You thought he brushed you off last night, didn't you?" I said.

"Yes, I did," Alberta said dreamily. "But you can see how wrong I was. And you can see what lengths he went to to make it up to me. Last night, he was just going to drop off dinner for us—but instead he came here and cooked. I love a man who cooks for me."

Under ordinary circumstances, I would have teased Alberta about that, but at the moment, I was a little too worried about Rafaela.

"So who do you think that was?" Alberta asked.

"What?" I said. I wasn't quite sure what Alberta was talking about.

"Who do you think was the delivery boy? Do you think it could be Joe? Maybe his modeling career isn't going so well?"

"I don't know," I said. "It could be. But I hope not. I don't want Joe to be having problems."

"I imagine that social media stuff can be pretty unstable."

"Maybe," I said.

"Poor Joe," Alberta said.

"I'm sure it's not Joe," I said. I wondered if she was getting back at me because I'd teased her about Peter earlier.

"Well, maybe it's no one we know. I'd better check on the state of things in the kitchen. I'm sure Peter did a good job cleaning up, but you know how men are—they always miss something."

Alberta bustled off happily to the kitchen—no doubt to relive Peter's presence there, and Rafaela and I were left alone in the living room.

"What's going on, Rafaela?" I asked quietly. "What's wrong?"

She looked at me with the polite look she sometimes gave me when she was trying to keep something from me.

"Nothing," she said.

"Come on," I said. "Let's have a seat."

I sat down on the couch, and Rafaela, with some reluctance, sat down beside me.

I gave her an earnest look.

"Please tell me what's wrong."

Rafaela shook her head faintly. "You already know what's wrong. It's the same thing that's been wrong all week now."

"It think it's something more than that. Something's changed. Please tell me what's going on."

I knew that Rafaela liked to keep things to herself, but I also knew that she really needed help herself sometimes.

"Please, Rafaela. Tell me, and we can work on whatever it is that's troubling you together."

She turned to look at me, and her eyes were wide and frightened—it was almost as if she couldn't see me.

"I had a dream last night," she said. "I saw you in a field, standing by a dark tree with golden leaves. The sky was full of lightning, and a bolt came down and struck the tree. It split open, and a crow flew out and flew away. There was another bolt of lightning and it struck you. You fell down and were still. Then I woke up."

Rafaela stared at me. "I'm worried about you."

"Why?" I said. "It was just a dream. I'm fine."

"I don't think it was just a dream. I think it was a portent."

"What do you think it means?" I asked.

"I think it means that someone you know has magic hidden inside them. I think someone you know isn't what they seem."

Chapter Nineteen

"None of us has foresight."

Alberta's words of the night before echoed in my mind the next morning as I went out to my car.

Right before I'd gone to bed, I'd told Alberta about Rafaela's dream, and she'd been dismissive.

And she was right—none of us had visions of the future.

But Rafaela's dream wasn't really a vision of the future. It was more like a statement of what was happening now—our current situation. Rafaela didn't have any psychic power—but she was very sensitive to the way people felt.

And she'd been saying all along that someone was out to get me.

I wondered—since we'd been talking about Joe and his potentially short career as a delivery boy right before Rafaela had mentioned her dream—did she think Joe was the potential culprit, hiding his magic?

The tree in her dream had had golden leaves. And Joe had golden hair.

Could Joe be hiding magic inside?

But whoever was after me—if Rafaela was right—was also after Bradshaw.

Why would Joe be after Bradshaw?

Then an even worse thought struck me, and I pushed it aside.

I resolved to just focus on what I had to do this morning.

I was working the late shift today, so I had the morning free to go interview a few people.

The first person on my list was Chris Young.

Thanks to Stu, I now knew where to find him, and sure enough, as I pulled into the parking lot behind Crabtree Bay Auto and Body, I saw Chris's distinctive blue-and-yellow car reposing quietly in the morning sunshine. The lot was huge and largely empty, and I parked my car at a little distance from Chris's.

I walked across the dusty parking lot to the auto body shop, and then I walked around to the front of the building.

The first door I came to was actually the workshop itself, and two garage-style doors yawned open, revealing a big room with a concrete floor.

A lone mechanic was leaning under the hood of a car, working on something. He was wearing beige coveralls that had been unzipped and thrown back so that the sleeves and the jacket could be wrapped around the man's waist. His torso was covered by a sleeveless white T-shirt, and I could see the gleam of diamonds in the mechanic's ears as he worked. There were grease stains on his shirt and the gray floor.

As I approached, the man stopped working and looked around. When he saw me, he straightened up and began wiping his hands on a dingy blue rag.

He wasn't wearing sunglasses this time, but the shaved head and the finely molded cheekbones were the same.

It was Chris Young.

His dark eyes were watchful, wary. I wondered if he recognized me.

"I'm sorry, ma'am," he said. "We're closed."

I realized then that I hadn't spoken to Chris since high school, and I found that I was uncertain how to proceed.

I decided just to be direct.

"Hi. I'm Chloe Bartlett," I said.

A slow smile spread over Chris's face.

"I know who you are."

"You do?"

"Yeah—you're the witch who's trying to kill my girlfriend."

I felt a little spark of temper. "And you're the drag racer who's keeping people in a quiet neighborhood up at night."

Chris's smile broadened, and he shook his head. "Is that why you came here? To tell me you know about my drag racing?"

"No," I said. So far this wasn't going well. "Tell me about Bradshaw. Are you sure she's your girlfriend?"

Chris stared at me. "I'm not stupid. Of course she's my girlfriend. We're together—just like we were meant to be."

"It's just that I thought Bradshaw was with Andrew Wyatt—everybody thinks Bradshaw's with Andrew."

Chris shook his head again. "No. That Andrew guy was a loser. That was just a passing phase. Now she's back with me."

"Some people don't think that," I said. "Some people think you're stalking her and she wants to get away from you."

Chris chuckled—it wasn't a happy sound. "You got a lot of nerve, you know that?"

"Andrew is a wealthy guy," I said. "He's got tons of money from his dad—everybody knows that. Maybe Bradshaw wants a guy who can give her some security."

"Andrew's a loser," Chris said angrily. "He's been cheating on Bradshaw for months now. He's been running around behind her back with her cousin. What Bradshaw needs is a real man. No one else can give her what I can."

"And what can you give her?"

Chris's slow smile returned. "I've got that voodoo, you know? She can't keep away from it."

"Voodoo?" I said.

"I got that certain something. She can't stay away from me."

He wiped his hands again and threw the rag down on the side of the car. "What do you care anyway? Why are you snooping around here? Are you trying to find a new way to get at Bradshaw? You think you'll get to her through me?"

I glanced down at Chris's wrist. He was wearing a metal bracelet with a black symbol stamped on it—it was a crow.

"What's that?" I said. "A gift from Bradshaw?"

He covered his wrist. "It's an old family heirloom. It's nothing you need to worry about."

"But it would be nice, wouldn't it?" I said suddenly. "Having a rich wife? Especially if she'd do everything you said? Maybe you could even get your own garage."

"I got us," Chris said evenly, but I thought I saw an angry flush creeping up under his tan. "Bradshaw doesn't need to worry about anything—not anymore."

"What does that mean?" I said.

"It means we're going up to her lake house this weekend. And everything's going to be all right after that."

"And what does *that* mean?" I said.

Chris shook his head. "That's none of your business."

"Where were you on the night Lisa Stroup was attacked?" I asked.

"You mean the night she had a spell put on her?" Chris replied with a sardonic grin.

"That's the one."

"I was out drag racing. Just ask your friends in their quiet neighborhood."

"That isn't funny," I said.

"Yeah? Well, neither is your showing up to my place of work and harassing me."

Chris suddenly stepped close to me.

"If you want to know who cast a spell on Lisa," he said, "you should look in the mirror, witch lady. Bradshaw and I are doing just fine, and we don't need you snooping around here asking questions."

"But Bradshaw is in danger," I said.

"Yes, she is—because of you. Now I'm going to have to ask you to leave."

"But—"

"Leave now," Chris said angrily. "Or I'll call the cops. Like I said, we aren't open yet."

I looked up into Chris's dark, flashing eyes. I wasn't going to get any further information out of him.

"Fine," I said.

I turned on my heel and walked away.

"Hey, wait!" Chris shouted after me.

I stopped and turned back.

"The shop was broken into Thursday night," Chris said, "and a bunch of stuff was stolen. And now my car is making a funny rattling sound and not handling right. You know anything about that?"

"No," I said flatly.

"Just so you know, we have cameras." Chris paused and looked puzzled for a moment. "We didn't catch anybody this time—but we will next time. I promise you that."

"I'll keep that in mind," I said.

I walked to my car and drove away.

I was royally irritated, but I had a few things to think over, including Chris's metal crow bracelet.

And I still had my second suspect to grill.

I turned toward Henrietta College.

Mike had said that he didn't want me bothering Tina Chandler—or Ariadne Frost—or whatever her name was.

But that was exactly what I was about to do.

I had seen Mike's class schedule online, and I knew that he had a class on Monday morning.

With any luck, Tina would be in that class.

I parked my car in a distant lot and hurried toward the building where the class would be held.

Once again, I wasn't sure if access to the building was controlled or not, but I managed to fall in behind a crowd of students, and I went in with them.

I hurried upstairs to the right classroom and then peeked inside. I was early, so the class hadn't started yet, and there were only a few students in the room. I walked down the hall and sat down on a bench. I tried to look nonchalant as I watched the hall for each new student that arrived and walked into the classroom.

I would also have to be on the lookout for Mike.

I didn't want him to find me here.

A new batch of students ascended the stairs and started down the hall, and I scanned them eagerly. At first I didn't see Tina, and I sat back in disappointment. But as the group passed in, I spotted a girl with black hair and a slash of red lipstick all the way at the back behind two tall young men in T-shirts and shorts. The girl had her head down, and she was staring at her phone—but it was definitely Tina Chandler.

I quickly looked down at my own phone, hoping she wouldn't notice me—but as far as I could tell, Tina never glanced in my direction.

Once she was gone, I grabbed up my stuff and hurried down the hall to the stairs on the other end.

I would wait on another floor until the class was over.

I went downstairs and slipped into an empty classroom.

Time passed slowly, but eventually, the clock on my phone told me that the class would be over in ten minutes, and I hurried up the stairs just in case the class let out early.

I sat down on the bench again.

After a few minutes, the door to the classroom opened, and students began to stream out. I watched the crowd carefully, and I soon spotted Tina—she was all the way at the back again. I fell into step behind her, and I followed her out of the building.

She continued on to a wide, grassy lawn, and I jogged a little to catch up with her.

I could see she was wearing earbuds, so I waved at her.

"Hey, Tina!" I said just a little too loudly.

Tina looked up, startled.

She pulled one of the earbuds out of her ear and let its slender white cord dangle.

"What did you say?"

"I said hi."

Tina looked at me for a moment and then glowered. Her black eyebrows drew together in her pale face, and her scarlet lips pressed together in a thin line.

"You're the one from the library," she said.

"Yes," I said, a little too brightly.

"What do you want?"

"I need to talk to you for a few minutes," I said.

"I've said all I'm going to say to you."

"Tina—"

"My name is Ariadne."

I sighed. "Fine. Ariadne, I really need to talk to you. And you came to see me first."

Tina's expression grew sullen, but she stopped walking.

"What do you want to know?" she said.

"What do you know about the Sleeping Beauty Curse?" I asked.

Tina became wary. "I've never heard of it."

"Never?"

"That's right—never."

"It's not even one of those secrets that wasn't supposed to be told?" I asked.

Tina drew in her breath sharply.

"Tina, please—"

"Ariadne."

"Ariadne, a girl is under a terrible curse, and another girl is afraid for her life."

"Maybe they deserve it," Tina said flatly. "Maybe one of them should be cursed. And maybe one of them should be dead."

"That's horrible," I said.

Tina shrugged. "Sometimes the truth *is* horrible."

"Why did you tell me Mike was the one who released those secrets?"

"Mike?" Tina asked blankly.

"Professor Fellowes," I said. "You told me that he had spoken about things that shouldn't be revealed. You said there would be consequences."

Tina's dark eyes opened wide and a look of genuine surprise spread over her face. "I would never be upset with Professor Mike. He's the best!"

"But he wrote the article," I said.

"Yes—but that wasn't his fault," Tina replied. For once she looked like a regular college student and not like a dark spirit. "Someone gave that information to him, and he was just reporting on it. That's his job as a professor. He's supposed to put knowledge out into the world."

"So you're not mad at Mike?"

"No, of course not."

"But when you came to the library," I said, "you were fuming about a friend of mine who had come to visit me. Wasn't that Mike?"

"No." Tina stared at me for a long moment. "And why do you keep calling him Mike?" Her eyes narrowed. "Do you like him?"

"What?" I said, startled. "No. I mean, maybe—I don't know."

Tina's red lips pressed into a thin line again. "You do, don't you?"

The words were an accusation.

"If it wasn't Mike," I said, "then who was it? Who was the friend who came to visit me and betrayed your trust?"

Tina stiffened. "I never said anyone betrayed my trust."

"Who was the friend?"

Tina smirked. "You ought to know who your friends are."

I quickly got out my phone and began to scroll through several social media sites.

I found a picture and held out my phone.

"Was this the friend?" I said.

Tina barely glanced at the photo.

"No."

I scrolled through some more.

"Was this the one?" I said.

"No."

"How about this?"

"No."

Tina had been staring at me stonily, and I knew she was angry, but none of the photos produced even a flicker in her eyes. I realized that I believed her.

"Who was the friend?" I said. "Describe the person to me."

"Like I said, you ought to know who your friends are."

I looked at her for a moment—took in the pale skin, the sooty black hair, the scarlet lips, the single pearl on a gold chain around her neck.

"Tina, the pearl, all the things you seem to know. I have to know. Did you—"

"No!" Tina shouted suddenly.

"Tina, please," I said. "Just tell me something."

"You want me to tell you something?" she said. "Then I will. Your family thinks they own this town. They think they can keep everyone else out. They think they're the only ones who have the right to use magic. But they're wrong—and so are you."

"Tina—" I said.

"It's Ariadne," she snapped. "You're all so ignorant. You didn't even recognize the signs the other night."

"The signs?" I echoed.

"The summer lightning," Tina said. "Didn't you see how bright it was? Did you think that was normal?"

"Summer lightning?" I said.

"Lightning—in the summer," Tina said distinctly. "No rain."

"Heat lightning?" I said.

"Yes—whatever you want to call it. That was a sign of a curse being cast. And it will come again."

"How do you—"

"It's coming," Tina said, clutching the single pearl. "When you see summer lightning again, it's happening."

Her red lips spread into a wide, malicious smile.

"There will be a day of reckoning."

Chapter Twenty

I watched as Tina stormed away across the lawn.

Then there was a voice behind me.

"Chloe?"

I turned to see Mike silhouetted against the summer sunshine.

He broke into a grin when he saw me.

"What are you doing here? Did you come to see me?"

He looked really hopeful—but I had to tell him the truth.

"I came to see Tina Chandler," I said.

Mike blinked. "What? Chloe, I told you my students are off limits."

"I know," I said.

"This is totally out of line."

"I know," I said. "But you didn't hear what she said."

I told him quickly about Tina's prognostications of doom.

"And she keeps insisting on being called 'Ariadne,'" I finished.

"So?"

"I think that could be her coven name."

"Her coven name?" Mike sounded exasperated. "Chloe, she's just a kid."

I wasn't so sure about that.

Mike went on. "I know you want to help your sister, but this isn't the way to do it."

"And what is the right way?" I said.

"Work with the police," Mike said. "Work within the bounds of the law."

"The police think we're guilty," I said. "All of us."

"They're just in a tight spot with all of the magical nonsense that's been floating around. I'm sure once everything calms down, that some real clues will emerge."

"Magical nonsense?" I said.

Mike sighed. "You know what I meant."

"No, I don't," I replied. "It's not nonsense to me—or to my family."

"I know. I understand. And I respect your beliefs. But this stuff that you're talking about now—two rival groups of witches battling for control of this town—"

Mike's voice trailed off.

"It's just a little hard to believe," he said.

"That's not what I said at all," I replied. "*Tina's* the one who thinks we're rivals, though she hasn't actually said whether she's a member of the Crabtree Coven or not. And I have to look into the coven because whoever is guilty of these crimes has been using magic. The coven is the only lead I have."

Mike's expression grew pained, and he pinched the bridge of his nose with his thumb and forefinger.

"Oh, Chloe. If only you could hear the way you sound. I want to support you—I really do. But you're not making this easy. If you would just focus on the facts and forget about the magic, I'm sure you would learn a lot more."

"Forget about the magic?" I said indignantly. "I—"

I stopped. I suddenly realized Mike was right. I did need to focus on the facts. And one fact in particular jumped out at me.

"Thanks, Mike," I said. "I've got to go."

I began to run across the lawn.

"Wait!" Mike called after me. "Where are you going?"

"I have to go to work!" I shouted back.

I kept running until I reached the remote parking lot where I had parked my car. Then I jumped in and drove to the library.

I had a full day of work to put in, and even though I usually loved my work, today I couldn't wait for it to be over.

I had a new lead to follow.

Rita was already there when I arrived, and I hurried down to our break room to grab a snack before I started working.

When I came back upstairs, Stu had arrived, and since there were two librarians to staff the circulation desk, I took a cart and began shelving books.

My allotment of books led me to the true crime section, and I paused as I saw the spines of the books I had been reading the other day—the books on murder and fingerprints.

I picked up one of the books and flipped through it.

I was vaguely puzzled. The new lead I was planning to follow didn't really fit in with what I'd gleaned from my research. But I would follow it just the same—it was a good lead.

But still, I was puzzled.

Joe stopped in and hung out with me for a little while as I shelved books, but eventually, he left, citing work. As I watched him head out the door, I wondered about Peter and the trouble he'd had with his delivery boy. I wondered if Alberta's speculation that Joe was the delivery boy was correct. I really hoped not—I didn't like the thought of Joe's online business being in trouble.

The hours flew by since Monday was often a busy day—and this one was no exception—and before I knew it, I was stepping out of the library to get a snack.

On the days when I worked the late shift, I usually just had a snack at my dinner break and then waited until I went home to Alberta's to have a full dinner. Since Rafaela was staying with us for the foreseeable future, I'd probably be having dinner with them both.

I wondered if Rafaela was cooking tonight.

After a cup of coffee and a muffin from a nearby coffee shop, I was back at work, and I took a turn at the circulation desk to spell

Stu—Rita had left right around the time I'd had my dinner break. The rest of the evening was also busy, and before I knew it, Stu was flicking the lights on and off and announcing to our grumbling patrons that the library was closing for the night.

Eventually, everyone was ushered out, and then Stu and I searched the library to make sure there were no stragglers. Once we were sure the place was empty, and after we'd shut everything down, we left the library for the night and locked the doors.

Stu walked me to my car.

"Have a good night, Chloe," he said. "I hope you and your sisters are okay."

"Thanks, Stu," I replied. "I hope you aren't troubled by the drag racers tonight."

He sighed softly. "Yes, the drag racers. Just once I'd like to have an entire week without them."

I suddenly thought of Chris and what he had told me.

"I heard one of the racers—the one with the blue-and-yellow car—is going out of town this weekend. So maybe it'll be quiet for you."

"Oh, I hope so," Stu said fervently.

I got in my car, and Stu waved and turned toward his vehicle, which was parked not too far away.

I drove home.

As I walked in the door, I was met by the most delicious aroma, and Alberta greeted me along with it.

"Mmm. What is that?" I said, setting down my purse. "I definitely smell cheese and tomato sauce. And there's something savory in there, too, unless I miss my guess."

"Rafaela's made lasagna with a meat sauce," Alberta replied. "And she knows how much you love cheese, so she's used at least three cheeses in the layers."

"It smells divine," I said, inhaling deeply.

I glanced then at Alberta—instead of following me into the room, she was standing awkwardly by the door.

"What's wrong?" I said.

Alberta began to fiddle with one of her emerald earrings—a habit she sometimes had when she was worried.

"It's Rafaela," she said in a low voice. "I don't think she's doing well."

"What happened?" I said quickly. "Was someone horrible to her again today?"

"It's not that," Alberta said, playing with her earring again. "It's just that she hasn't been going to work—they've let her take time off until this whole thing gets resolved."

"That's only right," I said. "I can't imagine Rafaela would be much good with her patients right now. She'd be too distracted to care for them properly."

"Well, that's just the thing. She has the whole day off, and she doesn't really know what to do with herself. And she just naturally gravitates toward helping others."

"So what has she been doing?" I said.

"She went to see Lisa Stroup again. I think she's trying to help her. But of course there's nothing Rafaela can do. A curse is a curse. No amount of medical expertise can fix that."

Alberta paused and lowered her voice still further. "Rafaela says that all Lisa does is stare straight ahead and get moved around like a doll. Rafaela wants very badly to help her, and it's weighing on her mind. I think she feels responsible."

"That's crazy," I said, lowering my voice also. "There's no way Rafaela's responsible for what happened to Lisa."

"I know," Alberta replied. "It's not so much that she feels responsible for the curse—it's more like she feels responsible for fixing it. You know how she always wants to save everybody."

"About the curse," I said. "Have you heard anything else from Mom? Does she know another way to break it yet?"

"I have heard from her. But no—she doesn't. A kiss from the person who cast the curse is still the only way."

Alberta paused. "Mom and Dad still want to come up here. I told them not to. We argued back and forth for a long time—but I think I convinced them eventually. They both want to come up here and fight for us—Dad especially is raring to go. But I feel somehow like it's safer if they stay where they are. I told them no one's been arrested, so they should just stay put."

"I agree," I said. "I feel the same way—it's safer if they stay where they are. It seems like if they're down in Florida, they're out of harm's way."

"I just hope we can convince them to stay down there," Alberta said. "You know how Dad gets when he's got an idea in his head—"

"Meow! Meow! Meow! Meow!"

I looked around, startled. "Is that Sibyl?"

"Meow! Meow! Meow! Meow!"

Alberta sighed. "Yes, that's Sibyl."

The loud meows disappeared as quickly as they had come.

"What is she doing?"

"She's chiming the hour," Alberta said. "Rafaela says she's been doing it all day. And I heard her myself at seven."

"She's chiming the hour?" I said.

"Come and see."

Alberta led me over to her grandfather clock, which stood by the wall near the stairs. Sibyl was sitting at the base of it, staring up at the yellow moon on its face.

"So Sibyl's meowing every hour?" I said.

"Yes," Alberta replied. "And she gets the number of meows right. At eight o'clock, she gave us eight meows—as you just heard. She's been doing the half hour and the quarter, too."

I stared at the cat. Her amber eyes remained placidly fixed on the clock's face.

"I didn't know she could tell time," I said.

"I don't think she can," Alberta said. "I disabled the chimes a long time ago, but the mechanism still works. I think she can just feel the vibrations."

"Has she ever done this before?"

"No."

"That's very odd," I said.

"Yes. Yes, it is," Alberta replied.

I heard the oven door open, and the two of us continued on into the kitchen. Rafaela was just taking a tray loaded with garlic bread out of the oven, and I could smell the garlic and the butter that had melted into the bread, turning it a rich golden brown. Sitting on the stove already was a pan of lasagna, and I could see its red sauce still bubbling ever so slightly.

My stomach grumbled just a little, reminding me that I'd only had coffee and a muffin a few hours ago.

Rafaela glanced up at us.

She looked tired and worn out, and there were definitely lines of strain around her eyes. I could see that Alberta was right—Rafaela was taking too much on herself. She was looking much worse than she had even this morning.

"Dining room again?" she said to us.

"Yes, the dining room," Alberta said firmly. "I've got great air-conditioning in the house, but even so, the kitchen's too hot. And you, Rafaela, need to go and sit down."

"I'm fine," Rafaela said. "I'm happy to do the plating. You two go and sit down. You've been working all day."

"No, *you* sit down," Alberta replied. "You're overcompensating. Because you can't save Lisa, you're trying to take care of everyone else. Which isn't to say that I don't appreciate this lovely meal you've cooked us, because I do. I know it will be marvelous. But you really should relax the rest of the night. Chloe and I will do all the cleaning up."

"We will," I said. "You don't need to worry about a thing."

Rafaela smiled at us wanly and then went to sit down at the dining room table.

"See what I mean?" Alberta whispered to me.

"Yes, I definitely do," I said.

Soon we had set the table and served out the lasagna and the garlic bread, along with a salad that we had quickly made.

The lasagna and the garlic bread were terrific—the garlic bread was warm and salty, and the lasagna was hearty and full of tangy Bolognese sauce.

We were all silent for a little while, just enjoying the food.

Then it was time to go back to business.

"So what did you learn about Geraldine?" I asked—that was what I was most eager to hear about. My new lead had to do with her.

Alberta frowned a little. "I was looking into Geraldine *and* Bradshaw. And my results were—inconclusive. You go ahead first."

"Did you get a look at the wills?" I asked.

"Yes, I did," Alberta said. "But my stuff can wait. You go ahead."

"All right," I said reluctantly. I told them quickly about my encounters with the surly Chris Young and the threatening Tina Chandler.

"Well, you've had quite a day," Alberta said when I had finished.

"You should be careful," Rafaela said, looking a little wide-eyed. "You could get hurt interrogating people like that."

"But I did learn a few things," I pointed out.

"You certainly did," Alberta replied. "And it sounds like both Chris and Tina have the potential to be magic workers—and members of the Crabtree Coven."

"Yes, I know," I said impatiently. "But what I really want to hear about is Geraldine. Does she get all of Bradshaw's money?"

Alberta sighed. "I really don't know that. I took a look at Charles Tyndall's will, and basically, he left the house, half his fortune, and his vacation cabin to his eldest son, who was Bradshaw's father. And his other son, Geraldine's father, received the other half of his fortune. And there was a proviso that the younger brother should be allowed to use the older brother's cabin whenever he wished."

"And then?" I said. "What about the brothers' wills?"

"I looked up the wills of both Bradshaw and Geraldine's parents. And both of their mothers and fathers left everything to their respective daughters. And Bradshaw's father did say that he wanted her to allow her cousin to use the cabin whenever she wished."

"So what does that mean now?" I asked.

"It means Geraldine should be in possession of whatever exists of half of her grandfather's fortune. And Bradshaw should be in possession of whatever exists of half of her grandfather's fortune, plus two pieces of property."

"And who gets Bradshaw's fortune in her will?"

Alberta shook her head. "That I don't know. She's still alive, so her will wouldn't have gone through probate, and it wouldn't be in the public records. And Bradshaw's young, so it's very possible she hasn't made one."

"But if there's no will, doesn't the next of kin just get everything?" I asked.

"That's usually the case," Alberta said. "But we don't know for certain that Geraldine is her next of kin. We don't really know her family history that well."

"What did you mean when you said what exists of the grandfather's fortune?" Rafaela asked.

"Well, that's the thing," Alberta replied. "We don't know how much money Bradshaw has at the moment. We know she still has the house because she's living in it. But we have no idea what remains of the grandfather's fortune on either side."

"So Geraldine could have lost all her money and be in need of more?" I said.

"Yes, that's possible," Alberta said. "Why the sudden interest in Geraldine?"

"It's just that she supposedly just arrived in town," I said. "But I think she's been here a lot longer. And I think I can prove it."

Chapter Twenty-One

The next morning I was working the early shift at the library, so I wasn't able to go out and tackle Geraldine right away. I didn't quite see how she fit in with the evidence I had discovered earlier, but an idea was still growing in my mind, and I could see something slowly taking shape.

And Geraldine was definitely part of that image.

I'd talked to Alberta again before I went to bed about doing more scrying, but she still didn't want to go prying into Bradshaw or Geraldine's finances just yet. She said she'd need more evidence before she would do something invasive like that.

And Rafaela still wasn't doing well. She'd gone to bed immediately after dinner, and I had gone up to look at her flower. The once-blue hyacinth had now been completely gray for several days, and it was drooping so badly that it now touched the table. The petals had continued to fall off, and now there were only a few left.

Rafaela claimed she was feeling fine, but she was actually doing far worse.

I didn't know how much longer she could stand the strain.

Time at the library passed really slowly, and I thought lunchtime would never arrive. After lunch, time seemed to pass even slower, and I found myself glancing at the clock often to discover that no more than a few minutes had gone by. But the end of my shift did eventually arrive, and Stu and Emily came in to relieve Rita and me.

Then I quickly drove over to Bradshaw's house—I knew Geraldine was staying there, and I hoped she would be home.

Bradshaw's house was a big red brick mansion with three stories and an attic, and two one-story wings that extended off on either side. The trim in all the windows was white, and the central part of the building had a border of white bricks on each edge. The white edges, along with a white balcony on the third floor, somehow gave the impression of iced tiers on a cake.

The house that Bradshaw's grandfather had built was a pretty building, and I admired its beauty in the early evening sunshine. But as I drove up the wide, paved path to the house, I noticed that the grass needed to be mowed, and there were brown patches in amongst the green. As I pulled around the circular drive and parked next to a black BMW, I saw that the four tall shrubs in the front of the building had some brown patches, also, and were starting to lose their shape.

Bradshaw's house was apparently in need of some groundskeeping.

As I stepped out of my car, I glanced over at the black BMW. I knew that Bradshaw usually drove a Jeep, and I wondered if the car belonged to Geraldine. Of course, the BMW could also belong to Bradshaw, or Bradshaw could have parked her car in the back somewhere—I assumed that a house this large would have a garage. But it was also possible that the presence of this one car meant that only one person was home, and I hoped very much that that one person was Geraldine and not Bradshaw.

I walked up to the heavy wooden double doors and knocked.

I waited a few moments, and then I noticed a doorbell set into the white stone around the doors. I pressed the button and heard chimes echoing on the inside.

After a little while, the door opened, and Geraldine Tyndall looked out.

She was dressed in sandals, a white polo shirt, and khaki-colored capri pants. Her short dark hair fell over her forehead and somehow made her look older than she was. Her dark eyes regarded me suspiciously.

"Hi, Geraldine," I said. "I don't know if you remember me or not—"

"Of course I remember you," she said. "I just saw you at the ice cream parlor, and you and your sister are trying to kill my cousin."

She paused and gave me a sardonic look. "It's Chloe, right?"

"Right," I said.

"Well, Bradshaw's not here right now, so you won't be able to finish her off. You'll have to come back later."

"I'm not here to see Bradshaw," I said. "I'm here to see you."

Geraldine's eyebrows rose. "So now you want to kill me?"

"No," I said, quelling my exasperation—I would have to remain calm if I wanted her to talk to me. "I just want to talk. I need to know what you know."

Geraldine's sardonic look returned. "I assume you want to explain to me why you and your sister aren't guilty."

"Something like that."

Geraldine looked at me a moment longer. Then she seemed to make up her mind.

"You may as well come in," she said. "I don't have anything better to do at the moment."

She stepped back so I could enter, but I paused.

"Where's Andrew?" I asked.

Geraldine gave me a sly smile. "Who knows? But he won't be showing up here tonight. Bradshaw doesn't know about us yet, so we can't meet here."

"I think she may know a little bit," I said.

Geraldine shrugged.

I stepped into the house.

It was the first time I had ever been to Bradshaw's grandfather's house. I had been to Bradshaw's house when we were both younger and her parents had been alive—but that had been her parents' house, and though it had been nice and very large, it had been nothing like this.

Geraldine and I were standing in a wide, marble hallway, and in front of us rose a big, ornate staircase, with stairs on either side leading up to a balcony that looked down on the lower level. Above us was a magnificent chandelier made of countless tiny crystal drops, and a red carpet rolled down the hall before diverging in two and winding up the central staircase.

I paused and looked around in awe. "It's beautiful."

"Yes, it is, isn't it?" Geraldine said. Her tone grew sour. "I wish Bradshaw would take care of it. A house like this can fall into ruin if you don't look after it properly."

She led me to a white door with silver-painted trim and ushered me inside.

"This is the drawing room," Geraldine said dreamily. "My grandfather used to receive visitors in here all the time. Please have a seat, and I'll be right back."

She turned to go.

"And don't mind the dust," she said with some asperity. "That's Bradshaw's fault, too."

"Wait," I said. "Where are you going?"

Geraldine stopped and looked back at me with a wry smile.

"I'm going to get some refreshments. Bradshaw may not know how to entertain a guest, but I do."

With that, she was gone.

I glanced around the room. There were several delicate chairs upholstered in a satiny fabric—some of them plain and some of them with stripes. There were also several larger pieces of furniture—similarly delicate but capable of seating more than one person—and I was uncertain whether they were known as settees or chaises or maybe even something else. There were also several fragile-looking tables sprinkled throughout the room, and there were quite a few mirrors and paintings in ornate frames adorning the walls.

The centerpiece of the room, however, was a mantelpiece with an enormous painting hanging over it. The mantel itself was painted a pale blue gray, and an antique, fabric fire screen in a wooden frame sat in front of the fireplace. And over the charming mantel was an immense painting of a man in a blue uniform with red trim. I recalled vaguely that the trim along the buttons and the cuffs might actually be known as "facings," and the uniform looked to me to be from the Revolutionary War. Under the painting was an empty oval board with two hooks on it—it looked as if something had rested there once on display.

I stepped closer and ran a finger over the mantel—it was indeed dusty as Geraldine had predicted.

I glanced at the oval board. There was the faintest indentation of a pistol in the dust.

"That's where the gun was," said a voice behind me. "But then again, you apparently already know that."

I turned to see that Geraldine had returned and was standing in the doorway with a silver tray.

"Excuse me?" I said.

"That's where the gun was," Geraldine said again, stepping into the room. "The one that was used to shoot my cousin."

She frowned a little as she set the tray down on one of the fragile-looking tables.

"But I'm forgetting—it's your sister who's supposed to be the one, right? She's the one who shot Bradshaw and then cursed Lisa Stroup, leaving her telltale witch's mark behind?"

Geraldine's tone rankled, and she was watching me with an unpleasant look on her face.

I felt the stirrings of anger, but I had to remain calm. I didn't have any official position, and I'd have to tread lightly if I wanted to convince her to talk.

"Won't you be seated?" Geraldine said with a wave of her hand.

She sat down on one of the delicate chairs, and I perched on the edge of one also.

Geraldine had brought us a flowered teapot with matching cups and a plate full of cookies.

"Tea?" I said.

"Yes," Geraldine replied. For just a moment, she looked apologetic. "I know it's after teatime. And Bradshaw doesn't have any proper tea kettles, so I just heated the water in the microwave. And she also doesn't have any material for sandwiches. But I did find two boxes of cookies in the pantry."

She wrinkled her nose. "They're just mass-produced ones from the grocery store. I'm not sure how good they'll be."

"So when Bradshaw's away, you're lady of the manor?" I said.

Geraldine looked up at me and smiled—she looked genuinely pleased. "Yes—I suppose you could say that."

She dropped two round tea strainers into each cup and then poured hot water over them. I could see a sinuous line of brown seeping into the water in each cup.

"What kind of tea is it?" I asked.

"It's an herb tea," Geraldine replied. "From the root of the black-eyed Susan flower. It's a Maryland specialty, and it's very good for you."

I waited patiently as Geraldine let the tea steep and then added milk and sugar. She handed me my cup and then offered me cookies, which I declined.

"That's probably just as well," Geraldine said. "I don't think they're very good."

She became brisk. "Now what did you want to tell me? I assume you're going to protest your innocence."

"When did you arrive in Crabtree Bay?" I said.

Geraldine's eyebrows rose. "What do you mean?"

"When you came down to stay with Bradshaw, what day did you arrive?"

Geraldine's sardonic look returned. "What are you—a cop?"

"What day did you arrive?" I said.

Geraldine answered, but it seemed to me that she hesitated just a moment.

"Friday," she said.

"And who inherits the house and all the money if something happens to Bradshaw?" I asked.

Geraldine's tone grew more sarcastic. "I take it back—you're no cop. They have much more subtlety."

"Then I'll be blunt," I said. "Do you get Bradshaw's money?"

Geraldine shook her head. "You're trying to pin this on me? How about you? Did you shoot my cousin? Put her maid in a trance?"

"No," I said firmly.

"Of course that's what you'd say." Geraldine's lips twisted into an unpleasant smile. "Andrew said you might come to see me. He says you're jealous."

"When did you and Andrew become a couple?" I asked.

Geraldine's eyes grew unexpectedly dreamy. "It was back in February—Valentine's Day, actually. That's not really when we became a couple. But that is when Andrew showed up at my door with a red rose."

She sighed. "It was so romantic."

I fought an urge to roll my eyes and pressed on.

"He came to your house in Annapolis?"

"Yes—he said he was working on a play in town." Geraldine frowned in thought. "No—he said his show had closed unexpectedly, and he couldn't stop thinking about me, so he'd hung around. We went on our first date that night."

"But you knew who he was, right? You knew he was seeing Bradshaw?"

"Of course I knew who he was," Geraldine said haughtily. "I would hardly go out with a stranger. And I'd known him ever since high school—back when he was going out with you."

She shot me a sly look as if she expected me to be offended—but I was long past the point of feeling jealous—the only thing I felt in connection with Andrew was embarrassment.

"So you knew Andrew from high school," I said. "But you also must have known that Andrew had been dating your cousin for several years."

"Of course," Geraldine replied. "But Andrew told me it was over. And I could tell it was ending for a long time—they were never really suited for one another. Bradshaw is too wild. Andrew is refined—like me."

"Bradshaw didn't seem to know it was over," I said dryly. "She said Andrew was sneaking around with someone. I'm still not sure she knows it's you."

Geraldine drew herself up stiffly. "I am *not* cheating with Andrew. His relationship with Bradshaw has been over for a long time."

"Then why doesn't Bradshaw know?"

Geraldine sniffed. "Bradshaw has a terrible temper. I can't blame Andrew for not wanting to subject himself to that. But she knows it's over—she really does. Besides, she's seeing that creepy Chris guy again. The two of them are really better suited for each other."

"So when would you say you officially became a couple?" I said.

Geraldine's dreamy look returned. "We were completely in love by April."

"And when did you start coming down here to visit him?"

Geraldine glanced at me, startled. "What?"

"When did you start visiting him here in Crabtree Bay?"

"I never said I came down to visit him here."

"But surely you must have," I said. "If you guys were so in love, surely you would have come down here, stayed at his house—met all his friends?"

Geraldine stared at me for a moment. "I didn't come down here."

"You always met up in Annapolis?"

It seemed to me once again that Geraldine paused for just a moment.

"Yes," she said. "We always met in Annapolis."

There was another slight pause.

"I have never once been to Andrew's house," Geraldine declared emphatically. "And that is a fact."

She stood up suddenly.

She seemed uncertain what to do with herself for a moment, and then she walked over to the mantel and stared up at the picture over it.

"Do you know who's in this portrait?" Geraldine said.

"No," I said.

"It's Arthur Tyndall," Geraldine replied. "He fought in the Revolutionary War, and that was his flintlock pistol that was mounted here. Bradshaw really loves this portrait, which always kind of surprised me. I wouldn't have thought she'd have the taste to appreciate it. But she does. Sometimes she comes down here and stares at it for hours—I swear she even talks to it."

She turned to look at me. "To answer your earlier question, Bradshaw loves this house too much to ever give it to me. I know she doesn't seem like it sometimes, but her heritage matters to her a lot. And when she loves things, she loves them fiercely. I think she'd sooner burn the house down than let me or anyone else have it after she's gone."

Geraldine gave me her unpleasant smile. "So there you have it. I'm not trying to kill Bradshaw, and Andrew and I aren't sneaking around. We're genuinely in love. Is there anything else you need to know?"

"That should do," I said. I coughed apologetically. "The tea's made my throat a little scratchy. Could I trouble you for some water?"

Geraldine stared at me for a moment. "Certainly. I'll be right back."

After she left the room, I waited for a moment and then slipped out into the hall.

I'd noticed Geraldine's big silver purse in the hall, and I wanted to see if I could get a look at her phone. I wanted to see if I could find any texts between Andrew and her that would prove she was in Crabtree Bay earlier than she'd said.

Sure enough, Geraldine's big purse was still sitting on the table in the hall. I rifled through it and quickly found her phone. Unfortunately, I also found just as quickly that her phone was locked, and I couldn't get in.

I made a couple of stabs at guessing her password, but none of them worked.

I put the phone aside and continued looking through the purse.

Maybe I could find a receipt—or something—that would prove she'd been in town earlier than she'd said.

As I looked through the purse, however, I found a handful of gray metal balls clinking together at the bottom. I pulled one out and examined it—it was about half an inch in diameter and the surface was rough. It was heavy for its size, and it looked to my untrained eye to be lead.

I was puzzled for a moment, and then I realized what it was.

Geraldine's voice floated down the hall.

"Chloe? Is that you?"

I quickly put the metal ball back in the purse.

Then I ran out of the house.

Chapter Twenty-Two

I was more convinced than ever that Geraldine had been in town longer than she said.

And I was going to prove it.

I was a little rattled by my encounter with her, and I hopped in my car and drove away.

I watched my rearview mirror to make sure she wasn't following me, and I was soon satisfied that I was safe. And really, there was no reason why I shouldn't have been.

Geraldine didn't know what I had seen.

I was pretty sure those metal balls I had found in her purse were the bullets that were used in Bradshaw's antique gun.

I considered turning for home. But Geraldine wasn't after me, and I wanted to follow this trail while it was still warm.

I thought for a moment, and an idea suddenly popped into my head.

I knew where I would go.

It was still a little early for barhopping, but I knew that Andrew's actor friends often had a drink before an evening performance. There was a little theater in town that was putting on a play by a local writer titled "Maryland Mayhem," and there was a bar around the corner that was known as an actors' hangout.

Andrew and Geraldine had clearly been dating for several months, and I was sure that if Geraldine had been here before she claimed, that Andrew's friends would know something about it.

And the bar by the theater was a good place to start.

I drove over quickly and parked a few streets away.

Then I walked to the bar.

Strictly speaking, the Stained Glass Tavern wasn't just a bar—it was a full-service restaurant that also had a well-regarded bar in it. The tavern had actually been in continuous use since the late seventeen hundreds, and the owners had tried to get it designated as the oldest bar still in use in the state. However, several other establishments had it beat by a few decades, so they weren't able to get the designation to stick.

As I stared up at the Stained Glass Tavern now, I thought about what a pretty place it was. It was a brick building with four stained glass windows made up of diamond-shaped panes of bright colors—blue, red, green, yellow. And there was something else about the building— something quaint and comfortable that gave it atmosphere.

It was no wonder that artistic types liked to hang out here—the tavern was the perfect place to get the creative juices flowing.

I went inside. I figured that if I could find Andrew's friends that I would question them carefully—I would bring him up casually, and see if I could get them to talk about him.

And then maybe I might be able to bring up his relationship status and see if they knew if he was dating anyone new—and if they'd met her.

I glanced around.

The tavern had one main room with wooden tables, and lights that were set into metal rings and hung down from the ceiling—they were meant to imitate the old-fashioned chandeliers. There were also lights mounted on the walls in sconces, and there were candles on all the tables. The light was low, yet soothing, and the entire room was bathed in a soft, golden glow.

The bar took up the back part of the room, and I could see a bartender with gray hair and a blue polo shirt tending to customers at a long counter that was full of warm bodies.

There were seldom any empty seats at the bar at the Stained Glass Tavern.

I spotted a familiar group of people, and I made my way toward them.

Three of local theater's leading lights were seated at the corner of the bar, and a sonorous voice greeted me as I reached them.

"Good evening, Mistress Chloe. To what do we owe the pleasure?"

The voice belonged to Robert Herriman, a robust man with thick gray hair who was seated right at the edge of the bar's counter. Robert appeared in many area productions, and he was known for his portrayals of many of Shakespeare's elder statesmen. I had known him ever since I was in high school—Andrew had been appearing in local plays even back then—and I had seen Robert on stage many times.

Before I could answer him, a clear contralto voice cut through the general murmur of voices that surrounded us.

"Chloe! It's a terrible shame what people are saying about your sister. The poor child is incapable of harm. Incapable! And the things they said about you, too. Witches! Spells! Shootings! Attempted murder! Scurrilous lies, all of them."

The speaker was Alice Wright—she had chin-length hair dyed a bright, unrealistic shade of red, and her ears, neck, and wrists were draped in glittering baubles and bangles. She was a director, well-known for founding the Women's Voices festival, which ran every summer and featured plays of fifteen minutes or less written by local playwrights. While the festival had originally featured only female writers, playwrights of both genders were now welcome to submit their work—as long as they remembered to give their female characters a distinctive voice.

Alice was seated next to Robert. And on her other side was Dale Brickle, a middle-aged man with black hair that was just starting to gray at the temples. He was well-known as a talented dramatic actor with a penchant for passionate, emotional scenes. He was also known for being shy and soft-spoken when approached in public.

Dale gave me a diffident nod over his glass of beer.

Alice was clutching a short glass containing an amber liquid that had both an orange wedge and a bright red cherry nestled in it. I realized I had no idea what it was.

She waved her drink at me.

"It's criminal the way people are treating your family," she said. "Criminal."

She waved her drink again.

"Have a seat, my child! Join us!"

Alice quickly stood up and offered me her seat, and Dale stood up at the same time.

"I don't want to steal your spot," I said to both of them.

"Nonsense!" Alice replied. "We sit here nearly every day. It's about time we gave someone else a shot at these seats. Besides, Dale and I can share a seat."

Alice sat down on the barstool vacated by Dale, leaving a space that was wide enough for a second person to sit on. Dale glanced at the barstool and blushed to the roots of his black hair. Then he perched gingerly on the edge of the stool beside Alice.

I sat down on the stool that Alice had left vacant—ordinarily, I would have brushed off the offer of a seat, but after the trouble that Alice and Dale had just gone through, it would have seemed ungracious to refuse.

"What can we get you, my dear?" Alice asked.

"Just seltzer and lemon," I said.

"Oh, come now," Alice said. "That's not a real drink."

"I know. But I need to keep a clear head."

Alice nodded sagely and winked at me. "You're up to something, aren't you? I can see it in your eyes. Say no more."

She lifted a beringed hand and placed an order with the bartender.

I looked around at the two actors and the director I had fallen in with.

"So are all you guys working on 'Maryland Mayhem'?" I asked.

"The two boys are," Alice replied promptly. "I'm just here supporting my friends in the theater tonight."

Dale acknowledged Alice's words with a brief nod, and another blush stole over his face.

"Alice is quite correct," Robert said, his whole face lighting up. "Both Dale and I are appearing in the play, and I have been gifted the most wonderful role. I am playing a character named Edward Lazar, who is at a crossroads in his life. It is an honor to bring Edward to life on the stage."

"How about Andrew Wyatt?" I said in the most innocent voice I could muster. "Is he appearing in the play?"

Dale suddenly sputtered, spraying a few drops of his drink on the counter. He then giggled and mopped at the spray with a napkin.

Alice waved a hand, causing her many bracelets to clink.

"Andrew!" she said in disgust. "I've no patience for him at all."

"Now, now," Robert said, beaming at Alice. "Andrew is really quite a fine fellow."

Alice snorted in disgust. "He isn't. He's nothing of the kind."

"Did something happen?" I said.

Dale giggled again.

"That's Dale's way of saying yes," Alice replied dryly. "Andrew, that cad, has been cheating on his girlfriend—again."

I leaned closer. This was exactly what I had been hoping to find out.

"How do you know?" I said.

Alice sniffed. "Andrew has been sneaking around, and Bradshaw, the poor girl, has been at her wits' end trying to catch him. And then she's had so much trouble lately on top of that. I don't know why she puts up with him. She ought to wash her hands of him entirely."

"But how do you know Andrew's been cheating on Bradshaw?" I said again. "What proof do you have?"

"That's easy enough," Alice said. "Andrew's been seen."

"He's been seen?" I said quickly. "By whom? By you?"

Alice shook her head, and Dale tittered nervously.

"I haven't seen him," Alice said. "But Dale has."

We both turned to look at him, and Dale looked down into his glass.

"Go on, Dale," Alice said. "Tell Chloe about it. Don't be shy."

"It wasn't me." Dale glanced up at us furtively, as if the attention embarrassed him. "It was Laila and Marian. They just told me about it."

"Laila and Marian are two of our actresses," Alice said to me. "Very fine ones, too. So tell us about it, Dale—what did they witness?"

"They saw Andrew and a girl going into a motel," Dale said. "In the middle of the day. And then they saw it again. They saw them three or four times total."

"They're sure it was Andrew?" I said.

Dale smirked. "Yes. Andrew's pretty recognizable. And they saw him more than once."

"And who was the girl?" I said.

Dale smirked again. "They didn't know. They didn't recognize her. But they said she had short dark hair."

That certainly sounded like Geraldine to me. "Do you know which motel it was?"

"No," Dale said. "They said there were a bunch of them all together in the same area—they usually pass by the place on their way to the theater."

"And how long ago was it?"

"I don't know. At least a month—maybe two."

"Why are they going to a motel?" I asked. "Why not just go to Andrew's town house?"

Alice sniffed. "He's probably trying not to get caught. Andrew's town house is right downtown. That stretch of road with all the motels is on the outer edge of the city. I imagine he figured no one would see them out there."

Alice added something under her breath that was decidedly uncomplimentary to Andrew.

"Oh, Alice," Robert said on the other side of me. "Andrew is really quite a good fellow."

"Nonsense," Alice said. "A good fellow doesn't cheat on the woman he's been dating for years."

"Andrew is quite a good fellow," Robert repeated in his sonorous voice. "I'm sure it's all just a misunderstanding."

"Andrew is a fool," Alice said. "And he's not nearly such a good actor as he thinks."

Robert smiled at Alice, completely unruffled. "Andrew is a remarkable actor—truly remarkable. I have always admired him."

"The trouble with you," Alice retorted, "is that you see the good in everyone—even when there's no good to be seen."

"Yes, indeed," Robert said, as if Alice hadn't spoken. "A fine fellow and a fine actor—anyone can see that."

Alice sighed. "You know who really was a fine actress? Bradshaw. She had such fire—such passion. If only she'd kept going with it. Instead, she's spent the last few years chasing after Andrew, trying to get him to stick with her. If he'd had any sense, he would have married her."

"He probably will," Robert said amiably. "I'm sure he's just waiting for the right time to pop the question."

"Robert," Alice said in frustration, "have you heard anything we've said at all? Andrew's been cheating on Bradshaw—he's found himself a new girl."

"Ah," Robert replied. "Then maybe he'll marry the new girl. He's doing quite well for himself, you know."

Alice looked at him sharply. "What do you mean? Last *I* heard, no one would cast him in anything anymore."

"What?" I said. "Why?"

"He's too unreliable," Alice said. "He shows up late for rehearsal—which is a huge no-no in the theater. And one night he didn't show up for a performance at all. His poor, nervous understudy had to step in for him at the last minute. Andrew got tossed from the show. Word about stuff like that gets out. We theater folks look out for one another."

Robert smiled benignly and shook his head. "No—that's not it at all."

Alice bristled. "Yes, it is. I heard it from the show's director myself."

Robert placed a finger next to his nose.

"What's that?" Alice said. "What are you doing?"

"It's a gesture that means I know a secret."

"No, it isn't," Alice said. "Or at least if it is, *I've* never heard of it."

"Well, whether you've heard of it or not, I do know a secret."

"Fine. Whatever. Out with it, then."

Robert beamed, and the whole bar seemed to light up with his happiness. "Andrew did it—he got his big break. That's why he's been so unreliable lately. He had to jump through hoops to get in with these people—but he did it."

Alice looked thunderstruck. "No! He got what he wanted?"

"Yes."

Alice leaned forward, displacing Dale, who had to hop down to the floor.

"Are you telling me," Alice said, "that Andrew got a movie role?"

Robert's smile grew even brighter, and he nodded ever so slightly.

"A real movie role," Alice demanded. "Not a part as an extra? An actual, sizeable speaking role?"

Robert nodded again.

After a moment, he glanced around and whispered. "He's the star."

"Well, I'll be." Alice sat back on her stool. "Where are they filming? Does he have to go to New York? LA?"

"They're filming right here on the Eastern Shore," Robert said. "It's all very hush, hush. Apparently, it's a big studio film—a *big* one."

"I'd heard they were doing something out there in the country," Alice said thoughtfully. "But I thought those were just rumors."

"You can believe them," Robert said.

"Well, well, well," Alice said. "Some people have all the luck."

She glanced over at me then and gave me an apologetic look.

"I'm sorry, my dear, about all the shop talk. This must be terribly dull for you. And I'm forgetting, aren't I, that you used to date Andrew several years back. This whole thing must have been quite awkward and uncomfortable for you. We never should have brought Andrew up at all."

I sipped my seltzer and tried to look noncommittal.

After a moment, Alice eyed me sharply.

"Wait a minute," she said, "we didn't bring up Andrew—you did."

She paused, and her bright eyes seemed to look right through me.

"You came here looking for information tonight, didn't you? You didn't really want to keep a bunch of old fogeys company."

I rushed to reassure her, but Alice interrupted me.

"It's all right, my dear—in fact, it's quite clever of you."

She smiled.

"I hope you found what you were looking for."

Chapter Twenty-Three

I stayed and talked for a little while after that, and eventually I had some french fries and an iced tea.

But the actors had to get over to the theater, and Alice had to go and take her seat.

And I had to go home and think over what I'd learned.

As far as Andrew's big break went, I thought that was nice for him, and it occurred to me that if he did become a big star, he would probably leave town and stop bothering me.

But whether or not Geraldine would go with him was a different matter.

Geraldine had had bullets in her purse, and I now knew that she had been in town before she said she had been. And she'd been keeping it secret—meeting with Andrew in motels rather than at his town house, which was downtown.

And while some people might think Andrew had insisted on secrecy to keep Bradshaw from finding out, it was also possible that Geraldine had been the one who had insisted—she didn't want anyone to know that she had been in town when Bradshaw had been shot.

And what about the ability to curse Lisa Stroup? I didn't know what, if any, magical abilities Geraldine possessed. But she was the granddaughter of Charles Tyndall, just as Bradshaw was, and he had been rumored to have been a member of the Crabtree Coven.

As I drove home, I wondered if there was some way I could look into that—perhaps Alberta could help.

Alberta herself actually met me at the door, and she studied my face as I walked in.

"Is everything all right?" she demanded.

Her eyes were bright with worry, and her red hair was tousled as if she'd been running her fingers through it.

"Everything is fine," I said. "I just stopped over at the Stained Glass Tavern on my way home."

Alberta was visibly relieved. "Oh. Is that all?"

"Yes—what did you think?"

Alberta exhaled. "Oh, I don't know. It's just that you're later than usual, and with everything that's going on—"

She let her voice trail off.

"Did something happen?" I said quickly.

"No," Alberta said. "I was just worried about you. I feel like anything can happen these days, and anything that's out of the usual routine gets my alarm bells ringing."

She glanced at me. "Did you eat already?"

"Sort of. I had french fries over at the tavern. I'm not really that hungry, but I wouldn't mind eating a snack."

Alberta began to walk toward the kitchen. "How does an egg salad sandwich sound?"

I followed her. "Sounds perfect."

I glanced around. "Where's Rafaela?"

Alberta sighed. "She's upstairs—sleeping, I hope. She went to see Lisa again today, and that really tires her out. She wanted to do some cooking, but I told her she should really get some rest instead. Besides, we have a problem in the kitchen."

I frowned. "What kind of problem?"

"See for yourself."

I glanced into the kitchen.

Sibyl was sitting in the sink, somehow looking very staunch and determined. I reached out to scratch her sleek, dark head, and she closed her eyes in response.

"How long has she been in here?" I asked.

"Ever since I got home," Alberta replied. "And every time I move her, she just jumps right back in. Having her in there makes cooking very difficult—I really need to use the sink."

The kitchen had a double sink, and I moved the faucet over to the other basin.

"Can't you just use the other half?"

But as I reached for the tap to turn it on, Sibyl's bright amber eyes snapped open, and she quickly jumped into the other basin.

I moved the faucet back to the first basin, and Sibyl immediately jumped over to the original basin to follow it.

"That's very weird," I said.

"You're telling me," Alberta replied.

She reached into the sink and scooped Sibyl out of the basin.

"Come on, Sibyl," she said. "Get your furry butt out of there."

Sibyl protested with a tiny mew as Alberta set her down on the floor gently, and she immediately hopped right up and crawled back into the sink.

Alberta sighed. "Crazy cat. I don't know what's gotten into her lately."

"Sandwiches are just fine," I said. "And you make a terrific egg salad."

Alberta smiled. "I do, don't I?"

We soon had our sandwiches, and we sat down in the dining room—it didn't seem right to sit in the kitchen and interrupt Sibyl's vigil in the sink.

"So what brought you to the Stained Glass Tavern?" Alberta asked, as we began eating. "Were you visiting friends, or were you investigating?"

Before answering, I paused for just a moment to savor my sandwich. Alberta really did make a good egg salad—it had just the right mixture of creaminess and spiciness.

"I did see some friends," I said after I'd finished my bite. "But I was mostly investigating. And before I stopped at the tavern, I went to see Geraldine Tyndall."

Alberta looked up at me, startled. "You saw Geraldine?"

"Yes."

"At Bradshaw's house?"

"Yes."

"How did that go?"

"I found bullets in her purse," I said.

Alberta grew wide-eyed. "What?"

"And at the tavern," I said, "I found out that she's been in town for longer than she claims. She said she just arrived, but she's actually been meeting Andrew at a motel here for at least a month—and possibly even two."

I paused. "I think you need to try scrying again. We need to find out if Geraldine inherits Bradshaw's money."

"Whoa, wait," Alberta said. "Let's go back to the beginning. You found bullets in Geraldine's purse?"

"Yes," I said. "They were big and round—like the bullets that would go with a Revolutionary War-era pistol."

"They weren't regular bullet shape?" Alberta asked.

"No."

"Then how do you know they were bullets?"

"I just told you," I said. "They were round metal balls like the kind that go with an old-fashioned flintlock pistol like the one that was used to shoot Bradshaw."

"Did you actually find the gun?" Alberta asked.

"No," I said.

"Then how do you know they're bullets?" Alberta said again.

I started to feel frustrated. "I just told you—"

"I know what you said," Alberta said impatiently. "And I understand what you think you saw. You think you saw the old-fashioned lead bullets that go with Bradshaw's antique gun. But my question is how are you sure? How do you know they were bullets and not something else like ball bearings?"

"Ball bearings?" I said. "Why would they be ball bearings?"

"Why not?"

I drew in breath to speak and then stopped. "Actually, I don't know why not. I don't even know what ball bearings are used for."

Alberta frowned a little. "I'm not sure what they're used for, either. I think they have something to do with wheels in skateboards and cars. My point is those metal balls *could* be bullets. But they could also be something else."

"I—" I stopped again.

"You do concede that they could be something else, don't you?" Alberta said. "Unless you've become a ballistics expert?"

I sighed. "Yes, they could be something else."

"And why were you going through Geraldine's purse anyway?"

"I was looking for evidence."

It was Alberta's turn to sigh. "Chloe, you're not a cop."

"I know," I said. "But I happened to have a chance they didn't."

Alberta looked disapproving. "So what was your next point?"

"My next point was that Geraldine and Andrew have been seen going to a motel here in town. They've been doing it for at least a month. And she claims she didn't get here until Friday."

Alberta looked at me sharply. "That does sound like real evidence. And you spoke to the person who actually saw them?"

I hesitated. "No—not exactly."

Alberta's next glance was equally sharp. "What do you mean not exactly?"

"I spoke to someone who heard about it from friends of his."

"Ah," Alberta said, sitting back. "The infamous friend of a friend."

"Dale's a good witness," I said angrily. "He's very trustworthy."

"I'm sure he is. But what about his friends?"

"That's why you need to use your scrying ability," I said. "That way we can substantiate some of these leads."

Alberta shook her head. "I can't do that. That would be prying—we don't have any real reason to suspect Geraldine. We use our powers to help, not to harm."

I stared at Alberta, but I could see that her mind was made up.

"I'll get the evidence," I said.

Sibyl mewed softly from the kitchen.

"I'll look into it if you do," Alberta said. "But not before."

Sibyl mewed again.

I continued to stew the rest of the evening, and Alberta and I spoke very little. In the morning, her refusal to use her scrying ability was the first thing I thought about when I woke up, and as I drove to work, I stewed a little more.

I was going to prove that Geraldine had been here earlier than she said.

And I had a plan.

Rita and I opened the library like we usually did, and then our typical stampede of patrons followed.

Shortly after the initial rush had died down, Mike walked in.

I felt a little flutter of excitement when I saw him.

He walked right up to the circulation desk, and I could see worry in his eyes.

"Are you mad at me?" he said abruptly.

"I'm sorry?" I said.

"Maybe I was a little harsh on Monday," Mike said. "But I had to be. I can't have anyone harassing my students—even if it's you. And I'm sorry about the magic stuff I said—but I had to say it. You really do need to start looking at the facts."

"You were right when you said that," I replied. "I did look at the facts, and I have a good lead now. I'm going to follow up on it today after work."

Mike stared at me. "Wait, what?"

"I've got a good lead." I lowered my voice. "But I can't really talk about it here."

Mike was clearly puzzled.

"You're not mad at me?"

"No, of course not."

"Then why did you run off like that? You just turned and ran away from me."

"I just had an idea," I said. "That's all. I wasn't running away from you. I was running off to follow a lead."

"So you're really not mad?"

"I'm not mad at all."

Relief seemed to flood through Mike.

"These last two days I've been so worried," he said. "Chloe, you don't know how—"

The front door flew open, and both Mike and I turned to look.

Bradshaw Tyndall stalked into the library, her long blond hair pulled back into an untidy ponytail with strands escaping. She was clad in a tiny tank top and very short cut-off jean shorts.

I began to wonder if she owned any other kind of shorts.

She saw me, and she marched up to the desk, pushing Mike out of the way.

"I told you to leave me alone!" she shouted.

I glanced around at my patrons, all of whom were staring at us. I didn't know if they'd noticed my conversation with Mike, but we certainly had their attention now.

Before I could reply, Bradshaw went on.

Her face twisted into a smirk. "I bet you're surprised to see me."

"I certainly am," I said. Out of the corner of my eye, I could see Rita running toward the front of the room.

"I just wanted you to know that your plan didn't work," Bradshaw said.

"And what plan is that?" I asked.

"Geraldine told me that you came to the house yesterday. She also told me that she told you how much I like that painting over the

211

mantel. And then—surprise, surprise! It came crashing down last night while I was in there and nearly crushed me. Unluckily for you, it missed, and I'm still here."

"What?" I said.

Rita arrived at the desk, a little out of breath, her kind face creased with concern.

"Bradshaw, I'm going to have to ask you to leave," she said.

Bradshaw jabbed a finger in my direction.

"She came to my house last night. Just ask her."

Despite herself, Rita glanced at me.

"I did go to her house," I said.

"And then she loosened the hooks or something on a huge painting in my parlor, hoping that it would fall down on me and kill me."

"I most definitely did not do that," I said.

"Why don't we let the police decide?" Bradshaw said. "I just stopped in here to let you know you didn't succeed before I went to see them."

"Go ahead," I said. "The police will find that I did nothing wrong."

"Speaking of police," Rita said, "I'm going to ask you to leave one more time, Bradshaw. And then if you don't, I'm going to have to call the police myself."

Bradshaw stared at her, startled. "Are you kidding? She tries to kill me, and you're calling the police on me?"

"In case you hadn't noticed," Rita said calmly, "this is a library. You're supposed to be quiet."

Bradshaw exploded. "This is unbelievable! Just unreal. You've got a wannabe murderer standing right here, and you're worried about some library rules?"

Rita moved toward the phone. "That's it. I'm calling them now."

"I've already got it," Mike said.

I looked over to see him with a cell phone at his ear.

"Hello?" he said. "Yes. I'd like to report a disturbance at the library."

"Unbelievable!" Bradshaw screamed. "You're all going to regret this!"

She stormed out of the library.

Rita looked around at the patrons that were staring at us.

"I do apologize for that, folks," she said. "The police will be here soon, and we'll take measures to make sure this doesn't happen again. We'll even file a restraining order if necessary."

She glanced over at Mike, and he nodded.

"They're on their way," he said.

The crowd gathered at the tables and computers grumbled, but they seemed mollified, and a few people even cast me sympathetic looks.

Rita gave me a friendly squeeze on the arm and then returned to her work in the back.

"Are you okay?" Mike asked, and I turned to look at him.

He was looking at me earnestly, and the concern in his face made me feel funny inside—in a good way.

"Yes, thanks," I said.

Mike went on. "The police should be here soon. I didn't call 9-1-1, since it wasn't a life-threatening emergency—but I did call the local station. They'll come by and have us all give a statement—I don't think they'll actually charge Bradshaw with anything, but at least this will give us a record of what happened in case you do have to file a restraining order."

Mike continued to stare at me, and I felt myself blushing a little under his gaze.

"Chloe," he said. "If you ever need anything in connection with this stuff or with anything else at all—just give me a call. I want you to know that you can depend on me."

He paused.

"Chloe, I—"

Two police officers came in the front door then, and Mike quickly stepped toward them.

Rita reappeared from the back, as if she'd been watching out for them, and soon all three of us were talking to the police.

Whatever Mike had been about to say was lost.

Chapter Twenty-Four

Mike, Rita, and I eventually wrapped up our talk with the police—Mike was right that Bradshaw wasn't going to be charged with anything. But the police did tell us it was important to report Bradshaw's behavior—especially since it had happened more than once, and a pattern seemed to be emerging.

With that, the police had left, and Mike had gone along with them. It seemed to me that the two police officers had been giving me funny looks—after all both my sister and I were suspected of having shot Bradshaw. And I knew, too, that Bradshaw was likely to go to the police herself and tell them that I'd tried to crush her with a painting. So even though they were polite and sympathetic in a professional way, I knew that they knew that the two of us had a history—and that this wasn't over yet.

It seemed to me, too, that Mike had been looking at me funny—but in a different way. I got the impression that he really wanted to tell me something—but somehow the moment had been lost.

After Mike and the police had left, Rita and I had returned to work, and the library had returned to silence with the occasional rustling or typing.

And I was left alone with my thoughts.

At the moment I was most interested in Mike, but I knew I'd have to leave that for another time—right now I had to focus on what I had just learned.

So the painting of Bradshaw's ancestor, Arthur Tyndall, had come crashing down and had almost hit her. And Bradshaw thought the incident was another attempt on her life—and it may well have been. But the accident hadn't been caused by me, and it seemed to me that the person who was most likely to have sabotaged the painting was the same person who had told Bradshaw about my visit—Geraldine. And I didn't know why she would make such an obvious attempt, but perhaps she thought she would take a chance while she had me as a scapegoat.

An insistent idea that I was missing something nagged at me, but I pushed it aside.

I would go ahead with my plan to prove that Geraldine had been in town longer than she claimed.

The day went by more slowly than I would have liked, but eventually it came to an end, and I hurried out of the library.

I began to drive toward a stretch of road that had quite a few motels when something made me want to take a detour.

I turned the car in the direction of the downtown area instead.

Crabtree Bay's downtown was the oldest section of the city, and many of the buildings dated back to the colonial era. The streets were brick, and in some cases even cobblestone, and the old brick buildings were a combination of businesses and homes. Fashionable attorneys' offices and restaurants sat right next to houses and apartments. Prices were high in the downtown area, and most of the real estate was owned by the well-to-do.

Andrew had a town house in this neighborhood, and I found myself driving over to it.

The streets were narrow and traffic was pretty heavy, so I couldn't do much more than slow down as I went past it.

Andrew's town house was red brick with black shutters like all the other houses on the block, and I could see that a piece of paper had been taped to the door. I was curious about it, but street parking was difficult to come by in this neighborhood, and I didn't know if there was parking in the back—Andrew hadn't had the house while I was dating him, so I had never actually been inside it. I figured that the piece of paper was just a notice about a local event—or maybe even one of the flyers from last week.

I didn't know what I'd expected to find by coming down here—even if I'd seen Andrew and Geraldine coming out of the house this very moment, it wouldn't prove what I wanted to prove—that she'd been here earlier than she'd said. I had to establish a witness that had seen her, and I certainly couldn't do that here.

I drove on.

Once I was out of the center of town, I drove back in the direction I had originally been going. On the outskirts of the city, out where the roads began to look more like country roads, there was a stretch where a lot of motels were grouped together, along with a sprinkling of restaurants. I didn't know for certain that this was where Dale's friends had seen Geraldine and Andrew—but at the very least, it was a good place to start.

The first motel I pulled into was a sprawling gray building with two levels and a parking lot that was badly in need of repair. It didn't look like the kind of place where a budding movie star and a wealthy heiress would stay, but I supposed that they'd wanted to stay as hidden as possible—or at least Geraldine had.

The man behind the counter in the office was very pleasant, and he listened patiently to everything I had to say and looked at the photo I showed him of Geraldine. But he politely declined to answer any of my questions and wouldn't even tell me if he'd seen Geraldine or not.

I left the office and hoped that this was simply the wrong place.

I went to two more motels, both very much like the first one, and I talked to a man and a woman in their respective offices. Like the first motel manager I'd spoken to, they were both very polite, and they both refused to answer any questions. I'd scrutinized both of their faces as

I showed them the picture of Geraldine, but I couldn't tell if they really didn't recognize her, or if they were just hiding their reactions.

In any event, they wouldn't admit to having seen her, so I was forced to move on to the next motel.

It began to dawn on me that even if Geraldine had stayed at one of the motels I'd visited, that the managers might not remember her. The motels must get a hundred customers in a week, and remembering just one was probably difficult—if not impossible. Then, too, multiple people probably worked the counter in the offices—even if Geraldine had booked a room at one of the motels I'd visited, it was possible the people I'd spoken to hadn't been there when she'd come in.

I made myself push on anyway—I told myself I just hadn't found the right motel yet. And if none of these motels worked, I would simply move on to the motels and hotels that were closer to the center of town.

The next motel was a little smaller than the others. It only had one level, it was much more compact, and there was a small restaurant attached to it.

I went into the office.

The man behind the counter had thick white hair, and he was humming along to an oldies tune that came from a speaker that sat next to him. He was wearing jeans and a crisp white shirt, and a red badge placed just over his shirt pocket read "Len."

When he saw me, he turned the music down and smiled at me.

"What can I do for you, doll?"

I smiled back. "Hi, Len."

Then I launched into my story as I had before—I told him I was looking for a girl and that finding her was very important.

I also told him that I wasn't with the police and that this wasn't any kind of official business.

I could see the polite mask descending over Len's face.

I quickly pulled out my phone and showed him the picture of Geraldine.

"This is the girl I'm looking for," I said.

Len's face transformed.

A distant anger showed itself for just a moment, and then he covered it.

"She didn't pay her bill," he said. "Are you here to pay it for her?"

I quickly seized on his words. "You recognize her?"

"Yes, I do," Len said. "Like I said, she didn't pay her bill."

"How long did she stay here?"

Len shrugged. "She's been here a few weeks. She has some fellah with her. They paid their bill at first, but this time the card was declined."

"A few weeks?" I said. "You're sure about that?"

"Yes—I'm positive. Like I said, if you want to pay her bill, you're welcome to."

"Thank you very much, Len," I said. "I really appreciate it."

I turned to go.

"Hey, wait," Len said. "You're leaving, just like that?"

"Uh, yes," I said. "I just needed to establish Geraldine's whereabouts."

Len looked disappointed. "You're a friend or something, right? Are you going to see her again?"

"Maybe," I said carefully.

"Well, you tell her from me that I'll put her stuff out if she doesn't pay. I mean it—I'll put it right out on the street."

I paused, momentarily at a loss for words.

"If I see her, I'll tell her," I said at last.

Then I left the motel. I stood outside in the early evening heat for just a moment—I could feel the image that had been growing in my mind shifting and changing shape. And I was a little stunned that I had actually found the information I was looking for.

Then I got in my car and drove home quickly.

As I walked in the door, I smelled the delicious aroma of pizza. I saw Alberta sitting on the couch, and she was flipping through channels on the TV without really watching anything.

She looked up as I set my purse down.

"I thought we'd just have pizza tonight," she said.

"Pizza is good," I said. "Pizza is always good. From Armando's?"

"Yes."

"Even better, then."

I glanced at Alberta—she looked tired, which was rare for her. Even when she worked long hours, waking up before dawn and going to bed after midnight, she was always full of energy and purpose.

"How are you doing?" I said.

Alberta stood up and gave me a wan smile. "I'm fine."

She walked to the dining room, and I followed.

"How's Rafaela?" I said.

Alberta sighed, and I sensed that our sister's state of mind was the source of her weariness.

"She's not doing well. She's sleeping now, and I think she's been sleeping all day."

I glanced around. "Where's Sibyl? She's not in the sink again, is she?"

Alberta smiled a little. "No—she's actually upstairs with Rafaela. I looked in on them just before you got home."

She raised the lid on the white pizza box that was sitting on the dining room table.

"Are you hungry?" she said.

"Sure," I said. I went into the kitchen to get some plates.

Alberta followed me and pulled a big bowl out of the refrigerator.

"I made a salad for us, too," she said.

She set the bowl on the counter and then returned to the refrigerator.

"And I know you're going to want milk with your pizza."

Alberta shot me a glance that had a little of her usual energy in it, and I smiled back at her.

"Weirdo," she said.

We were soon seated at the dining room table—me with my glass of milk and Alberta with a glass of iced tea, and I glanced over my shoulder toward the stairs.

"Should I go wake Rafaela?"

"No," Alberta said. "Let her sleep. The only thing that will really help her at this point is to get this all solved."

"Speaking of getting this solved," I said, "I really think you need to do another scrying session."

Alberta shook her head. "Chloe, I told you about this already. I don't like prying into—"

"I know," I said. "Just hear me out."

I told her quickly about my conversation with Len.

Alberta stared at me for a long moment.

"You're positive he recognized the photo of Geraldine?" she said.

"I'm one hundred percent sure," I said.

"And he said she hadn't paid her bill?"

"That's exactly what he said," I replied.

Alberta was thoughtful. "That does sound like someone who's in a fair amount of financial distress."

She was silent for a time.

"All right," she said at last. "I'll do another scrying session—but only because we have enough evidence to make Geraldine a genuine suspect."

"And that's not all," I said. "There was another attempt on Bradshaw—this time a painting almost fell on her."

I told Alberta quickly about the way Geraldine had pointed the painting out to me. And then I told her about how Bradshaw had shown up at the library and accused me of trying to kill her with it.

Alberta frowned. "And you think Geraldine is actually responsible?"

"Well, I certainly didn't do it," I said. "And no one else knew about our conversation."

"But she couldn't have planned it ahead of time," Alberta said. "She didn't know you were coming over. There's no way she would have known she'd have a chance to set you up."

"Maybe it was a spur of the moment kind of thing," I said. "She saw an opportunity, and she took it."

I glanced over at Alberta. "Are you saying that you don't want to do the scrying session anymore?"

"No—I'll do the scrying session. It's just that something seems a little strange about this."

I felt a tug at the back of my mind—I'd thought something similar. But the scrying session was important—I needed to find out if Geraldine stood to inherit from Bradshaw.

Alberta stood up and began clearing our plates away. "Just give me about twenty minutes—I need to get myself mentally prepared."

"Would you like me to make some tea again?" I said.

"No, I think I'm good. My energies have been so focused on this lately that I don't think I really need to do much preparation. Are you going to join me?"

"I'd like to," I said. "Is that okay?"

"Yes, it's fine," Alberta replied. "Your desire to find the truth will lend strength to my own abilities. Meet me in my room in a little bit."

She went upstairs.

After a little while, I went upstairs also. I found Alberta in her room in the dark, already seated with her mirror and her candle.

"Have you started?" I said as I sat down next to her.

"No, not yet," she murmured. In the candlelight, I could see that her face had a dreamy quality to it. "But my frame of mind is good for this—very good. I feel very in tune tonight—I think in some way I've been waiting to do this again."

"You have?" I said. "Why? Did you find something out?"

"Not exactly," Alberta said. "But after you brought up the question of who inherits Bradshaw's money, I did a little digging. It turns out Geraldine and Bradshaw both have their affairs managed by the same attorney. This guy's firm has managed the Tyndall family's fortune since Charles' time. I'll be able to focus on him."

"You found that out and you didn't tell me?" I said in exasperation. "Alberta, we could have done another scrying session ages ago."

I started to go on but then stopped myself. If Alberta was in a good mood for scrying, I didn't want to ruin it.

"I couldn't do another session," Alberta said. "Not without proof. But I've been preparing all along, and now that we have proof, we can go ahead."

"That doesn't make any sense," I said. "You've been objecting the whole time to doing any additional scrying. You were objecting all the way up to a few minutes ago. You're really exasperating, Alberta."

She smiled in the candlelight, and I could see her smile reflected back to me in the mirror also.

"I'm ready to begin now," she said.

Alberta stared into the mirror, and I saw the same intent yet calm expression steal over her face that I had seen before. She stared and stared, and a couple of times her brows drew together in consternation. Her eyes gazed searchingly into the mirror, and they roved over its surface, as if she were reading something from it that only she could see. Time passed, and eventually, Alberta seemed to come out of a trance and sat back.

She frowned. "Well, that's not what I expected to find at all."

"What is it?" I said quickly. "What did you find out?"

"Bradshaw doesn't have any money," Alberta said. "In fact, she's broke, and she's probably going to have to sell the house—she can't afford to keep it up anymore. And as far as Geraldine—"

"Yes?" I said.

"Geraldine is rolling in cash. There's no way she's trying to kill Bradshaw."

Chapter Twenty-Five

That night I had trouble sleeping.

I'd been so sure that Geraldine was after Bradshaw's money—but Geraldine was the one who had held onto her fortune, while Bradshaw had frittered hers away. So my pet theory had been proved wrong.

And yet the image that had been growing in my mind was undisturbed. It was still shifting and changing, but the basic outline was still there—somehow the information about Geraldine fit right in with the rest of the image and actually made it more complete. It definitely belonged.

I just didn't see how.

I would have to figure out what to do next—where to go to find the next clue.

The trouble was I didn't know how to keep going—as far as I could tell, I had exhausted every path.

So I lay in the dark, turning everything over in my mind, trying to figure out what I had missed.

Nothing came to me.

I continued to stare into the darkness, and eventually, I felt myself drifting off. Right before I slipped into sleep, I saw my mother's house before my eyes. I saw a big room full of books, and I pictured myself looking through them.

I'll go to Mom's house tomorrow, I thought to myself. *I'll start there.*

Then I slipped into the comforting darkness of sleep.

In the morning, I woke when sunlight touched my eyes. I hadn't set my alarm since it was Thursday, and I had the day off. But it was still early, and I could hear Alberta and Rafaela bustling around downstairs.

I sat up and frowned as I tried to remember what I'd been thinking about before I'd fallen asleep, and then it came to me—Mom's house.

I realized that if there was one place I had left to look, it was my mother's house with her books. She had taken some of them with her to Florida—mostly her rune books—but many of them she had left here, including the books that contained our family's knowledge of the Crabtree Coven.

I had to take a look at the magic once again.

I'd been forgetting my own original plan.

Mike had advised me to forget about the magic side and to just focus on the facts. And he had been both right and wrong. I did need to focus on the facts—but I'd been neglecting the magic side—not giving it equal weight—and that's why I wasn't able to see the whole picture. I had to delve into the past of the Crabtree Coven and discover not just who had the motive, but who had the supernatural means.

I had to investigate both the magical and the mundane.

I went to take my shower quickly, and then I hurried downstairs.

But by the time I'd made it to the kitchen, both Alberta and Rafaela had gone, and the remains of their breakfast had been cleared away.

There was, however, a note on the table.

I picked it up and read it over.

Chloe—Alberta has gone to work, and I've gone to see Lisa again. I know you're both worried about me, but you don't need to be. I've been sleeping a lot lately, but I believe it's necessary. I've been looking for an answer in my dreams. So far, I haven't found one, but one thing comes across very clearly. I believe you're in danger, and I want you to be very, very careful. Please, Chloe, please be careful today.

It was signed by Rafaela.

I stared at the note for a long moment.

Rafaela had written me notes before, and I wasn't surprised that she had done so on this occasion. She wrote notes sometimes when her emotions became too much—she actually found it hard to talk at those times, and writing was the only way she could get the words out.

I looked the note over again—Rafaela seemed genuinely worried about me. But I still didn't know why. And then the image that had been growing in my mind shifted a little, and one part of it came into sharper focus. I wondered for just a moment—but the idea didn't lead anywhere. I decided to think about it later, and I went to get a bowl of cereal.

I ate breakfast quickly, and then I went outside and got in my car.

The drive to my parents' house took about fifteen minutes. Mom and Dad lived out in the countryside, and their house sat on a quarter acre on one side of a two-lane road that was sparsely sprinkled with homes. Across the street sat a farm, and a gray pony and a brown horse grazed in a meadow directly across from their house.

I parked my car in their gravel driveway and got out.

The morning was already hot and humid, and I stood for a moment looking at the two-story white house with its well-trimmed lawn. Even though Mom and Dad intended to be gone for months, they had a neighbor look in on their house every few days, and they'd hired a local teen to take care of the lawn and water the flowers.

Though the house wasn't currently occupied, it didn't look abandoned—in fact, it looked friendly and inviting—as if my parents had just stepped out for the morning and would be back any moment.

Mom had left a spare key with us, and I drew it out of my purse as I walked up to the front door.

I unlocked it and went inside. As I did so, my phone buzzed.

I looked at it, surprised—Mike was calling me.

I answered quickly. "Hello?"

"Hey, Chloe," Mike said.

His voice was rich and warm on the phone.

He continued. "I'm sorry to bother you at work."

"It's okay," I replied. "I'm not at the library today—I have the day off."

"Oh," Mike said. "That's good."

Then he hesitated.

"Is something wrong?" I asked.

I could hear Mike sigh.

"I know I'm a professor of folklore," he said. "So you would think that I would be more open-minded about the supernatural and mystical things. But I'm really not. I'm not open-minded at all."

"I'm not sure where you're going with this," I said. "You called to tell me you aren't open-minded?"

Mike sighed again. "That's not what I meant at all. I believe I'm very open-minded—I just believe in the facts. I believe in things I can see. That's why I like to study folklore—I'm interested in all the wild stories people tell themselves when they can't explain what's happened to them. Then I like to break those stories down and see where they really came from—what the facts are behind the fiction."

"I'm still not sure where you're going with this," I said.

"Chloe, I've got a terrible feeling," Mike blurted out. "I can't explain where it comes from or what its factual basis could possibly be. And it's against everything I believe in—"

"Mike," I said. "What are you talking about?"

"I have a bad feeling," he replied. "Like a premonition. I have a terrible feeling that someone is out to get you. Someone wants to destroy you."

I felt a chill spread through me—Mike's words were eerily similar to Rafaela's.

"Chloe?" he said. "Are you still there?"

"Yes," I said. "I'm here."

"Chloe, I'm sorry. I just realized how terrible that sounds. I'm sure everything is going to be okay. And I didn't mean to scare you. I just want you to look out for yourself. Where are you right now?"

"I'm at my mom and dad's house."

"Any suspicious-looking characters around?"

I had to smile at that. "Hardly. They're both in Florida. There's nobody here at all."

"I meant have you seen anyone following you today? Have you seen any cars that seem to go everywhere you go?"

I glanced out the window. My parents lived on a quiet street, and there was hardly ever any traffic on the road at all. I could only see my own car parked in the driveway.

"No—there's no one outside," I said. "Why would you ask that?"

"I'm sure it's nothing," Mike replied. "It's just part of my bad feeling—I've got this idea that there's this dark shadow after you all the time."

"Mike!" I said.

"I'm sorry. I shouldn't have said that. I shouldn't have said any of this. I'm being completely irrational. Forget I said anything."

Mike paused. "But promise me one thing."

"What's that?"

"Promise me that if you get a weird feeling about somebody that you'll call me immediately. I don't care if it turns out to be purely your imagination and the poor guy is completely innocent. Just give me a call, and I'll come to you right away. Just call me if anything or anyone gives you a funny feeling."

I found myself at a loss for words.

"Chloe?" Mike prompted.

"You really feel that strongly about this?" I said after a moment.

"I really do. Just promise me you'll let me help you."

"Okay," I said. "I will. I'll call you if anything comes up."

"You will?" Mike sounded hopeful.

"I will," I said. "I promise."

"Oh, Chloe." I could hear the relief in his voice, and the warm tone it had held when he'd first called returned. "I'm so glad. I'm sure I'm being completely ridiculous, and I'm sure there's nothing in it. But it makes me feel better knowing you won't be alone. I'm just a phone call away."

"Thanks, Mike," I said.

He paused for a long time, and I suddenly got the feeling that he didn't know what to say.

"Well," he said at last, "I'm glad we had this discussion. With any luck, you won't need to call me—in fact, I'm sure you won't. So if I don't hear from you, I'll assume everything's okay. At least, I hope everything will be okay. In any event, don't be a stranger."

"I won't be," I said. "Don't you be one, either."

"Okay," Mike said. "Bye, Chloe."

"Bye."

The connection was broken, and the phone went quiet.

I stared down at it for a moment. Rafaela was worried about me, and now so was Mike—who had no belief in the supernatural whatsoever.

I had to wonder if maybe they were right to be worried.

But at the same time, I had come here with a purpose, and I needed to focus on that right now.

Though the morning was bright outside, it was dark in the house, and I switched on a light in the hall.

Mom had a room on the ground floor that she actually called her library, so I went in there first. The room was small and had two walls lined with bookshelves. There were several notable gaps on the shelves, and I assumed those were the spots where Mom's rune books had been. Seeing the gaps reminded me that I still needed to find a way to lift the curse off Lisa—the curse had been sealed by a rune—and I thought of Rafaela going to see her every day—I knew she was working tirelessly to figure out how to cure her.

I stepped closer to the shelves and ran my fingers along the spines, reading each title carefully. When I had exhausted the books that I could reach easily, I pulled a step stool out of the corner and climbed up to examine the books on the top shelf.

When I had looked at every book, I stepped back down—I hadn't found anything on the first wall that related to the Crabtree Coven.

I went to work on the second wall. I did find one book titled *A Brief History of Witchcraft and Magic* that I took down and perused—but it turned out to be a general history of witchcraft rather than a history of witches in our particular corner of the world. Other than that, I didn't find anything that might relate to our current situation, so I turned my steps back toward the hall.

I knew Mom kept more books in the basement.

Looking for books in a basement about a coven might have sounded like a spooky undertaking, but in reality, it was nothing like that at all. The basement, like the library, was Mom's domain, and it was bright and cheerful and scrupulously clean. There were big windows up by the ceiling that let in a lot of light, and when I flipped the switch on the wall, an array of decorative lamps sprang to life.

Mom had more books on three large bookcases over by the far wall, and she also had a stack of colorful boxes that held even more books.

I started on the bookcases first.

But just like with the shelves upstairs, I didn't find anything.

I turned toward the boxes with some trepidation—I was running out of places to look.

Inside the boxes were books stored in individual clear plastic bags. I sifted through them without finding anything I could use, until I came across a book that had no title on the cover or on the spine. I didn't know if I could use this book, either, but at least it was a little different-looking.

I drew it out of its bag.

The book had a blue cloth cover with a fake blue jewel in the center—it appeared to be handmade.

I opened the book and found the title inside: *Witches of Crabtree Bay.* And there was a further note below it: *Copied from the original.*

The book appeared to be handwritten.

I began to read, and I discovered that the book was a history of the Bartlett family in Crabtree Bay. I leafed forward several chapters and found out some scandalous things about my great-grandmother that I'd never known. I kept leafing forward and found a section titled "Other Witches in Crabtree Bay." I read again about Ezekiel Rapp and his disastrous election strategies, and how he had sworn his followers to secrecy after that. I read once again about how one of his descendants had failed to heed that call to secrecy and how they had been run out of town.

I read again, too, that the coven's symbols were the crow, the pearl, and the eye.

I paused. I remembered the pearl necklace that Tina had worn—and the crow bracelet that had adorned Chris Young's wrist. Tina, I was pretty sure, was a member of the coven. And Chris I wasn't sure about—but it wouldn't have surprised me. And the coven typically had three members—and if, for the sake of argument, Tina and Chris were both members, then who was the third?

And which one was the leader?

I wondered, too, about the eye. I'd always assumed that "the eye" referred to the evil eye or something similar. But as I read on, I discovered that the eye actually referred to the black-eyed Susan, a local wild flower. The dark, round spot in the middle of the showy yellow petals did indeed look like an eye.

But there was nothing sinister about it, and I wondered why the coven would have chosen it for their symbol. And then I realized as I should have from the beginning, that plants were very valuable ingredients in potions and spells—I wondered what kind of potions the coven had used the black-eyed Susan for.

It suddenly popped into my head that Geraldine had given me tea that was made from the black-eyed Susan.

But Geraldine had been cleared of the attacks on Bradshaw and Lisa—she didn't have any motive.

Or did she? Maybe she had a motive I knew nothing about.

I continued to read, and I reached the end of the section on the Crabtree Coven.

The chapter concluded with a warning—it said that even though the coven had been banished, they weren't gone, and they were always looking for a way back into town. Secrecy had become their most important tenet, and they had learned how to hide in plain sight. They had learned from the election debacle and from their banishment. It went on to admonish the witches of Crabtree Bay to be alert.

And then there was a further warning—the dangerous one is the one you don't see.

Chapter Twenty-Six

I went out to lunch after that, and I then drove all over Crabtree Bay—
I even went downtown. I needed to think, and the driving helped me.

As I drove aimlessly through the streets, I stopped several times,
and I saw something that puzzled me—it was just where I'd last seen
it, and I thought it might have been moved by now.

But it didn't puzzle me nearly as much as the image in my own
head. The idea that had been growing there continued to grow, and I
could see several pieces of it clearly—but I didn't see how they all fit
together.

I went down to the water then to think.

Crabtree Bay had an actual bay, of course, and I drove down to my
favorite spot and parked. It had rained a little while I was in the
restaurant eating lunch—just enough to leave all available horizontal
surfaces damp—and I was content at first to stand and look out over
the bay with the sunlight dancing on the water.

Eventually, I spied a large rock under a group of trees that wasn't
damp, and I went to sit down on it.

The image in my mind continued to turn and twist and change.
Soon it was almost complete—I could almost see the shape in its
entirety.

But there was still one thing that was missing—one piece that
would make the puzzle whole.

I didn't know what that one thing was.

I sat for a long time staring out over the water and thinking. But time passed, and nothing came to me.

The day continued to wear away, and eventually, it was approaching dinner time.

I got up and drove home.

Alberta met me at the door and wrapped me in a hug.

"Thank goodness you're okay," she said.

"Of course I am," I said. "Why wouldn't I be?"

Alberta stepped back. "It's just that Rafaela's been talking about how worried she is about you again. And Sibyl's missing."

"Sibyl's missing?" I said sharply. "What happened?"

"I don't know," Alberta replied. "I can't find her anywhere in the house. I think she just got out when one of us left this morning."

"Are you sure she's not just hiding?" I said.

Alberta frowned. "She could be—but somehow I feel an absence. I can feel that she's not here. And her food still hasn't been touched. She's got both wet and dry—and she never lets the wet food go to waste."

"Do you want to go out and look for her?" I said.

Alberta shook her head. "I've been out in the yard, but other than that, I don't know where she'd go. She's always been an indoor cat—this isn't like her at all. I just hope she comes back soon."

"Did you add that protective charm to her collar?" I said. "I know you'd mentioned doing that once."

"No," Alberta said. "I really wish I had now."

Her eyes dropped down to my purse, and she frowned.

"I thought you said you were going to add a black knotted cord to your bag for protection."

I looked down also.

"I did," I said.

But as I looked at my bag, I could see that the cord and my little "Chloe" charm were both missing.

"That's odd," I said. "It was clipped on pretty tightly."

"Everything's odd these days," Alberta replied.

I made macaroni and cheese, which was my favorite comfort food, and all three of us had a quiet dinner together.

Afterward, Rafaela went up to her room, and Alberta went outside from time to time to search the backyard.

She didn't find Sibyl.

Eventually, I went up to my room also, leaving Alberta downstairs.

I hoped very much that she wouldn't stay up all night, but I was afraid she was going to.

I slept fitfully, troubled by dreams that were full of conflicting ideas and images and by a puzzle that I couldn't solve.

And then, as the night wore on and dawn approached, I fell into a heavy sleep and was suddenly roused by the loud beeping of my alarm.

I had the volume all the way up—otherwise I tended to sleep through it—and I grumbled angrily to myself as I shut the insistent beeping off.

It seemed to me that the alarm had come at the worst possible moment. I felt like I'd been about to solve something—the image that had been growing in my mind had loomed large in my dream—I'd been following it, and I was just about to turn a corner and see it in full light.

And then I'd woken up, and the image had vanished. I tried desperately to grasp onto any little bit I could remember, but the solution I'd been about to see faded fast.

I got up grumbling to myself and got ready for the day.

As I took a shower, however, it occurred to me that it was very possible my dreams hadn't had any genuine answers—just a tantalizing feeling that what I couldn't see would soon be revealed.

If only that were true.

I went downstairs for breakfast and found that both Rafaela and Alberta were already gone. Rafaela, I assumed, had most likely gone back to the hospital to visit Lisa, and Alberta had presumably gone to work.

There was, however, a note on the dining room table at a place that was set for me.

Be very careful today, Rafaela had written. *My bad feeling is getting worse.*

Below Rafaela's note, on the same sheet of paper, was a second note.

Remember none of us has the gift of foresight, Alberta had written. *Rafaela doesn't know what she's talking about.*

I put the note aside and got some coffee.

After letting the caffeine seep into my body and wake me up properly, I grabbed an apple and an energy bar for breakfast and then drove to work.

As I drove, I was surprised to see heat lightning lighting up the sky—for some reason, I'd thought that that was a phenomenon that only occurred in the evening. I flipped up my sun visor and ducked my head a bit to get a better view through my windshield. But the sun was shining brightly, and there wasn't a single cloud in the sky—the lightning was definitely not a sign of an approaching storm.

I drove the rest of the way to work and went into the library with the strange, silent heat lightning flashing all around me.

Rita was working with me in the morning, and our regulars walked in as soon as we opened the doors, and the day seemed to be progressing as usual. And then there were several pops, followed by a crackle and a fizzle, and then the lights went out. There was a collective moan of dismay from our patrons as books became unreadable, and computer screens went dark.

"Hang on, everybody," Rita said. "I'm going to check the circuit breaker downstairs."

We all sat in the dark as lightning flashed in the windows.

Soon people began texting and calling on their phones, and it became obvious from the snatches of conversation I could hear that the lights were out all over town.

Rita returned after a few minutes with her own phone in her hand, her face worried in the dim light.

"Sorry, ladies and gentlemen," she said, her voice firm and professional. "The problem's not with this building—there seems to be a city-wide blackout. I've called our main office, and they'll call me back soon to let us know how we should handle this."

Crabtree Bay Library was actually run by the town of Crabtree Bay, and we had administrative offices downtown that were responsible for our library and the smaller library annex on the outskirts of town. Whenever there was a severe weather event—like a snowstorm or a hurricane—they were the ones who decided if the library would close—they were the ones who decided what we did in an emergency.

Of course, our patrons could leave any time they wished. But at the moment, they all seemed inclined to stay put. Many pairs of eyes watched Rita anxiously in the dim light.

After a few minutes, her phone rang.

Rita answered and then listened. She was silent for a long time, and the voice of another speaker could be heard buzzing through the phone. Eventually, she made a few brief replies and then turned to address the room.

"All right, folks," she said. "If the power doesn't come back on in ten minutes, I'm going to have to close the library and ask you all to leave."

Our patrons groaned once again.

"I know—I'm sorry," Rita said. "I appreciate how much you guys like being in the library. But no electricity means no air-conditioning, and it's going to get very hot in here soon. It also means no lights in the bathrooms or the stairwells, and we don't want anyone to get hurt."

We waited the requisite ten minutes, and the electricity didn't return.

"Okay, everybody," Rita said. "The library is officially closing now."

There was a lot of grumbling and rustling as our patrons began to gather up their things. The circulation system wasn't working, of course, so Rita and I weren't able to check any materials out for people who wanted to take items with them. This caused further grumbling, but we placed a sticky note with each person's name on all the materials people wanted to check out, and we promised them that everything would be waiting for them tomorrow.

Then our patrons began to shuffle out, and Mrs. Ludlow threw me a particularly baleful look as she left.

Once everyone was gone, we locked the door.

Then Rita and I got out flashlights and swept the library carefully with their beams to make sure that nobody was hiding out anywhere.

We were soon satisfied that the building was indeed empty, and the two of us left, locking the door behind us.

Rita told me that she would let me know if the library would be open tomorrow, and we both went to our cars.

I drove home in the sunshine with the weird lightning flashing all around me.

I let myself into the dark house, which was still cool, and I closed the door quickly so as not to let any of the cool air escape. The house was eerily quiet, and I could tell that neither Alberta nor Rafaela were home.

Both of them soon texted, however. Alberta said her office was closing for the day, and she'd be coming home soon. Rafaela said the hospital had back-up generators, and she'd be staying at the hospital—she said she had a bad feeling today and she wanted to keep an eye on Lisa.

I stared down at Rafaela's words.

A bad feeling...

Alberta had pointed out that none of us had visions—and that was true. But Rafaela *was* very sensitive—I was sure she had noticed something.

I thought of Rafaela's flower upstairs. It had still been drooping and gray when I'd left this morning—there was no sign of improvement.

I didn't know what to do to make her or her flower feel better.

I sighed and went into the kitchen.

I had a vague idea that I would get Rafaela's plant some water, but I knew very well that the plant didn't need water, and that adding water to it would actually harm the magic that supported it.

I thought then of getting some water for myself—I typically drank quite a bit during the day—but I didn't want to open the refrigerator and let the cold air out.

I stood in the dark kitchen and looked out on the bright, sunny day with the weird flashes of silent lightning.

"When you see summer lightning—" Tina had said.

I froze.

I thought of Tina Chandler's single-pearl necklace, Chris Young's crow bracelet, and Geraldine Tyndall's black-eyed Susan tea.

I thought of the bullets in Geraldine's purse and the fact that Chris's car wasn't working. I thought about all of the pieces of the puzzle that almost fit into one clear image.

There was a scraping sound then, as of a key fitting into a lock, and Alberta's voice floated into the house.

"Chloe? Are you here?"

I walked out into the living room.

"I'm here," I said.

"That's good," Alberta replied. "Because your car's outside. It would be disturbing if your car was here and you weren't."

She was holding the door open, and her long red hair spilled over her face as she bent down and struggled with something.

"Can you help me with these?"

I could see that Alberta had four cardboard boxes full of paper sitting just outside.

"What is all this?" I said.

"Work," she said shortly.

"Can't you just work with all this stuff electronically?"

"Apparently not. Are you going to help me with these or not?"

I hurried outside, and the two of us dragged the boxes into the house. Alberta was just turning to close the door against the heat when a small, black blur streaked past her into the house.

"Sibyl!" she cried.

The dark blur was indeed Sibyl, and she ran through the living room, climbing all over the furniture, and then she took off for the kitchen.

She was apparently spooked about something, and she was also wet—she was leaving muddy paw prints all over Alberta's white furniture and beige carpets.

"Sibyl, honey! Are you okay?" Alberta cried.

I heard Sibyl's claws scrabbling on the kitchen's linoleum floor, and then she ran back into the living room and headed for the stairs.

She turned sharply and then galloped up them, making a ton of noise and leaving a muddy paw print on each individual step.

"Sibyl, honey!" Alberta called after her. "What's wrong, baby?"

Sibyl replied with a yowl and then a calm, normal meow, and Alberta went up the stairs carefully, stepping around the paw prints.

"Crazy cat," Alberta muttered.

Sibyl suddenly reappeared at the top of the stairs, her amber eyes glowing as she looked down at us. Then she began to walk down the steps calmly and met Alberta halfway.

She meowed softly, showing her white teeth, and Alberta kneeled down to examine her.

"Everything okay, Sibyl?" she said.

From where I was standing, I could see that Sibyl's legs, back, and chest were liberally covered in mud, but other than that she looked fine.

Alberta seemed to come to the same conclusion, and soon she was scratching Sibyl behind the ears—one of the few places where dark mud didn't cover her.

"How did you get so dirty?" Alberta asked.

She sighed and stood up.

"She's been acting so crazy. I don't know what's gotten into her lately."

"She's been acting crazy," I murmured.

A strangled cry came out of me.

Suddenly everything shifted into place.

I could see it all clearly.

"What was that?" Alberta said.

"She's been acting crazy," I said again. "Yes, she has. She really has. I don't know why I didn't see it before."

I hurried to grab my purse.

The image that had been growing in my mind had suddenly popped into my head, clear and complete. I saw it all—and I did mean all of it.

I quickly moved to the door.

Alberta looked around at me. "Where are you going?"

"Me?" I said. "I just need to go out for a moment."

I stopped suddenly.

"Do you have any stationery?"

Alberta stared at me blankly. "Stationery?"

I hurried up the stairs past her and Sibyl and ran down to her room.

"Yes—stationery. Do you have any girly cards or note paper? Maybe something pink and flowery?"

"Did you transfer your crazy to Chloe?" Alberta's voice floated up the stairs.

I ransacked Alberta's desk, and I came up with a handful of notecards that had sunsets on them.

I figured that was close enough, and I ran back down the stairs past Alberta—Sibyl had disappeared.

"Seriously, where are you going?" Alberta said.

"I'm going to get some—ice," I said as I headed toward the door.

Alberta started down the stairs. "I'll go with you."

"No!" I said quickly. "You can't go."

"Why not?"

"It could be dangerous."

Alberta frowned. "Dangerous? Getting ice? Maybe Sibyl's crazy really did get into you."

"I—just want to be by myself," I said.

Then I ran outside and jumped into my car.

I put the car in drive and peeled away from the curb.

Then I put my phone on speaker and called Mike.

"Hello?" Mike's voice crackled to life.

"Mike, it's Chloe," I said quickly.

"Yes, I know," he replied. "Is everything okay?"

"I need you to help me out," I said. "I need you to come with me somewhere."

There was a slight pause from Mike. "Okay. Where?"

"We're going to Bradshaw's lake house. Bradshaw is in danger, and Chris has got a gun."

Chapter Twenty-Seven

I'd thought at first that Mike could just drive straight up to the lake house—the two of us could race up there, and maybe one of us would arrive in time. But then I realized that Mike didn't actually know where the lake house was. Luckily, he was still over at the school—even though the power was out—and I drove over there to get him.

But first I made a detour downtown—something there had puzzled me, and I wanted to take a look at it. If I was right about everything, I had a pretty good idea what I would find.

I drove over quickly, and I found what I was looking for.

I was right.

Then I quickly drove in the opposite direction over to Henrietta College.

Mike was standing outside his building, waiting for me.

He got into the car, and I sped off once again.

"So what's this all about?" he said.

"Bradshaw's in danger, like I said," I replied.

"And Chris Young has a gun?"

"Yes."

"How do you know?"

"I deduced it."

"You deduced it?" Mike looked at me, incredulous. "You didn't actually see it?"

"No."

Mike ran a hand over his hair in exasperation. "Chloe—"

"I know I'm right," I said. "I know it. And you said you'd help me."

"Yes. Yes, I did."

Mike paused.

"What do you want me to do exactly?"

"Just come along," I said. "Be a witness. I've figured everything out, and I'm going to reveal everything."

Mike frowned. "Isn't that dangerous? Especially if Chris has got a gun?"

"Yes," I said. "But I can handle it."

I expected Mike to object further, but he seemed strangely calm about the whole thing.

Instead, he shot me a sidelong glance.

"So you didn't tell your sisters about this? I notice you didn't bring anybody else along."

"No—I didn't want to put them in danger."

Mike grinned. "But you don't mind putting me in danger?"

"I—" I stopped. "I—"

"It's okay. You don't have to answer that. I'm glad you called me."

"You are?" I said.

"Yes. I've been worried about you, like I said. If you're going to do something, I want to be in on it."

I felt warmed by Mike's support. He probably thought I was crazy—and I knew that he didn't believe. But all the same, he was here, and he was going to help me.

I looked over at him, and I was struck once again by just how handsome he was.

"So how do you know where this place is?" Mike asked.

"I've been there a few times," I said. "Back in high school when Bradshaw and I sort of got along. Besides, everybody knows where it is. Around here it's a famous local landmark."

"Ah—that explains it," Mike said.

"Explains what?"

"Nothing important. I just heard about it recently."

Mike glanced out the window.

"There sure is a lot of lightning."

"Yes, there is," I replied. I ducked my head to glance at the sky myself. "There's really more than there should be. Even if—"

"Yes?" Mike said.

"Never mind. You'll hear it all soon enough."

I drove a little faster.

Bradshaw's vacation home was known as the Tyndall Lake House, and it sat thirty minutes outside of Crabtree Bay. The house had been built by Bradshaw's grandfather, and it sat in a heavily wooded area on the top of a little hill. The hill sloped gently down to a man-made lake that had also been created by Bradshaw's grandfather. He'd named it Prosperity Lake in honor of his success in business.

As I'd told Mike, I'd been to the lake house a few times—mostly for parties—and I remembered the place well. The house was sort of an enormous cottage—all one level with one wing that was nothing but guest bedrooms. Charles Tyndall and his sons had done quite a bit of entertaining in their time, and Bradshaw kept the tradition up—on a slightly smaller scale. After about a half an hour, we reached the very long driveway that led to the Tyndall Lake House and its attendant lake.

A gate had been drawn across the driveway, closing it off. And from its rails hung a sign that read "Private Property."

Mike and I both stared at the gate.

"Are you sure about this?" he said. "Maybe it's better if we just turn back."

"No," I said. "We need to keep going."

I turned the car toward the trees on the side of the gate. The gate itself wasn't attached to anything—it was just four metal bars and two metal posts sitting in the driveway.

It was easy enough to go around.

"If we go on," Mike said, "we could get in trouble for trespassing."

"And if we don't go on, Bradshaw's going to die," I said.

I thought I heard Mike sigh gently as I maneuvered the car through the trees and back onto the driveway and kept going.

So he hadn't necessarily believed me when I'd said that Bradshaw's life was in danger.

But at least he was here—that was what really mattered.

I drove on.

The driveway was unpaved, and it seemed to be made up entirely of dirt and very large rocks. Mike and I were bounced and jostled as we rode along the lengthy, winding path, and as we hit a particularly large rock, my phone began to buzz insistently.

I glanced over at it. I had a text—or rather a series of them.

"Can you read those for me?" I asked as the car continued to shudder and bounce.

Mike looked at me uncertainly. "You want me to read your texts?"

"Yes—read them out loud to me."

I quickly gave him my password.

Mike continued to look uncertain, but he picked up my phone, which was lying on the seat between us.

He frowned. "These appear to be from your mother."

"Read them anyway," I said.

"Chloe, honey, you're in danger," Mike read. "You all are. The runes are telling me that someone is casting a spell right now. It's a big one. It's not actually in Crabtree Bay—but it's so big that it's pinging our rune stones anyway. And a forget spell was cast earlier today inside the town. Again—it was a big one."

Mike broke off. "So your mother believes this stuff, too?"

The phone buzzed again, and I ignored him.

"Does she say anything else?"

Mike tapped the phone and began to read again.

"I'm texting your sisters, too. I want you all to go home and stay there. Dad and I are coming home now, and I'll take care of this. We'll be there soon. Whatever you do, don't go outside."

Mike stopped.

"Is that it?" I said.

"Yes," he replied. He paused. "It sounds like your mother wants you to stay out of this—whatever this is."

"I can't wait for her," I said. "This has to be done now."

Something suddenly struck me.

"My fingertips aren't tingling," I said.

"What was that?" Mike said.

"When the runes ping, I'm supposed to feel—"

I glanced over at Mike.

"Never mind."

I drove on, and mercifully, we soon reached the end of the driveway.

We broke free of the trees, and the Tyndall Lake House came into view.

As I remembered, it looked like an overgrown cottage, and it was actually quite a pretty building. It was blue and white and a little rambling, with one long wing poking out of the side, and it sat at the top of a little hill that gradually sloped down to the lake. Sunlight danced on the water, and a little brown pier extended out into the lake.

There was nothing tied up at the pier at the moment, but as I recalled, there was a boat house around somewhere that housed all the boats.

The house itself sat at the end of a wide gravel yard that almost looked as if it could be a parking lot, and closer to the house, there was a proper lawn that had a few flower beds with a smattering of blue and yellow flowers.

The driveway just kind of disappeared into the gravel yard, and there were two cars parked in its wide expanse—a blue sports car with yellow lightning bolts on the side and a black BMW.

I parked close to the edge of the driveway, and Mike and I got out of the car.

Lightning was still flashing high in the sky all around us.

"That's Chris's car," I said, pointing to the blue-and-yellow sports car. "And the black one belongs to Geraldine."

Mike frowned. "Were you expecting her to be here?"

"Oddly enough, yes," I said.

I started toward the house, and Mike followed me.

"What if the door's locked?" he said.

"Then we'll find another way in."

Mike frowned again, but he didn't say anything.

I walked up to the door, and just as I was reaching for the doorknob, Mike put out a hand.

"Wait. What's your plan?"

"Plan?" I said.

Mike looked at me, incredulous. "You're just going to barge in there with no plan?"

"Yes."

"I thought you said Chris had a gun."

"He does."

I opened the door and went in.

Luckily, it was unlocked.

We found ourselves in a big open room—sort of an entrance hall. There was a short set of stairs to our right that led down to a big room with a fireplace. I could hear raised voices coming from the room, and Bradshaw's angry tones floated out to me.

"What are you even doing here?" she shouted.

"I've been wondering that myself," Mike muttered.

I ignored him and strode boldly into the room.

There were four people standing on the other side of the room next to a sliding glass door. The door opened onto a path that led down to the lake, and from the looks of things, two people had just entered from that direction and had been confronted by two other people.

The two people who had entered were Andrew and Geraldine. And the two people who were confronting them were Bradshaw and Chris.

Bradshaw whirled to face me.

"What are *you* doing here?" she demanded.

"I came to save you," I said.

"What?" Bradshaw looked startled. That was clearly not the response she expected. "What are you talking about?"

"I suppose you've never asked Chris about his bracelet?" I said.

Bradshaw glanced over at Chris, and he suddenly looked nervous. He moved to cover the bracelet with his other hand.

"You mean the crow bracelet?" Bradshaw said. "No, I never asked him. Who cares?"

"Would it interest you to know that the crow is a symbol of the Crabtree Coven?" I said. "You seemed to be interested in them. After all, you made enough fuss over the article about them."

Bradshaw glanced over at Chris again, and he seemed even more nervous.

"Would it also interest you to know that he brought a gun here?" I said. "In fact, it's the same gun that was used to shoot you earlier. And it's going to be used again."

Bradshaw glanced down at the cast on her arm. Then she looked over at Chris.

"Is this true? Did you shoot me?"

Chris took a step back. "What? No. She's a crazy chick. I have no idea what she's talking about."

Bradshaw glanced from Chris to me, uncertain where to look. "Where is the gun?"

"Don't look at me," Chris said. He practically squeaked. "I don't have any gun."

"That's true. He doesn't," I said. "He brought it here, but he didn't know he had it. Someone else planted it on him."

I turned. "Didn't you, Geraldine?"

It was Geraldine's turn to look shocked, and I thought she did it very well.

"Me?" Geraldine said.

"I suspected you early on," I said. "I thought at first your motive was money—but then I realized it was family pride. So you returned to your roots—you'd heard your grandfather was a member of the Crabtree Coven, so you turned to them for help."

"That's crazy," Geraldine said.

"Is it?" I said. "Bradshaw has squandered her fortune. She's allowed the family mansion to fall into disrepair, and you couldn't stand to watch everything crumble. So you shot Bradshaw and you cursed Lisa."

"That's ridiculous!" Geraldine cried. Her pale skin had turned a bright red, and she took a step toward me.

Andrew stepped in front of her.

"That's enough, Chloe," he said. "This really is pathetic. You're trying to hurt Geraldine because you're jealous. And I won't allow it."

"Then how did I know you two would be here?" I said. "And how do I know that Geraldine has bullets in her purse right now?"

"What?" Bradshaw said sharply. She turned to her cousin.

I'd long suspected that there was tension between the two, but now I knew it for sure.

"Let me see your purse," Bradshaw demanded.

Geraldine had her big silver purse on her shoulder, and she clutched it reflexively.

"No," she said.

Bradshaw lunged toward Geraldine and scooted around Andrew, who tried to stop her. Bradshaw successfully pulled Geraldine's purse off her shoulder and retreated to a corner with it. Andrew moved to go after her, and Chris stepped in his way.

"Just a moment, my friend," Chris said.

Bradshaw rummaged through Geraldine's purse, and she soon came up with a handful of round metal pellets.

She held them in her hand for a moment and then moved toward her cousin.

"What are these?" she demanded.

Geraldine's angry flush faded, and she turned pale once again.

"I—I don't know."

"I'll tell you what they are," I said. "They're bullets. They fit in the antique gun that was hidden in Chris's car—the same one that originally shot Bradshaw. That's why the car's been running funny."

"Wait, wait, wait," Chris said. "You messed with my car?"

I turned to him. "That's what the break-in at the auto body shop was all about. It wasn't really about the money. It was to distract you so you would pay a little less attention to your beloved car—which was the real target. The gun was hidden behind the engine firewall. The plan was to plant the gun on you and have you drive it up here. That way Geraldine wouldn't have possession of the gun and you would."

Chris looked over at Geraldine. "And then what were you going to do next?"

Geraldine's face had gone even paler. "I wasn't going to do anything."

"I can tell you what she was going to do next," I said. "She was going to shoot you, kill you. Cast a spell on Bradshaw, get her to sign over the mansion and everything else in a will. And then she would shoot and kill Bradshaw. She'd make it look like a lover's quarrel—a murder-suicide."

"She'd need witnesses for the signing of the will," Mike interjected quietly.

I turned to look at Mike—he'd been so quiet, I'd almost forgotten he was there.

"She could get witnesses to sign and date it later," I replied. "Someone who's going to commit murder isn't going to worry much about falsifying a date."

"This is outrageous!" Geraldine said. Her face flamed red again. A vein stood out on her forehead. "No one is going to believe these flimsy accusations!"

"And that's exactly what your attempts were, weren't they, Geraldine?" I said. "Shooting at Bradshaw so many times and hitting her only once. Trying to drop a heavy picture on her head. Not very inspired—or very effective."

Geraldine took a step toward me. "I never—"

"Which is why I knew it wasn't you," I concluded. "There was a reason Bradshaw was still alive. Bradshaw was the culprit."

"What?" Bradshaw screeched.

I thought for just a moment that she was going to rush toward me, but instead she stayed right where she was.

"Though I suspected Geraldine," I said. "I'd wondered about you, Bradshaw, for a while. That wound to your arm reminded me of something—but I couldn't figure out what it was at first. And then I remembered Nancy DeVault. She shot her husband and killed him, then shot herself in the arm. She told the police that intruders had broken in, killed her husband, and wounded her. She did it to make her story more credible. She tried to make her crime look like self-defense."

"You think I shot myself?" Bradshaw demanded. "Are you insane? Why would I do that?"

"To cover up the crime you were planning to commit," I said. "Like I said, I was puzzled by the gunshot wound, and I thought there was a possibility that it was self-inflicted. At the time, I believed that you had all the money and that Geraldine was planning to kill you for it, so I didn't know what your motive could be. And then that painting came down in a very lame attempt to kill you, and then shortly after that, I learned that Geraldine had all the money, and you were at risk of losing everything—including your house. That's when everything clicked."

"You really are insane," Bradshaw said. "This is a total fantasy."

"No, Bradshaw," I said. "It just makes sense. You were planning to use the Sleeping Beauty Curse to get Geraldine to sign over all her money to you. Then you were going to kill her and pin the whole thing on me—you would say it was a case of mistaken identity. That's why you sent those emails to Mike. That's why you encouraged him to publish what you sent him. And that's why you came to the library and made such a big scene—why you made a big fuss all over town. You wanted everyone to link me to witchcraft and to think that I was jealous of you. That way when you killed Geraldine, everyone would think it was me—I'd been trying to kill you for weeks, and I accidentally killed Geraldine instead of you—just like I accidentally cursed Lisa instead of you."

Bradshaw did rush toward me then.

"Liar!" she screamed. "Liar! You're trying to pin your own crime on me! You're the one who's guilty!"

I ran away from Bradshaw, and Chris went after her and wrapped her in his arms.

"It's okay, baby," he said quietly. "She can't prove a thing. You're safe here with me, and no one's going to listen to her crazy talk."

"You always were a little ham, weren't you, Bradshaw?" I said. "Always acting, dancing, always in beauty pageants. Always the center of attention. All of that came in useful when you wanted to frame me for murder."

"Shut up!" Bradshaw screamed.

"But there was one thing I didn't quite understand," I said. "I believed you could shoot yourself. I believed you could steal your cousin's money. But I didn't believe you could wait."

Bradshaw had begun to sob.

"What are you talking about?" she choked out.

"I couldn't figure out why you had cursed Lisa," I replied. "I figured you did it for practice, but that didn't seem quite right—you're not the type of person to wait. Once you'd learned the curse, you'd want to use it on Geraldine right away. And then it hit me—"

Bradshaw wrenched herself away from Chris.

"Shut up!" she screamed, tears streaming down her face. "Shut up!"

Andrew stepped forward then.

"Stop it!" he said. "This has gone on long enough."

I looked at Andrew. His face was unusually serious.

His mesmerizing eyes bored into mine, green and compelling. There was an aura of command about him.

"Chloe, you don't have to do this," he said. "I know you're jealous. I know your heart's broken. But hurting the women I love won't help you."

"It won't?" I said.

"No."

He took another step forward.

"Do you know what will help you?"

"What?" I asked.

"Confess," Andrew said. "Confess that this was all you. It always has been. You're the guilty one."

"I'm the guilty one," I said softly. I got a tissue out of my purse and wiped it across both of my eyes.

Then I broke down. Tears began to stream down my face.

"I'm the one," I said. "I did it all."

"What?" Bradshaw said.

"What?" Mike echoed.

"I did all of it! All of it!" I sobbed.

I turned to Andrew. "Can you ever forgive me?"

"No, Chloe," he said. "You know I can't do that."

"You can't?"

"No. But there is something you can do."

"What's that?" I said.

"Turn yourself in."

I took in a long, ragged breath.

"All right," I said. "I'll do that."

"Chloe—" Mike said.

"I have to own up to what I've done. This has all been an elaborate sham. I've been guilty the whole time, and I've lied to you all."

I turned to go.

Then I turned back.

"Andrew," I said. "Would you do me one last favor? Would you do one thing for the sake of the love we once shared?"

Andrew looked at me warily. "I no longer love you, Chloe."

"I know," I said. "I understand that. It's just one small favor."

"What's that?"

I reached into my purse. I pulled out a card and swiped it with lipstick.

"Would you press a kiss to this card?" I said. "Like you did once so long ago?"

"You remember that?" Andrew said.

"Yes," I replied. "Please—just one small kiss. It will comfort me in my jail cell."

Andrew's expression softened. "All right, Chloe. I'll do this one last thing for you. I'm sorry you couldn't let go—I'm sorry your obsession with me led you to attack innocent people. I hope this last kiss will help to heal your broken soul."

He took the card from me and pressed a kiss into the rosy smudge left by the lipstick.

Then he handed it to me.

"Treasure this always."

I took the card quickly, and I stared at him through tear-filled eyes.

"Thank you," I breathed. "This is just what I wanted."

Then I stashed the card in my purse and stepped back, wiping my eyes.

"As I was saying," I said in a more normal tone of voice. "And then it hit me."

"And then what hit you?" Andrew said. He looked confused.

"You'll see. To finish what I started to say, Bradshaw was always a little ham. She was fond of causing scenes. But her cursing Lisa as practice didn't make sense—she wasn't the type to wait."

"I don't understand," Andrew said. "Why are you talking about Bradshaw again? You just confessed."

"You'll understand in just a moment," I replied. "Then I suddenly realized that someone in this town was an even bigger ham than Bradshaw was. And that person is you."

"Me?" Andrew said.

"Yes, you. You're the one who cursed Lisa and shot Bradshaw. And you came here today to kill Bradshaw and finish what you started."

Andrew stared at me with his mesmerizing green eyes again.

"Chloe, you don't know what you're saying."

"Yes, I do. Bradshaw may have money troubles, but you have even bigger ones."

Andrew shook his head. "That's not true. I'm onto something big."

"No, you're not," I said. "That's what you've been telling everyone, including your friends down at the Stained Glass Tavern. But you lied about getting a big gig—or at the very least you misled them. Your big break is actually your involvement with the Crabtree Coven—your career is going nowhere."

"That is absolutely, positively, one hundred percent not true."

"Oh—but it is. You're the unreliable delivery boy Peter was talking about, not Joe. You begged him for the job because you needed the money."

"Joe?" Andrew said, puzzled.

"Never mind," I replied. "The point is you hoped to use what you learned from the coven to further your career eventually, but for now, you just needed money and a place to live. And for that you needed both Bradshaw and Geraldine."

Andrew looked up at the ceiling. "Oh, Chloe. This is so sad."

"I agree," I said. "It is."

"I'm doing fine."

"Then why is there an eviction notice on your town house?"

Andrew's head snapped back down.

"What?"

"I saw it myself today on my way over here," I said. "And I'll tell you what it means. Your father finally got fed up and stopped paying for everything."

"That is *not* true."

"Which part? That your father was paying for everything or that he stopped?"

Andrew stared at me.

I went on.

"Everything I said about Geraldine and Bradshaw was actually true of you. You're the one who broke into Chris's auto body shop, and the one who hid the gun in his car. And yes, Geraldine had the antique bullets that go with the gun—but you put them there. You wanted other people to have them so you wouldn't be suspected if they were found. And you're the one who put a curse on Lisa and shot at Bradshaw."

Andrew folded his arms. "And why would I do that?"

"In your case, placing a curse on Lisa really was practice," I replied. "You wanted to get it right before you used it again. And you were shooting at Bradshaw to establish a pattern before you shot her for real and killed her. And you were planning to frame me for her murder."

"Nonsense," Andrew said. "Why would I need to curse a girl I'd never met? And why would I kill Bradshaw? I have found new love with Geraldine, and I'm much happier."

Andrew was still staring at me with his piercing green eyes as if willing me to agree with him—but it wasn't going to work.

"It's simple," I said. "Your plan is to force Bradshaw to sign over her house to Geraldine and then kill her. And then you'll cast the Sleeping Beauty Curse on Geraldine to force her to marry you. Bradshaw's house will go to Geraldine, and then you'll get both the Tyndall mansion and Geraldine's half of the fortune, which she's apparently managed quite well. I don't know what will happen to Geraldine after that. The Sleeping Beauty Curse will make Geraldine an extremely amenable wife, but it's entirely possible that you'll kill her, too, once she's made a will signing over everything to you."

I turned to Geraldine. "That's why he got that 'G' tattoo. It wasn't because he loves you and he wants to have your initial on him always—it was so he could convince you to have a rune painted on you in return. I bet he told you it was a design he came up with, and that you could just do the body paint first to see how you liked it—the real tattoo could come later. But the paint was always what he wanted. It's the final part of casting the curse."

Geraldine stirred uneasily, and she looked over at Andrew.

But Andrew simply laughed.

"You think I would cast a curse? How would I even know how to do that? You're the witch around here."

"You learned it from Tina Chandler—otherwise known as Ariadne Frost. You charmed her like you've charmed many women before. You got her to tell you all the Crabtree Coven's secrets, and then you used their magic for your own plans."

Andrew shook his head. "This is so sad, Chloe. So sad. Your jealousy knows no bounds."

"No—your jealousy knows no bounds," I said. "You've claimed all along that I'm jealous of your new relationships, but I'm not. I was hurt back when you left me as a teenager, but I haven't felt a thing for you in years. And deep down you know that. Deep down you know that I've moved on, and you can't stand that. You're the one who's jealous—you're the one who wants me to be in love with you, and your vanity can't handle the fact that I don't want you anymore. You're projecting your feelings onto me, and that's why you chose me to take the blame for your crimes."

"Oh, Chloe, Chloe, that's so not—"

"If it's not true, then why do you have my black cord in your bag?"

"What?" Andrew said.

"The black cord I'd made for protection went missing," I said. "It's a cord with knots that has a charm with my name on it. You took it off me back at the ice cream parlor. You were planning to leave it here after you killed Bradshaw—and I'm assuming Chris, too, now. It was going to be evidence that linked me to the crime scene."

Andrew had a small black backpack hanging from his shoulder, and he held it tighter to his body.

"That's ridiculous," he said.

"Then you won't mind if we have a look?" I said.

"Absolutely not. This is my private property. You have no right to look in there."

"You know what else we would find in there?" I said. "We'd find the antique gun that you retrieved from Chris's car and the paint you were going to use on Geraldine. Of course there are no bullets in the gun yet, so it's safe enough at the moment."

Geraldine moved uneasily again, and Chris walked toward Andrew.

"Let's see the bag, my friend," Chris said.

Andrew stepped back. "No—it's just vacation stuff. Just stuff I packed for the weekend."

"If it's just clothes and shave gel," Chris said, "then why not let us see it?"

"Because it's none of your business."

Chris lunged forward then and grabbed for Andrew's bag.

Andrew jumped back and reached into it.

In one swift movement, he pulled out a gun.

But it wasn't the one I was expecting.

Instead of an antique flintlock pistol, Andrew was holding a very sleek, black, modern-looking gun.

I didn't have any idea what kind it was, but I had a terrible feeling that this gun—unlike the other one—was loaded.

Chris quickly moved back.

"Okay, friend. Okay. Don't get excited."

Andrew pointed the gun at him, and Chris continued to move back.

"Get back!" Andrew shouted.

He pointed the gun at all of us.

"Everyone, get back!"

We all did as he said, and Andrew glanced over at Mike.

"What are you doing?" he said. "Why do you have your cell phone out?"

"No reason," Mike said. "I was just—"

"Drop it!" Andrew screamed. "Drop it right now!"

"Okay," Mike said.

He let the phone fall from his hand, and it clattered on the floor.

"In case you're wondering, Andrew," I said, "this behavior doesn't make you look very innocent."

"Shut up!" Andrew screamed, and he pointed the gun at me.

"Andrew—"

Geraldine had been standing nervously by his side, and she reached out a gentle hand to touch his arm.

259

"Andrew, please—"

Andrew switched the gun to his other hand and grabbed Geraldine by the arm.

"Come on. You're going outside. And then I'll finish with them."

She twisted in his grasp. "Andrew, let me go!"

He grinned at her. "Don't worry, darling. You won't remember any of this ever happened."

Suddenly, the front door flew open, and out of the corner of my eye, I saw Mike rushing toward Andrew.

Andrew turned swiftly as if trying to cover all of us.

And then the gun went off.

Chapter Twenty-Eight

"How much longer?" Mike asked.

The two of us were sitting in the waiting room of Crabtree Bay Community Hospital.

Shortly after Andrew had pulled a gun on us, police had swarmed into the lake house. At the same time, Mike had thrown himself at Andrew, trying to get the gun away from him.

And so had Geraldine.

In all the confusion, Geraldine had been shot, and after Andrew had been apprehended, and the gun taken away from him, Geraldine had been rushed to the hospital.

She'd needed surgery right away, and Mike and I had followed the ambulance to the hospital.

Bradshaw and Chris had followed also, and since Bradshaw was family, she was the only one who was likely to get any information. But Mike and I waited anyway, hoping to find out something.

"How much longer?" Mike said again.

He was sitting with his elbows on his knees and his head down.

I thought fleetingly of rubbing his back to comfort him, but I decided against it.

"I'm really glad you called the police," I said quietly. "I certainly didn't think of it."

Mike looked up at me and gave me a small smile.

261

"Actually, I called them right after you called me," he said. "I called your old friend Detective Mia. I had her and her team on speaker phone the whole time."

"The whole time?" I said.

"Yes."

"So they heard everything?"

"Yes, they did."

"Well, that's a relief," I said.

I paused. "How did you get them to listen to you? Detective Mia never seemed to believe anything when I said it."

Mike gave me a sly grin. "Perhaps it's because I never talk about magic. Being realistic has an upside."

I thought of a retort, but I stifled it—this wasn't really the place for an argument. And I realized that Mike was only teasing—he wasn't angry about magic like he once was.

But he still didn't believe in it.

I heard footsteps clacking down the long hall then, and I looked up to see Detective Mia walking toward us.

She stopped in front of us, and Mike and I looked up expectantly.

"I just wanted you to know that Geraldine is all right," she said. "She pulled through her surgery, and she's expected to make a full recovery."

Detective Mia's voice was soft, and her brown eyes were full of sympathy.

"What was it?" I said. "Was it her heart?"

"No," Mia said, and she sounded relieved. "No—she was shot in the chest, but it was higher up. The surgery was mostly to repair her collarbone, which was shattered. But as I said, she did very well, and I won't be charging anyone with her death today."

She looked for a moment as if she were going to sit down next to me, but then she seemed to think better of it.

"Thanks for telling us," I said. "Even though we aren't family."

Mia nodded. "I thought you would want to know."

"I don't suppose you can tell us anything else?"

Mia smiled. "Not a chance. But I will admit that things don't look too good for Andrew Wyatt. Though it will take quite a while for us to untangle all of this. And I am grateful to you for running up to that lake house as recklessly as you did. Otherwise, we would never have known what Andrew was up to."

She paused. "How did you know he had a gun?"

"Well, I didn't know about the modern one," I said. "That one was a complete surprise. The only one I knew about was the antique gun."

"That's the one," Mia said. "We looked all over town for it. How did you know it was in Andrew's possession?"

"Are you saying you found it in his little black bag?"

Detective Mia gave me another small smile. "Possibly."

"It *wasn't* in his possession for a while there," I said. "He'd hidden it very well. He didn't want to get caught with the gun or the bullets. But I knew he'd have to retrieve them both eventually—he needed the gun to finish out his plan. And what better way to retrieve his weapons than to have someone else bring them to him? It only made sense. That's how I knew he'd have the gun."

Mia looked at me for a moment—it was impossible for me to tell what she was thinking.

Eventually she drew in a deep breath.

"Well, as I said, thank you for your help. We never would have known to look at Andrew if it weren't for you."

She turned to Mike. "And thank you for being the sensible one and calling us."

"Wait, what?" I said.

Mia winked at Mike and then turned to go.

She soon disappeared down the hall.

"So how did you know?" Mike said to me.

"About the gun?" I said.

"About the gun, about Andrew, about all of it."

"It was Sibyl, really."

"Sibyl?" Mike said.

"Sibyl is my sister Alberta's cat. She's been acting strange lately—and that's what finally made me realize it was Andrew."

"Your sister's cat?" Mike was incredulous.

"She was acting *really* crazy," I replied. "Really, exceptionally crazy—sitting in the sink, yowling in time with the grandfather clock, marching around the house."

"That does sound a little unusual," Mike said.

"And I'd been thinking for a little while that Bradshaw might be faking the whole thing, so I already had the idea in mind that someone might be putting on an act here."

"You did?" Mike said. "You never told me."

"Well, it was only half-formed in my mind," I replied. "I suspected Chris Young for a little bit—just because he was acting so creepy—and he *was* stalking Bradshaw. And then I suspected Geraldine—but it looked like she'd been out of town when all the trouble started. And then I began to suspect Bradshaw—I thought her gunshot wound could have been self-inflicted, and I remembered the case of the woman who shot herself to cover up the murder of her husband. But no one had been murdered yet, and Bradshaw didn't seem like the type to wait—or to practice. So then I was back to suspecting Geraldine."

"You did seem pretty determined to find out what Geraldine had been up to."

"I was determined, wasn't I?" I said ruefully. "And then when I discovered that Geraldine had been staying in town much longer than anyone realized, I was sure it was her. But when I found out Geraldine had all the money, and Bradshaw was going broke, I no longer had a motive for her. But once I realized Andrew was behind everything, it all fit."

"Does it?" Mike said. "I don't see it."

"I'd seen Geraldine paying for lunch back at the ice cream parlor," I said. "And then I thought, what if Geraldine's been paying for everything else? When I went to the motel, and found out that Geraldine had been staying there, the manager made it sound like

Andrew had been staying there, too. And the manager threatened to put all their stuff out if they didn't pay their bill—and that didn't make any sense to me, because I knew Geraldine was staying at Bradshaw's house. But it suddenly *did* make sense if Andrew was really the one who wanted to stay there. If he was out of money, and needed a place to stay, he could have persuaded Geraldine to come into town and put him up in a motel. I'm sure he gave her a plausible reason."

"And you knew this because of a cat?" Mike asked.

"It's just that she was acting so crazy," I said. "And it suddenly occurred to me that Andrew was acting equally crazy—he took every opportunity to make a public scene about how jealous I was—about how scared he was for Bradshaw and Geraldine. And then I remembered that little scrap of paper with our symbol on it. I had no idea how that slip of paper had gotten into Lisa Stroup's hand—but I knew someone had planted it. And since Andrew had been trying to incriminate me all along, it made sense that it had been him. He broke into my sister's house, stole a few small items, and thought he could use one of them to incriminate me."

"But it didn't incriminate you," Mike said. "At least not after the police lifted the prints off it. It incriminated your sister."

"And that was a mistake of Andrew's. He didn't think about the prints on the paper. Even I didn't realize you could get usable fingerprints off paper. I had to look it up."

"Why didn't he just steal something of yours?" Mike asked. "Why go to your sister's house?"

"He did steal something of mine eventually," I said. "He took my black cord off my purse—I hadn't had it very long, and I remembered how he wrapped his arms around me. He must have pulled the cord off then—and it had the added bonus of having a charm with my name on it."

"But why not just go to your house? Why break into your sister's house?"

"Oh, right," I said. "You wouldn't know about that. I don't have a place of my own yet—I'm staying at my sister Alberta's house. And her house is basically a fortress. Breaking into Rafaela's house was really his best bet."

"So how did he know all that alleged magic stuff about you and your sisters and that symbol?" Mike asked. "Did you tell him back when you were dating?"

"Oh, no," I said. "No. I would never have told him about that. That was all a secret—at least until your article came out in *The Morning Cider*."

"Then how—"

"He learned about it from Ariadne Frost."

Mike frowned. "Ariadne? Oh, you mean my student Tina Chandler."

"Yes," I replied. "I believe she's actually a member of the Crabtree Coven."

Mike frowned harder, but I went on anyway.

"Andrew must have charmed her like he's charmed many other ladies. He found out she was a member of the coven, and he got her to tell him all their secrets. And in telling him their story, she ended up telling him about my family, too. Our two groups were linked since the very beginning. And then he got her to show him how to do magic and work spells—and curses."

"You really think he learned how to do magic?"

"Yes."

"Don't you need some kind of affinity for that for it to actually work?"

"Yes—and that's what makes this even worse. And now I understand what Tina was so upset about."

"What?"

"She gave him special knowledge—sacred knowledge—and he betrayed her. Andrew's the one who sent you the emails—he's the one who spilled all their secrets."

"Wait," Mike said. "Andrew sent me the emails?"

"Yes."

"The ones that were supposedly from Charles Tyndall?"

"Yes."

"Why?"

"He did that because he knew it would inflame Bradshaw and make her act out when it became public—he knew she would come after me, and that would help to make me look guilty."

I took a deep breath.

"And that's what Tina meant when she said 'my friend' had sent the emails—she was talking about Andrew. She'd seen him when he'd come to the library to harass me. And he'd been to the library quite a few times before that. That's when he was sending you emails from my place of work—trying to incriminate me. And that's why Tina didn't ID him when I asked about him. One, she was embarrassed that she'd fallen for him. And two, I showed her pictures of my friends, and she obviously didn't recognize any of them. I didn't show her a picture of Andrew because I would never have thought of him as my friend."

"And you believe he used what he learned from Tina to place a curse on Lisa."

"Not only do I believe it," I said, "I *know* it. That's what all the lightning was. Tina told me about that. Summer lightning was a sign that the Sleeping Beauty Curse was being worked on. I saw it the night Lisa was cursed, and we all saw it today when Andrew was preparing it for Geraldine."

Mike gave me a sardonic smile. "The lightning was a sign of the curse?"

"Yes," I said. "It appears when it's being prepared."

"And Tina had to tell you? Why didn't you know already? I thought you were a witch."

"Well, I don't know much about curses," I said. "We don't do stuff like that. And I haven't really been learning and studying like I should. For example, I didn't realize at first that the recent power outages were caused by Andrew casting forget spells."

Mike's eyebrows rose. "Forget spells?"

I nodded. "The first one occurred while I was at the police station last week. I didn't realize it at the time, but Andrew must have been at the station at the same time. And I bet I know why he was there. Since he was the one who broke into Chris's shop and then tampered with his car, he probably showed up on some surveillance footage, and all they had to do was haul him in. Since the police had caught him, and they had proof, he had to cast a pretty big forget spell. And the by-product of that was that all the lights went out."

"He put the power out in the police station?" Mike still sounded skeptical.

"Yes—and he's the reason the power went out all over town today. Andrew must have been casting spells on lots of people as he prepared his curse. And he may even have been casting them on Geraldine, too. You heard what he said back at the lake house—he said Geraldine wouldn't remember any of this."

Mike looked thoughtful. "He did say that, didn't he? But then why—from your perspective—did he go to all of the trouble of setting up a curse for Geraldine? Why didn't he just marry her without the curse?"

"Maybe she didn't want to marry him," I said. "Running around with a bad boy is one thing. But actually marrying him is another. And even if they did get married, she might not dispose of her fortune the way he wanted—the money is hers, and he wouldn't have control over it. Besides, he wanted the mansion, too, and he had to kill Bradshaw to get it. I'm not sure Geraldine would be too kindly disposed toward the person who killed her cousin."

Mike sighed. "I guess that all makes sense—assuming you believe in the magic aspect of it."

He paused. "What was that thing you did at the end there with the fake confession and the crying? And why did you ask Andrew to kiss that card?"

"All of that was for a *very* good reason," I replied. "I did that to save Lisa."

Mike looked puzzled. "And how would that help exactly?"

"I knew I had to catch Andrew in a piece of drama," I said. "Otherwise, he would never do what I wanted."

"And what was that?"

I smiled wearily. "I'll tell you if it works."

I heard the clack of footsteps in the hall once again, and I looked up to see my sister Alberta hurrying toward us.

When she saw me, she broke into a run.

She rushed right up to the chair where I was sitting and pulled me into a hug.

"Oh, Chloe, Chloe! Are you okay?"

Then she stepped back and stared into my face searchingly.

"I'm fine," I said. "It's Geraldine we have to worry about at the moment."

"You're sure you're all right?" Alberta said.

"Yes, I'm sure."

"Oh, Chloe," Alberta said again, though this time her voice held a different note. "I can't believe you did something that reckless and dangerous—and you didn't invite me. And why did I have to find out through Rafaela? Why didn't you text me yourself?"

"I just didn't think of it," I said. "Rafaela is always good about thinking of things like that. She said she'll tell us when they're ready."

I realized then that Mike had risen and was hovering near us uncertainly.

I turned to him. "Mike, this is my sister Alberta."

Alberta stared at him.

"This is Mike?" she said. "Oh. Oh!"

Whatever reply Mike was going to make was lost, as both my phone and Alberta's started buzzing at the same time.

Alberta got to her phone first. "They're ready. Let's go."

She started off down the hall, and Mike looked at me uncertainly.

"I think it might be better if you stay here," I said to him gently. "We had to get permission from her family, and I think they might be uncomfortable if we brought you with us."

"Yeah, sure," Mike said. "Whatever you need to do." He paused. "What are you doing, by the way?"

"With any luck, I'm going to lift the Sleeping Beauty Curse off Lisa," I replied.

Mike's eyebrows rose. "Oh, okay. I hope that goes—well."

I had a sudden urge to stand up on tiptoe and kiss him on the cheek, but instead I just smiled and turned to follow Alberta.

She led me down the hall and then into another wing to Lisa's room. I already knew the way, since I had stopped in to see Lisa and Rafaela earlier, but Alberta was walking so fast that I had trouble keeping up with her and was forced to walk behind her.

Soon we reached Lisa's room, and the two of us came to a stop in the doorway.

Lisa was lying in bed under a plain white hospital sheet, and her head was propped up on several pillows. Her eyes were closed, and a tiny smile sat on her lips, as if she were smiling in a beautiful dream. With her golden hair cascading down her shoulders and the look of peace on her face, Lisa truly did look like Sleeping Beauty herself.

Sitting by the side of Lisa's bed were a man and a woman who looked like older versions of Lisa. The woman had a faded version of Lisa's golden hair, and the man had her same soft smile.

I figured these were Lisa's parents.

Rafaela was standing quietly at the foot of the bed.

"Do you really think this will work?" Alberta whispered to me.

"I don't know," I said. "But I have to try."

Lisa's mother—Mrs. Stroup, I presumed—looked up at me and smiled sadly.

"The doctors have tried everything, and nothing's worked," she said. "I'm happy to try one last thing—especially if it's as simple as Rafaela says."

"It really is very simple," I replied. "We'll know very soon if it works."

"What do you need us to do?" Mrs. Stroup asked.

"You and Mr. Stroup don't really need to do anything," Rafaela said quietly. "Chloe just needs a little space by Lisa's side."

Mr. and Mrs. Stroup rose and came to stand beside Rafaela.

"What is she going to do?" Mrs. Stroup asked nervously. "Is it some kind of ritual?"

Rafaela gave her a reassuring smile. "You'll see." She turned to me. "Lisa's usual nurse shut her eyes. She thought that might make it easier for you."

I approached the bed and pulled Andrew's card from my purse.

Then I sat down next to Lisa and stared at her peaceful face.

I really hoped this would work.

I took a deep breath, and then I carefully pressed the spot with the lipstick and the lip print to Lisa's own smiling lips.

I waited for a long moment.

Then I removed the card.

I stared at Lisa.

She still looked very still, and the peace of her slumber didn't seem to be disturbed.

I wanted to try again, but I knew that if the card hadn't worked the first time that it certainly wasn't going to work the second time.

I sat back and watched and hoped.

But Lisa didn't wake.

Eventually, I turned to Lisa's parents.

"I'm sorry," I said. "I thought the lip print would be enough—"

But Lisa's parents weren't looking at me.

They were looking at their daughter.

"It's Lisa," Mrs. Stroup breathed. "Her eyes."

I turned. Lisa's eyes were indeed fluttering open.

I leaned forward, and Mr. and Mrs. Stroup crowded in beside me.

"Lisa, honey, we're right here," Mr. Stroup said.

Lisa blinked a few more times, and then her eyes seemed to focus on us.

"Mom? Dad?" she said. Her eyes focused on me for a moment, and then she looked back at her parents. "What's going on?"

"You're okay, sweetie," Mrs. Stroup said. "You're in a hospital. But you're okay."

Lisa nodded groggily. "Could I get some water?"

I moved out of the way to give Lisa and her parents some privacy, and then I hurried over to hug my sisters.

"It worked!" I cried. "The Sleeping Beauty Curse is lifted!"

Alberta and Rafaela hugged me back tightly, and then we all turned to look at Lisa.

She was sitting up in bed now, talking to her parents and sipping a little bit from a glass of water.

Even though I couldn't see it, I knew the rune was fading and would be gone entirely soon.

"Oh!" I said suddenly. "I've got to tell Mike."

I hurried out into the hall and ran all the way to the waiting area where I had last seen Mike.

He was waiting there still with his head down and his elbows resting on his knees. He looked up at my approach.

"Mike!" I cried. "Mike, it worked!"

I ran toward him, and he stood up.

I threw my arms around him and gave him a hug.

"It worked!"

Mike looked down at me. "What do you mean it worked?"

"I lifted the curse off Lisa. She's fine now."

"What? How?"

"Well, back when I was researching the crime that Bradshaw's wound reminded me of, I also did some reading about fingerprints. And while I was reading about fingerprints, I also read about lip prints. It turns out that lip prints are like fingerprints—each lip print is unique to the individual and no two in the world are alike. And then suddenly it occurred to me that maybe I could break the curse with Andrew's lip print rather than with an actual kiss from him. Luckily, Andrew was just vain enough to fall for it."

"Wait. What?" Mike said.

"We needed a kiss from Andrew to break the curse that was on Lisa," I replied. "Since he was the one who placed the curse, only a kiss from him would do. And it turns out that as far as the curse was concerned, a lip print from Andrew was just as good as an actual kiss."

"I didn't follow any of that," Mike said. "But speaking of lip prints—"

"Yes?"

And then all of a sudden, Mike and I were kissing.

After a moment, we both stepped back.

Mike looked a little stunned. "Did I do that? Or did you do that?"

"It wasn't me," I said.

"Well, it wasn't me, either."

"Should we try again?" I said. "Just to see who may have started it?"

"I could do that," Mike said.

"So could I," I replied.

And so we did.

Other Books by Catherine Mesick

Pure, Book 1 of the *Pure* series

Firebird, Book 2 of the *Pure* series

Dangerous Creatures, Book 3 of the *Pure* series

Ghost Girl, Book 4 of the *Pure* series

Coming soon!

Little Sun, Book 5 of the *Pure* series

A Maryland Witch in Arthur King's Court, Book 2 of the *Witches of Crabtree Bay* series

About the Author

Catherine Mesick is the author of *Pure*, *Firebird*, *Dangerous Creatures*, *Ghost Girl*, and *A Maryland Witch*. She is a graduate of Pace University and Susquehanna University. She lives in Maryland.

Visit the author's website at catherinemesick.com and her Facebook page at facebook.com/PureBookSeries. You can also connect with her on Twitter at twitter.com/CatherineMesick.

Sign up for Catherine's newsletter at http://eepurl.com/cXS5_z.

www.ingramcontent.com/pod-product-compliance
Lightning Source LLC
Chambersburg PA
CBHW031704170626
46808CB00005B/1610